THE
CAT'S MAW

by

BROOKE BURGESS

Illustrated by
COLIN MOORE

– with Dani Singer and James Curcio –

Publisher's Note: This is a work of fiction. Names, characters, places, and incidents are a product of the author's imagination. Locales and public names are sometimes used for atmospheric purposes. Any resemblance to actual people, living or dead, or to businesses, companies, events, institutions, or locales is completely coincidental.

Book design © 2014, BookDesignTemplates.com & James Curcio.

Ordering Information: Special discounts are available on quantity purchases by corporations, associations, and others. For details, contact the publisher at the address above.

CREATESPACE – SEATTLE, USA / Second Edition

ISBN: 1500971650 / ISBN-13: 978-1500971656

THE

CAT'S MAW

— The Shadowland Saga —

BOOK I

For Kitchener,

It wasn't in vain.

"Devouring time, blunt thou the lion's paws,
And make the earth devour her own sweet brood;
Pluck the keen teeth from the fierce tiger's jaws,
And burn the long-lived phoenix in her blood"

WILLIAM SHAKESPEARE, Sonnet no. 19

THEN

"IT'LL BE ON US 'FORE WE HAVE TIME *to pray and pass water!*" yelled a voice from high in the rigging.

Lightning crashed in the distance, and a tide of black clouds swallowed the stars behind the ship. The Captain paced the deck. Half his men were starving and threatening mutiny. The other half were spilling their guts over the side, or fouling up the hold below.

The sickness was spreading. The storm was closing in. And Death waited on all sides, laughing in the shadows.

"*Then skip the prayer, hold your piss, and dump everything,*" he yelled back, gripping the hilt of his dagger.

"Sir," the Steward said, holding his swollen stomach, and doing his best to stay standing as the boat lurched. "Are you sure you want to–?"

"Dump it all," said the Captain, inching the blade from its silver scabbard. "The cannons. The bags. The liquor. The food that's turned. Even the rats, if you can catch 'em. Anything that could slow us down."

The Steward winced and gagged as the deck dipped, and clutched at the arm of the Captain's salt-stained coat. "But the *haul*, sir? What we almost died for? What of the thing that's cursed us since we left?"

The Captain looked to the cabin door. A bearded priest stood in the shadows, shivering in his ashen robes. The holy man moved to block the door with darting eyes and a considerable girth.

"There's more to fear than *curses*, boy," the Captain hissed, slapping the young man's hand away. "Touch that box, and you'll know. *All* of you. Go!"

"Yes, sir," the Steward said, stumbling off towards the bow. "*You heard the Captain – dump it all!*"

The Captain turned and gripped the back rail. He watched the lightning dance and slice through the heavens. He saw the darkness creep towards him, like oil spilled across the sky.

I'm in a race with the Devil, he thought. *But when we're light as the whiskers on His face, we'll see who gets there first.*

With fingers full of splinters, he twisted the ring of gold on his left hand. It slid easily across his taut, pale skin, leaving smears of brown and red. Dirt and blood.

It won't be for nothing, I swear. To the edge of the Earth, the end of Time, and whatever stands between. We will raise a glass again in the New World, and laugh in its face. Together.

He looked up at the stars as the storm closed in and saw them extinguished, one-by-one, until just two remained. They glimmered and shone through gaps in the clouds like two great eyes in the darkness, burning on a demon's face that chased him across the sea.

Rest now, my love. For soon, you shall sleep no more.

With a gust of wind the eyes blinked out, shut tight in the storm.
Far below, a lone man tilted back his head, and howled at the darkness.

I

Of Boys and Bones

BILLY BRAHM WAS HAVING A NIGHTMARE.

Now, there's nothing the least bit peculiar about a ten-year-old boy having a bad dream. Be it fanged beasts, or exploding volcanoes, or having to go up in front of the entire school to give a speech in your underwear, there isn't much call for alarm.

Just remember that you're dreaming. Run away as fast and as far as you can. And then wake yourself up.

But this boy's dream was different. It was different because there was no way to escape from it. It was different because he was already wide-awake.

Elizabeth and Stanley Brahm stood over their adopted son with masks of concern and frustration on their weary faces. For years, Billy's mother had scolded him for being accident-prone, causing them so much unnecessary worry (not to mention the implied expense).

"You could trip on a whisker, or cut yourself in a rubber room," his mother would say, removing her glasses with a heavy sigh and furrowed brow.

Stanley Brahm would nod in agreement, keeping the fragile peace. As his mother continued to scold, Billy would watch his father turn and inch quietly from the room. The bald patch on top of his head would bob out the back door and gleam its way across the lawn, disappearing behind the doors of his workshop.

Billy couldn't argue with his mother. He may have been a smart boy – frighteningly smart, according to the standardized tests they gave at his school each year – but no amount of brain could dispute the boy's storied history of profound clumsiness.

When Billy was three he fell down the stairs with a double-scoop strawberry cone. Shag carpet softened the blows and absorbed the ice cream and blood, limiting the boy's suffering to two chipped teeth, a fat lip, and the ridicule of his three foster siblings.

When Billy was four he ran out of daycare, tripped on his untied shoes, and met the shale-and-gravel driveway face-first. At the doctor's, he shrieked as the little man with the lazy eye slid a needle and thread four times through his upper lip. The boy's siblings (down to two now) were no less cruel with their laughter.

When Billy was five, a hulking sixth grader – lunging to avoid a dodgeball throw of vicious intent – slammed him into a tetherball pole. Six weeks in a sling, and a broken collarbone to add to his 'scorecard'.

Billy's sole sibling at the time – a shy blonde girl with a love for stuffed bears and a tendency to cry – asked him in all seriousness if he was *cursed*, or just had really bad luck. Three weeks later, Billy watched from the kitchen window as the girl was packed neatly with her bear into a long grey car that would whisk her away to another home.

As he waved goodbye to her and remembered her words, he began to wonder the same thing.

A jolt of pain brought him back to the present. Back to the living room and the squeaky, lump-infested cot. Back to the plaster cast on his leg, and the reason he was trapped.

His mother unfolded a newspaper, sat down beside the bed, and began clipping a piece from a page near the front. For a minute Billy forgot his pain, hoping she had found a coupon for ice cream, or for the movies. His mother loved coupons as much as Billy loved ice cream, and movies, and dreams. Probably more.

"Do you have any idea how *lucky* you are?" his mother asked, though she wasn't really asking. She waved the strip of paper in front of his face. "You could've been killed! People must think we're *awful* parents."

The news story was titled: 'SUMMER RUINED FOR LOCAL BOY'. That's all he could make out, aside from his school photo. The unflattering picture showcased his prominent overbite, bulging brown eyes, and a lopsided mop of chestnut hair. Billy never saw himself as a handsome boy before and now, after the accident, even less so.

The throbbing in his leg made it hard to focus and reading only made him dizzy. But the memories were slowly returning. They came to him in flickers of blood, and flashes of screeching metal.

Three weeks earlier, the boy had turned ten.

Two weeks ago, he got a perfect report card.

And last week?

Last week, Billy Brahm was hit by a car.

Billy's mother had had enough.

She was tired of the lounging in front of the TV, of the comic books strewn around the living room, and of the toy-soldier wars that threatened to engulf the entire house.

In short, her son's tendency to dream was fraying the tip of her last working nerve.

"Silly Billy," she said, "I'd really like it if you found something to do outside. Something *productive*. Ask your father for a chore. Or build something. Or, maybe you could find a friend..."

She unscrewed the cap from a fat green bottle, and poured red wine up to the rim of a juice glass on the counter. After a long sip, Billy watched her putting extra muscle into kneading the pizza dough. Her face reddened, and began to resemble an heirloom tomato from their garden.

That's when the boy decided it was unwise to stay and risk losing his special 'perfect report card' dinner.

Billy shuffled to the front hall. Arranged for him on the low hall table were the blue wristwatch and matching running shoes that he got for his birthday. He put them on, opened the door, and stepped out into the heat of the first Sunday of summer.

Find a friend.

It's something she had said many times before. This only convinced the boy that his mother didn't have the best grasp on their geographical reality.

The Brahms lived in Appleton, a tiny rural town in the heart of the eastern valley. It had a year-round population that hovered just shy of 800.

The kids anywhere close to his age lived far away – past the sprawling orchards and sweet-corn fields and dairy farms – on the other side of the hills. A trek like that was a daunting prospect in the heat of late June with only a slim chance of success. Besides, after the year he'd had, Billy wasn't exactly keen to see anyone from his school anytime soon.

He circled the house and wandered back to his father's workshop. It was a small grey shack with white trim and topped with tarry black shingles.

The square door yawned open and Billy peered inside. Paint-flecked ply-board walls were lined with hanging tools, and a set of old golf clubs was hoisted high in a shiny black bag near the door.

Billy liked to watch his father work. Sometimes the man would spend all weekend in the shop cutting and sanding pieces of sweet-smelling wood. The shop was filled with projects in various stages of build and design – *unfinished masterpieces*, as his mother called them.

But that didn't seem to bother Stanley Brahm. He looked happy just pushing the circular saw through a fresh plank of cedar, as he was doing at that moment.

"Can I help?" Billy said.

The boy wasn't eager to follow through on the offer, but it was cooler there in the shade of the shop. He waited for an answer, but the man kept on cutting. Billy knew his father was focused because his tongue was still sticking out the side of his mouth.

"Dad! CAN I HELP?" Billy shouted.

Stanley jerked his hands at the sound, shearing the wood at an ugly angle. Unlike his mother, Billy's father wasn't one to show big emotions. This made the boy nervous, because the man's moods were harder to read. But it didn't take a psychic to see the annoyance hanging in the air just then with all that wood dust.

"*Busy* right now, son," his father said. He clicked off the saw and it whirred slow, stopping with a sudden *CHUK*. "How about you help your mom with the pizza? I'm sure she'd appreciate it."

"She sent me *outside*," Billy said.

"Of course she did," Stanley said, sliding off his safety goggles and wiping the sweat from his brow.

As his son stood in the doorway, still and unblinking, Stanley fought the urge to turn away. There had always been something he just couldn't place with the boy. Something unsettling. Something in his eyes that seemed to look right through people and take them apart.

"It's a gorgeous day," his father said. "Summer vacation, right? Go find a friend and kick the ball around. Just don't get those new shoes too dirty. You know how your mother is." Stanley winked, put his goggles on, and set the saw in motion. His tongue slid back into its sideways work groove. The conversation was over.

Find a friend.

Billy was starting to get the hint. His parents weren't keen on tripping over him constantly for the next two months. But they were also drawing the line on their son becoming what the parenting books had described as 'borderline antisocial'.

Pickings were slim in the valley if you weren't after apples. Plundering anthills in the sandpit with toy trucks and a magnifying glass wasn't going to cut it. Neither would a summer spent daydreaming in his favourite place – Billy saw the looks his folks shared when he spent too much time there.

That left only one option. Thankfully, it was a good one.

Billy would make a point of crossing the road to visit the old Thomas place as often as he could. It was a big two-storey house with a stone foundation, chipped white siding and dark, dusty windows. It seemed to sag in the middle, as if the weight of its age had made it exhale and refuse to stand tall again. Yet it looked perfectly comfortable with its bad posture, peeling trim, and balding roof. The plants around the yard had grown tall and wild, defying the trimmed bushes and tidy squares of manicured lawn across the road.

It was *old*, to be sure. Billy had read in the paper that it was probably built in the early 1800's, but his father – whose job it was to inspect buildings and assure the township that they measured up to municipal codes – had been in the basement to help with a plumbing mishap. He placed the stonework in the foundation at fifty years older than the paper's estimate, maybe more.

The 1700's. Back to the days of the first settlers. The beginning of Appleton. It was part of the reason the boy loved it so much. But only part.

Billy had a ritual. First, he'd hop the ditch instead of using the driveway. Then he'd sit on the plank swing hanging from the huge elm out front. After a few swings he'd leap into the grass, hunt for four-leaf clovers, and then make his way around the side of the house.

He'd move through the garden then, and approach the old stone arch. Its curious shape was cracked and sun-bleached, and covered in snaking vines and wildflowers. It had grooves and markings on its smooth surface, but they were too shallow to share any secrets.

It was there beneath the stones – near the rose trellises and swaying sunflowers, with the sound of seashell wind chimes clattering in the breeze – that he would stop. And it was there that he would kneel in the grass, take a deep breath, and then call to *them*.

Billy was there to see Mrs. Thomas' cats. Which was all fine and good, because the old lady's attention was divided in countless furry directions.

There were fat cats and skinny cats. The long-tailed and the bobbed. The daring young leapers, and the old windowsill sleepers. Balls of waddling fluff, smooth-coated prowlers, and hairless ones that looked fragile and wise. The tiger-striped, the ring-tailed, and the ones with matching coloured socks and mittens. There were tabbies and calicos. Manx and Persians. Siamese and Bombay. Ragdolls and Birmans. Maine Coons and Russian Blues. There were Snowshoes and

Somalis, Tonkinese and Turkish, and many, many more. Brown and beige and orange and grey and black and white and silver cats, each with gleaming eyes of emerald, or sapphire, or amber. A rainbow of precious stones.

On that fateful afternoon, a white tabby with black spots (or was it black with white ones?) had caught the boy's eye. It had just slipped out from one of the basement windows and was wiping its paws on the foundation.

Billy crouched low, as he had learned to do, and called to it. *Wsss, wsss, WSSS.* He forced the air gently between his teeth and tongue, extended his hand along the ground, and rubbed his thumb in circles against the index and middle fingers.

The cat stopped what it was doing, dropped to all fours, and turned to face him.

Billy was struck by its golden gaze, the blacks of its eyes narrowing in the sunlight. The cat looked as if ink had been spilled upon its head, painting a black helm that dribbled a dark spear down the bridge of its nose. This made its gleaming eyes and pink nostrils stand out all the more on its narrow face. The cat's ears, jet-tipped and pointy, stiffened and curled towards the sound. It crouched as it stared with its black tail flattened, swaying across the loose dirt.

This is not for you, child.

Billy thought that if the creature could speak, that's what it would say. This was clearly a foolish thought. As anyone with sense will tell you, cats can't talk.

Yet Mrs. Thomas had claimed many times (over homemade apple pie with chunks of cheddar that she shared with her furry beggars) that cats could talk perfectly well, thank you very much. The problem was that most of us had forgotten how to *listen.*

The cat blinked and scampered off. Billy gave chase, following it through the long grass. He ran past the crumbling gazebo and the stone well and around the giant elm, whose lowest branch still held the swing in a lazy embrace.

He followed the cat all the way to the property's edge, watching it weave through the ditch and onto the road. He kept on following until it stopped in the middle of the far lane. The cat sat down on the pavement with half-opened eyes and measured breaths, and turned its head down the road to the north.

There was a growing shape in the dusk, faint and grey like a shadow. It was moving fast, and coming straight towards them.

Billy heard a voice.

'*No more...*'

The moments that followed were an insane blur. Shock and agony. Blood and breathlessness. Waves of sheer terror, not all of them Billy's.

His mind flashed, and his parents stood over him. They were shaking and crying, and waving traffic through as they called for help.

As he lay there, crumpled and bloody on the ribbon of asphalt, the boy remembered running out to help a cat for some reason. And when he heard his mother's wail over the hushed chatter of those who stopped to gawk, Billy tried very hard to convince himself that it was all just a terrible dream.

When the ambulance arrived, he was loaded onto a stretcher with a sickening jolt. He thought he heard someone say that he had slid across the road so fast that the soles of his new shoes had melted. His wristwatch was smashed, and his best jeans were beyond the help of any seamstress or commercial cleanser.

But those were just *things*. Far worse were the shattered bones and dangling tendons poking through the side of his shin, the flesh failing at its job of keeping them all in place.

Siren blaring, the ambulance sped north. Darkness was quick to descend, transforming the vehicle into a wheeled firefly that darted and flashed as it steered through the night.

Inside, the red lights set an eerie scene. The attendant's face was shadowed and grim as he steadied the boy's stretcher. Stanley Brahm crouched in silence beside him. Through a pained haze, the boy thought he saw tears running down the man's cheeks.

It must've been a dream, for Billy had never seen his father cry.

It took 45 minutes to reach the Middleton emergency room. The driver had radioed ahead and the on-call doctor met them at the door – a pasty man with thinning hair, a wide jaw, and small, precise eyes. His voice was steady as he directed everyone inside, and remained calm when he saw the extent of Billy's injuries.

As a nurse dabbed stinging liquid at the wounds on Billy's face, the doctor removed the boy's melted shoe and cut through the blood-soaked denim on his leg. Billy screamed as the jeans peeled away from his shin, and the pale man whitened another shade.

He shouted something at the nurse, and Billy moaned as a large needle jabbed into his hip. There was a muddle of voices as a numbing relief swept through his body. The boy tried to thank them, but the words wouldn't come and the room went black.

Another burst of pain, and Billy slid from the wooden carry-board and onto a cold, stiff bed. Two hours had passed, and he had been taken to the children's hospital all the way up in Bridgeton.

The attending physician had an angled face and shaggy hair, and seemed flustered by all the screaming. He asked the boy's father for some details, shook his hand, and had him sent from the room.

Thus began Billy's week in the hospital – a fuzzy, melted jumble of memories. There was the initial operation to set his leg. Painkiller drips and soiled bed-sheets. Dry meat and warm Jell-O. Bedside rounds of cribbage, where the boy would skunk his mother twice with a miraculous 29-point hand.

Then came *physio*.

The nurses wrapped his cast in plastic, and had Billy swim in a too-blue pool that stung his eyes. They gave him a pair of creaky wooden crutches, and had him practice moving in the halls between meals. They massaged his face with sticky liquids, and used tweezers to pull off the crusty scabs from his cheeks, chin, and forehead.

The hospital staff all gave the kindest smiles, used the gentlest touches, and spoke in the friendliest voices. They were nice when Billy cried, or when he was lazy, or even when he had a tantrum.

This confused the boy, even more than the painkillers did. Each day, his black-brown stare searched their faces for clues. Probed for secrets. Scanned for lies.

Something's wrong, he thought.

It was a long drive south on that rainy morning in early July. Little was said, as Billy had been given a sedative before they departed. When the Brahms finally arrived home, Stanley carried his son inside. Elizabeth went straight to the kitchen, poured a glass of milk, and filled a plate with chocolate chip cookies.

Billy's heart sunk when he awoke, finding himself on the musty cot downstairs. It was too far away from his comics, and his toys, and his wallpaper adorned with pirate ships and treasure maps. It was too far from his bedroom window, which looked out upon the rolling fields and weeping willow trees. It was too far from the view of his favourite place in the world.

Another jolt brought Billy back to the present.

He had been home for several days now, and things didn't feel much better. He was still downstairs. The cot was still lumpy. The cast was still heavy, and scratched his thighs raw.

Then there was the horrible tingling – the maddening *itch* where the bones had pushed through the flesh – that he was unable to scratch. The more he thought about it, the more upset he became, and the more the itch spread.

It was creeping up his leg, moving higher every second. It finally made camp in his ears, and went to work in his brain. Billy's eyes welled with tears, and the low groan that was born in his belly grew to a howl in his lungs.

"It's okay, Billy, I'll be there in a second. I've got your favourite!" his mother shouted from the kitchen.

She shuffled across the linoleum and onto the living room carpet, carrying a tray of food that was piping hot. He was soothed a little as the smells worked their magic – tomato soup, a grilled cheese sandwich, and a glass of chocolate milk.

She propped up the cot and tilted the glass of milk into her son's mouth. She couldn't help but sigh as much of it ran down his chin, splashed on his chest, and soaked into the sheets.

"Drink it down," his mother said. "It will all be better soon."

"No, it won't," the boy said.

Billy met his mother's gaze as he drank. He watched her pupils dilate and contract. He drank more and saw her nostrils flare, and tiny beads of sweat glisten on her upper lip. He swallowed the rest, and was suddenly aware of a bitter, metallic taste that lingered on the back of his tongue.

A sound grew in Billy's head then, distant at first, yet strangely familiar. It was something he hadn't heard since that terrible day, just before the accident.

A *voice*.

As the milk swam through his belly and into his veins, it grew louder. Billy's vision blurred. The sights and smells and pains of the waking world drifted away in the drugged ether, until only the voice remained.

'*No...*' it hissed.

'*No more...*' it cried in the darkness.

'*WE SLEEP NO MORE!*'

And that's when the real nightmare began.

I I

Of Cats and Catastrophe

HIS FEET ARCED UP INTO THE SKY.

They looked as if they could scrape the clouds. He felt weightless. Light and fast and free. The cool breeze of each swing whipped through his hair and against his face, and when he fell backward he would look up at the tree, transfixed by the tangled canopy rushing overhead.

There was something else in the branches, looming a little closer with each downward swing. Through the dark of the leaves he could see its eyes shine like tiny suns, and its lithe body weave in and out of the tree's limbs.

Billy closed his eyes as he swung upward. A sound struck his chest like a thunderclap, or the roar of a mythical beast. He opened them. The swinging continued, the sky tilting and spinning as it does in a dream, but his vision stayed fixed. It was drawn to one thing.

The cat.

It was perched on the lowest branch, snaring the boy in its golden gaze. It twitched its whiskers and swished its tail.

And then the cat spoke.

"You shouldn't have come here," it said.

The words didn't come from its mouth. They didn't make sound in the air, as words do. Instead, they seemed to rise in Billy's mind like ghostly balloons, popping gently to reveal themselves.

"It's *my* dream," Billy said, reaching out to pet it. As his hand moved closer, the cat blinked. Its pupils swelled, engulfing the gold in blackness.

"Are you sure, child?"

The cat dissolved into smoke. Wisps of black and white swept through Billy's fingers and down the trunk of the great elm.

"That's not fair," said Billy, stopping the swing. "It's not fair that you can do that, and I can't."

He spun around looking for some trace of it, and saw smoke coming from the old Thomas house. From the windows. And there, on the sill of one, was the cat.

"Is that what you want?" it said, eyes aglow in the haze. *"To do what I do, and know what I know?"*

Billy stumbled towards the house. His legs felt heavy and weak, especially his right one. The wet ground seemed to be sucking at his feet, and he stiffened as he reached the window and met the cat's gaze.

"That's why I followed you," the boy said.

Suddenly, he was no longer standing by the house. He was on the road now, one foot on either side of the faded yellow line that cut down the middle of it.

"We're so sorry." An elderly voice came from somewhere behind him.

Billy turned to meet it. He saw a silver-haired couple, finely dressed. Their heads were bowed, faces creased with age and regret. Behind them sat a vintage chrome and powder-blue sedan.

Blood dripped from the front fender.

"It happened so fast," said the old man. *"You were looking the wrong way."*

"Yes," said the old woman, *"you were looking down there."* She lifted her hand. It was clad in a crisp white glove, and pointed north.

Billy turned again.

The whole world opened up, like he was seeing in all directions at once. There was a large bonfire in the front yard of the Thomas house. It crackled and popped, and a column of dark smoke rose into the sky. The smoke drifted and formed black clouds over the far mountain range. The clouds flashed, and jagged bolts of lightning crashed into the highest peak.

He heard a *howl* then, like the baying of a wolf. The mountaintop exploded, sending plumes of stone and fire hurtling into the air. The clouds themselves *fell,* as if wounded by the burst, striking the horizon. They splashed and rolled and swept down the highway in a black, colossal wave.

Billy spun back around. The old couple were gone.

The wave swept forward, tearing the trees and farms and houses from the earth in its wake. It began to crest and the vast blackness of it *unfolded,* spreading in the sky like the wings of a giant bat.

The wind howled and the sky went dark. Lightning crashed and the wave stretched higher, billowing like the sails of a great black ship.

'NO MORE!'

The boy heard the voice and tried to run, but the water held him fast. He cried out, which did nothing to slow the rising tide or the mammoth shape upon it. He stood helpless as the sky burned, and the earth shook, and the black wave swept over him.

A pain shot through Billy's leg then, and he remembered. He took a deep breath, covered his ears, and clamped his eyes shut.

This is only a dream.

The storm collapsed around him in the darkness, vanishing like warm mist. A soft, empty silence filled the oasis in his mind.

Billy breathed.

With each breath the darkness was pierced like pinholes in the fabric behind his eyes, filling his vision with a shimmering ocean of stars. Billy scanned the constellations, searching for the cluster that had always called to him, the one that held vigil in the lonely night skies of the waking world.

Orion.

The stars blinked and then trembled. The sky shook, as if gripped in a pair of celestial hands. There was a *CRACK* of thunder, a frightening *HISS*, and a *BUZZ* that grew to deafening. And then the voice returned.

"NO MORE!"

The scream flooded the void. The stars died with it, their light toppling like glittering rows of dominoes. The last to fade were a pair of distant golden orbs, burning to their last before blinking into nothingness.

"LISTEN," the voice hissed, and buzzed, and gurgled. *"You are with USsss now.""*

The sound was low, and wet, and treacherous. Billy felt it closing in and began to panic. He tried to concentrate, to breathe and remember.

It's just a dream, he repeated. *It's only a dream.*

"A good trick, BOYyyy," said the voice. *"But you'll have to live a long, long time to know what WE knowww."*

The air grew hot and foul. Billy had had hundreds, maybe thousands of dreams before, but none of them had ever *smelled*. He choked when he took another breath, and felt the sick rising in his chest. It was a reek of filth, and garbage, and utter decay. It was a smell so awful, so dense and noxious and violent, that Billy feared he would lose his mind.

It was the smell of Death.

"Let USsss see that pretty skin..."

The hissing grew louder, like a thousand hungry mouths sucking air through rotten teeth. Billy opened his eyes, and for a moment he thought the stars had returned. The darkness had given way to hundreds of tiny blinking lights.

But he was wrong. They weren't stars. They glowed red. And they were in pairs.

In the cruel and hellish light, Billy saw that he was in a cramped room. Its floor and walls were stone slabs covered in thick, putrid slime, and there were things twitching in the dense shadows. Things with eyes. Things that *moved*.

Rats.

Billy spun around and saw the mouth of a giant tube – a pipe – with more rats gathered at the opening. They crawled over each other, lashing their hairless tails in frenzy. The wriggling, oily mound grew and grew, eyes blazing like hot embers in smothering smoke.

"We have waited so long, We have forgotten. It was LOST–" said the voice, and Billy looked up to its origin. Something emerged from the darkness above and crouched on the rim of the pipe. Something big. *"Now We FIND it."*

The thing looked human. It had arms and legs and what appeared to be a man's body. It was clothed in a quilt of soiled rags, like a cloak that had been sewn together from countless old garments. A filthy patchwork hood concealed its face.

"Where am I?" Billy cried. "What do you *want?*"

The room filled with hissing. The shadowy thing lifted a limb and raised a skeletal hand to its face. Its eyes flared with crimson fire like the rats' eyes did, and the sudden light revealed the true horror of it.

Sallow, rotting flesh. A gaping hole where a nose should be. An impossibly wide mouth filled with jagged, broken teeth. Black, cavernous eyes cradling stars of angry fire.

It was the terrible face of the Grey Man.

"*LISSSTEN,*" hissed the Grey Man, pressing a bony finger to diseased lips. "*That is what you DO! You will listen, and WE will remember. Then you will help us FIND it.*"

The rats squealed and shrieked in chorus, and the room rumbled. Billy backed away from the thing, and the rats, and the ominous sound coming from the pipe. It was only a few steps before he felt the cold, slimy stones against his back. Again, Billy was trapped.

Water burst from the pipe, sweeping the frenzied mass of eyes and teeth towards him. The water rose, and the rats with it, churning the flow as they swam. They clung to him – to his arms and his legs, to his skin and his hair – and as the water passed Billy's knees, they began to bite.

"Get off me!" the boy screamed, "*I want to wake up!*"

The Grey Man stood to his full height, eyes ablaze and arms outstretched. His hands tensed and his body went rigid. From the darkness above him, something descended. Four squares of stone. The shapes hovered in the air, forming an arc above his head.

"*We can SMELL it on you. The KEY is close. The GATE shall open,*" the Grey Man snarled, his voice drowning out the rising water and squealing vermin. "*The one who HEARS through the Veil of Tears, with the FANG o' the Great Cat's Maw! You will help USsss!*"

The water was up to Billy's chest, and the rats had doubled their attack. They swarmed around his face and dove underwater to gnaw on his injured leg. He swatted and squeezed and hurled as many as he could but they kept coming. The stench in the air, the sight of his own blood, and the thought of his imminent drowning crippled the boy with dread.

"I WILL," Billy shouted, "just make it *stop!*"

The air grew hot, and the stones floating above the Grey Man's head burst into flames. In the fiery light, Billy could see carved shapes on the four slabs. *Symbols.*

The Grey Man grinned, clapped his hands twice, and the stones vanished.

The rats continued to tear at the boy's flesh. The flood rose up to his chin. Billy choked and cried as he struggled in vain. He was alone in the dark, at the false mercy of a demon from his dreams.

"PLEASE!" he begged, fearing that his next breath would be his last. "*Please...help...me...*"

That's when Billy heard it over the rush of water in his ears – the *scratching* – just to the left of his head. He turned and gulped at the air, willing to use his last breath to show them that a boy's bite could be just as fearsome as a rat's.

A chunk of rock wiggled in the wall. The rock popped free in a spray of dust, and splashed into the chamber.

"*Follow,*" urged a voice from within the hole. "*Hurry.*"

The words gave the boy a glimmer of hope, and that was enough. Billy closed his eyes, swallowed his fear, and changed the rules of the dream. With a thought, his body shrank to a fraction of its size, and the rising waters lifted him into the hole in the slimy stone wall.

"*Faster,*" a shadow called from deep in the tunnel. "*You have to come back.*"

Billy clutched at the loose earth and began to crawl.

"*We KNOW you can hear Usss...*"

The tunnel shook with the Grey Man's bellow, and dirt fell around Billy's head. He lunged forward, dragging himself on his hands and knees. The way quickly grew more narrow and steep. He stopped to catch his breath, and the voice hissed again. Closer.

"We CURSE you, Listener!"

This will never end, Billy thought, fresh fear exploding in his chest. *I'm doomed.*

Something clamped around his wrist and pulled. It felt like a very strong hand, rough and soft at the same time, and much larger than a man's.

"WE CURSE YOU!"

The hand squeezed, and then dragged the boy fast through the tightening passage of dirt and stone. Billy hurtled through the end of the tunnel, squinting as he tumbled onto a clean, smooth surface.

The air smelled amazing. Billy *knew* that it was the most amazing smell from the most amazing meal he would ever eat. He took a deep breath. A beautiful warmth filled his belly, draining the fear from him.

He rubbed his eyes and saw that he was back in his house – in the kitchen, to be precise – but a much better version of it. It had mosaic tiles, cherry cupboards, and a large wooden island in the middle. It looked just like his mother had always wanted it to.

Billy looked around the room and saw that he wasn't alone. The kitchen was full of people making a feast. He saw his mother and father, and even some kids from his school. There were adults that he knew and others that he didn't recognize.

Mrs. Thomas was there. She was standing off to the side by the kitchen window, the sun making a halo of her silver hair. She wore a bright white dress that flowed in the breeze as the window swung open. She held out her hand, as if waiting to catch something.

A white bird flew into the room and landed on her fingers. Mrs. Thomas lifted it to her ear and listened to it chirp. She nodded, and turned to look at Billy with a bittersweet smile.

"*It's alright,*" she said. "*Whatever happens, we just wanted to thank you.*"

Everyone in the kitchen turned then, as if suddenly realizing he was there.

"*Welcome back,*" they cheered.

His father poured a glass of beer and raised it to him. Others followed suit, and his mother wiped gleaming tears from her cheeks as the room burst into applause.

Billy stared up from the floor in disbelief. He wanted to cling to this moment as long as he could. To bask in their unexpected kindness. But he knew it wasn't real. He was still dreaming. At any moment, even this perfect one, the nightmare could return.

He felt something brush against his leg. The thought of more rats sent him sprawling backward, kicking at the air as he fell to the floor. The room laughed, and applauded some more.

"*You're safe now,*" Mrs. Thomas said, calming him with the creamy jade of her gaze. "*Close your eyes and rest.*"

Billy did as she asked, and the room hushed as he lay down on the floor. He felt something brush against his leg again and put its weight upon it.

The weight moved, shifting to his groin then his belly, until coming to rest on his chest.

"*You can wake up now.*"

Billy opened his eyes and jerked his head up with a gasp. He rubbed his face, caught his breath, and even bit the inside of his lip to make sure that he was awake.

His parents stood beside the cot. It was clear by the confusion on their faces that they saw it too.

It was right there in black and white on the boy's chest, still and silent and staring right at him. Just like it did the day of the accident. Just like it did in his dream.

The cat with the golden eyes.

III

Of Pie and Pleasantries

THE DOORBELL RANG, its cheery *bing-bong* echoing through the house and drifting out the windows.

Billy was on the patio, propped up on a padded chaise lounge beneath a cloth umbrella in the shade. It tilted just enough to keep the sun off his upper half, leaving his bare leg free to tan or burn as he saw fit. The boy wasn't too concerned either way – a lump of fur stretched out between his knees commanded his undivided attention.

"Enid, thank you for coming over," his mother's voice carried from the front door and through the kitchen. *"Oh, isn't that lovely! You didn't have to go to the trouble of bringing anything. Let me help you with that."*

Billy could hear the muscles in her face straining with the weight of such politeness.

The cat cocked an ear, tilting it towards the kitchen sounds like a fuzzy sonar dish. Its eyes were half-open, pupils thin as pins in the sunlight, with the second fleshy lids retracting slowly to the corners of its eyes.

"*No trouble at all,*" Mrs. Thomas said. A musical humming accompanied her laboured shuffle into the kitchen.

Billy perked up. Enid Thomas – still spry and sharp, and the fastest apple-corer around at 88 years young – was known as 'the Cat Lady of Appleton'. In a town as small as theirs it wasn't that hard to stand out and Enid, with her feline brood, certainly did that.

People came from all over to see the cats, but mostly to *bring* them. Locals would drop off litters of kittens they couldn't find homes for. Some folks brought in strays. Others abandoned the injured or 'temperamental'. These were all kinder fates than the pound in Middleton, where their days would surely be numbered.

Whatever the case, Mrs. Thomas loved them all, and all were welcomed in her home. And, every so often, that love rubbed off on visitors – on quiet children, or lonely souls seeking a special bond – and someone would make an adoption. Billy understood them the best.

There was a clinking of china and glassware in the kitchen, and the sound of ice cubes cracking and tumbling into a glass pitcher. Painkillers and hospital food had played havoc with the boy's appetite, but Billy sensed that was about to change.

The cat stirred and stretched its limbs, hind paws jutting straight back and front ones lunging ahead, with toes spread and claws out. Its eyes clamped shut as it yawned, a curled pink tongue unrolling between rows of sharp, pearly teeth. As it lay prone on the soft blue cushion, it looked less like the descendant of a dangerous beast and more a like an overgrown kitten that was trying its best to fly.

"Look who's come for a visit," said his mother, carrying a crowded tray out to the patio table. She placed it down and Billy drooled at the sight – fresh lemonade, scoops of vanilla ice cream, wedges of cheddar cheese, and three huge slices of Enid Thomas' brown-sugar-and-cinnamon-crusted tart apple pie.

"Oh goodness, will you look at that," Enid said, stepping gingerly onto the deck. "Lounging in the sun like a movie star. The way you spoke, Elizabeth, I was prepared for much worse!"

"It's been up and down," his mother said, arranging the plates and glasses and utensils in the most orderly fashion. "But he's been good today. Since he woke up."

Mrs. Thomas spread out her arms and slowly shuffled towards the boy, soft green eyes twinkling behind a pair of horn-rimmed glasses. Billy did his best to be patient. He adored the old lady, but, like the cat sniffing at the table's edge, he had other things on his mind. Edible things.

"There we are," Enid said, finally within range to bend down and give the boy a long, loving embrace. "I'm overjoyed that you're alright, young man. I was *so* worried when that ambulance took you away. Let me pinch you and make sure I'm not dreaming."

"You're not," Billy said, as he hugged her and breathed in her sweet, flowery perfume. "If you were dreaming, would you put this stupid thing on my leg?"

"*Manners*," his mother looked up from the table, pausing the folding of napkins and straightening of forks. Billy hadn't said anything particularly rude, but he heard the warning in her tone – a firm reminder of how he was expected to speak with adults.

"I'm sorry, Mrs. Thomas. I didn't mean it like it was *your* fault or anything," Billy sighed. "I'm the stupid one. I ran into the road without looking."

"You're not stupid, dear boy. The furthest thing from it." Enid leaned back and held his face in her wrinkled hands. She smoothed his hair to the side, and skimmed her fingers across the scabs and faded skin on his brow. "These things happen."

"It didn't *have* to happen," his mother said, pouring the lemonade. "You're smarter than that. We taught you to look both ways, remember? But you've never been the best at paying attention. You're so easily distracted…"

"Perhaps," Enid said, seeing the shame flicker in Billy's moist brown eyes, "but I think it's harder to keep the attention of the brightest ones. They're curious by nature."

The old woman reached down and dragged a finger across the cushion by Billy's knee. The cat spun its head from the table to the shiny pink fingernail tapping on the fabric. It flattened its body and tail as it took a step, haunches flexing, pupils widening in a swath of shade. Enid wiggled her finger, making a *vit-vit-vit* sound on the cushion.

The cat pounced. It clutched her wrist in its paws, and looked every part the ferocious beast as it gnawed on her finger without breaking the skin. She scratched under its chin and massaged its cheeks, signaling her unconditional surrender.

"You're not so different," Mrs Thomas said, winking at the boy.

"Well, you know what they say about cats and curiosity," his mother said, plating the last slice of pie, cheddar, and ice cream. "And speaking of…will our little friend be going back home with you today?"

Billy knew that tone, too. It wasn't a question. It was a *request*.

Mrs. Thomas shifted the chair to face the table. She made no move towards it, instead remaining by Billy's side. "No pie for me dear," she said. "At my age, the joy is in the making, not so much in the eating. But I'll have some lemonade."

She reached for a glass, but Billy's mother was quick to hand her one of her own choosing. The old woman took a sip, and gave Billy's hand a soft squeeze.

"I ask," his mother continued, "because we aren't really in the market for a pet right now."

The cat's ears twitched and it rolled on its back. Billy gently rubbed its warm, white belly. It yawned again, peered up at him with a satisfied look on its spotted face, and blinked.

"You see that, Mom," Billy said, "It trusts me. A cat doesn't show its tummy like that unless it feels safe."

"Quite right," Enid smiled, "and when it blinks like that, it's saying *'yes'*. It looks like you've been paying attention during our visits at least." Mrs. Thomas took another sip of lemonade, watching the boy's mother search for the most polite way to disagree.

"That's an interesting theory," Elizabeth said, "but after all the time Billy's spent across the road, I'm sure they're *all* comfortable with him. *Across* the road. The cats, I mean."

The cat wrapped its paws around Billy's hand and began to lick his fingers. Its tongue was sandy and rough, but in a way that tickled.

"Come on, Mom," Billy said. "Can't we keep it?"

"I'm sorry," his mother took a long drink of her lemonade. "It's an extra expense, and you're in no condition to care for a pet. Besides, you know how sensitive you are. What if you develop an allergy? Or what if it makes your skin even worse?"

Billy blushed. She was right on all counts.

It was obvious that the cast made him anything but a good playmate, for felines or otherwise. As for money, his parents were always arguing about it. He didn't realize how bad things were until his mother started separating the two-ply toilet paper, and then re-rolling the sheets into separate rolls. He also knew that the loss of his birthday presents in the accident drastically reduced his bargaining power.

His skin problems were another matter entirely. When the Brahms adopted him as an infant, Billy had an ugly rash on his torso – itchy, scaly spots that peeled every few weeks, leaving raw red skin underneath. Sometimes they bled on his clothes, or on his sheets as he slept.

The doctor called it *psoriasis* – something the boy would have for life. He prescribed a smelly ointment, and advised against using cheap cleansers that could make it worse. So, the Brahms had to buy better soaps and shampoos and detergents because their son was so 'sensitive'.

Mrs. Thomas put her lemonade down, cleared her throat, and used a napkin to wipe her glasses. When she put them on again, she straightened her back and sat up to her full height.

"Elizabeth, if I may," she locked eyes with the Billy's mother. "Your son has just been through a terrible trauma. Who knows how this will affect him, or what scars it will leave beyond the ones we can see...?"

"Well, yes, but what does that have to–?" his mother tried to interject, but Mrs. Thomas spoke over her.

"You said he was *sick*, Elizabeth." Enid continued, "That he was sad and weak. I heard the concern in your voice. But seeing him now, with that wee creature? I see *happiness*. In the end, isn't that what we all want?"

Billy had not seen Mrs. Thomas like this in all the times he had visited her – not when he was playing 'time bomb' and broke her antique egg timer, or even when he spilled a whole bag of flour on her kitchen floor (she was still finding powdery paw-prints to this very day).

This wasn't the charming old woman who spent her days clipping roses, and baking pies, and whistling forgotten tunes from another century. This was a woman ready to fight for something.

"Of course," his mother stammered, draining her glass down to the ice cubes. "What parent wouldn't want that? I'm just saying that the practicalities of having a cat right now, the *commitment*–"

"Nonsense," Enid said. "First, if the boy were allergic, we'd know it by now. He'd be wheezing, puffy-eyed, and there wouldn't be enough tissue on earth to plug his precious nose. And second, do you really think, at my age, that I could care for all those furry dears if they weren't so darned *independent*? A little food, freedom, and affection– that's all they need."

Billy leaned forward, picked up the cat, and held it as she had taught him years before. It lay there in his arms, back and neck supported, with its tail hanging over his elbow. The cat looked up at him, eyes narrowing in the sunlight, and blinked.

"Please, Mom," Billy said. "You can keep my allowance." It wasn't much at five dollars a week, but he knew that she had to be *sold* on the idea. "Oh! And I bet it would keep the rabbits and squirrels away from the garden!"

"That's...interesting," she said, and Billy saw the wheels turning behind her eyes. "Still, I'd have to speak with your father about it first."

"Awww c'mon, Mom," Billy sensed that this was his chance. "You're the boss. He'll do whatever *you* say."

"That's not true, young man," she said, half-bristling and half-proud at the truth of it. "He'll be home soon and we'll talk about it then. After dinner."

"Where is Stanley? Such a lovely day for a family to be together," Enid said, rubbing the cat's chin and throat. It began to purr with a strong, deep thrum that seemed to make the whole chair vibrate.

"Golfing," Billy sighed.

"That's not *true*," his mother said, her sharpness returned. "You know how we feel about that. It is the absolute worst thing you can be – a *liar*." She collected the plates and glasses, and began stacking the tray. "We decided it was best for the budget if he didn't golf today. Besides, he's working on a surprise."

"Another 'masterpiece'?" Billy said.

"Don't be *smart*," she mouthed through a sheen of sweat. "It'll be finished by next weekend. I hope you appreciate it."

Elizabeth picked up the tray and waddled to the kitchen. Billy heard the water turn on and the dishes clanking in the sink. The clamour made the cat squirm in his arms, so he set it down on the deck before it got the notion to claw its way free.

"Do you think they'll let me keep it?" he asked, brushing the strands of white and black fur from his sleeves. The cat twisted its head and hunched to the side, licking and gnawing at the dark spot on its flank.

"Oh, I wouldn't be surprised," Mrs. Thomas shimmied her chair closer to him. "They haven't been shy to adopt before, and look how well *that* turned out." Enid tried to pinch Billy's cheek but he lowered his head and leaned away, curly bangs obscuring his eyes.

She reached for her purse on the table. For as long as the boy had known her she had had the same purse. It was shiny and black, and had a white cat embroidered on the side. The cat stood on its hind legs, swatting at a white butterfly that was just out of reach. They looked like pale shadows, frolicking in the dark.

Mrs. Thomas flicked the clasp, dug through the tattered folds of the purse, and pulled out a black marker.

"I'm so lucky," she said, twisting the cap off and releasing its sharp licorice scent. "I get to be the first to sign your cast." She adjusted her glasses and bent down, hovering close to the plaster before marking it with lines of black ink.

Billy's mother emerged from the kitchen with a damp cloth in hand. She had every intention of cleaning the patio table, but paused to watch the old woman draw.

"She's signing my cast," Billy said, smiling as he put on his sunglasses.

"Like an autograph, but in reverse," Enid smiled.

His mother watched her scrawl and squiggle on the boy's leg. As Billy basked in the sun and sipped the last of his lemonade, she couldn't help but think that the crazy old lady was right — he *did* look a bit like a movie star.

"Finished," Mrs. Thomas sat up and capped the marker. "Keep it in the sun and it'll be dry in no time."

Billy tilted his head to make sense of the drawing and the words surrounding it. The curves and angled lines made a familiar shape on his leg, like a symbol you might find in an ancient history book.

It was the face of a cat.

ONE TO WATCH OVER YOU.
AND THIS ONE TO HEAL YOU.
LOVE ALWAYS, ENID

"Thank you, Mrs. Thomas. Thank you very much," Billy said, reaching out and wrapping his arms around her.

"My pleasure, Billy," Enid rubbed his back and kissed his forehead. "My pleasure."

"That's very sweet," his mother said as she spritzed and wiped the tabletop. "But remember...we haven't said you can *keep* it yet. There's still a lot to talk about."

"I understand completely, Elizabeth," Enid said, shifting back to her delicate, honeyed tone. "So, let's give it a week, shall we? I'll supply the food and the litter. If it doesn't work out, then he'll probably come back on his own. But if he likes you? You couldn't keep him away if you tried."

"It's a *he?*" Billy said, spying the cat hop into an empty flowerpot. It disappeared, save for the tip of its tail.

"Yes dear, he's been fixed," Enid said. "No bad behaviours to worry about, even though he's still a boy." She went to pinch Billy's cheek again and this time he didn't resist.

"Fine. We'll talk about 'him' tonight," Elizabeth said, wiping the table to a shine. "But *he* won't have much say in the matter."

"You might be surprised, dear. Cats are special," Enid gave Billy another covert wink. "More often than not, they adopt *us.*"

Mrs. Thomas was slow to stand, and they could all hear the clicks and pops of her joints. Billy's mother led the old woman to the kitchen door, saying kind words about her hair and her sundress, and thanking her for the pie.

"Thank *you* for the hospitality," Enid said, pausing in the doorway to look over her shoulder. "And you, take care of yourself, young man. I expect to see you dashing through my sunflowers in no time. In fact, how long *is* it until the cast comes off?"

Billy's mother smiled weakly, and took a measured breath before she spoke. "Well, a watched pot never boils, and all that. There'll be a follow-up in Middleton in a month or so, and we don't want to rush things. I'm sure the doctors know best."

She patted the old woman on the back, urging her back into the kitchen. Billy watched through the windows as his mother escorted Mrs. Thomas all the way to the front door.

The cat peered over the rim of the flowerpot, spying the shadows that moved behind the glass. Its whiskers quivered, and the dark flesh of its lips pulled back from its teeth. Its eyes narrowed, its ears stiffened, and its mouth drooped open.

There was an unexpected thought that whispered in the boy's head then. He didn't know where it came from but it was there nonetheless, itchy and unavoidable, as the ladies bid their fond farewells.

My mother is hiding something.

Billy heard the door shut. The cat turned its golden gaze upon him, and slowly blinked once.

I V

Of Clouds and Claws

IN THE WEEK THAT FOLLOWED there was a change in Billy. He wasn't moping on the cot anymore, crutches unused at his bedside. He didn't leave his trays of food half-eaten. His eyes were no longer glassy and distant, and only interested in TV.

Instead, the boy had some spark, a growing appetite, and a resurrected smile. And it was obvious to anyone with a pair of eyes and a whisker of common sense as to the reason why.

Billy had made a friend.

From the hour he woke until the hour he slept, (and often the hours through the night), the cat stayed close to the boy. It would sit on the bed and clean itself, or follow a few feet behind as Billy practiced navigating the house on the crutches. But mostly it slept, curled in a warm mound of white and black by his side.

A few times each day, the cat would disappear. Billy would ask his mother to look for it, but she would just sigh and assure him that it was probably off doing what cats tend to do.

To her mounting dismay, she'd stumble across it nosing around the house, rubbing against furniture to mark its new territory, or sharpening its claws on cardboard boxes in the den. As the days wore on, the woman would prove to be less than delighted at the discovery of bits of fur in increasingly strange and hard to reach places.

But Elizabeth Brahm was one to count her blessings. She smiled with relief when she saw the thing paw at the back door, demanding to be let outside to engage in its bathroom business. The litter-box that Mrs. Thomas had delivered, along with a bag of dried corn litter – 'It's practically odourless!' Enid had said, with Elizabeth crinkling her nose – sat unused in the basement, between the furnace and the laundry machine.

More importantly, the creature was quiet. During that first week it didn't meow, or screech, or hiss even once. The only sound it made was a gentle purring when it was stroked. And that would only happen when it was in direct contact with her son.

When Billy would call to it with a generic 'Here kitty – here kitty, kitty', the cat would eventually trot into the room, spring up on the cot, and sit at the boy's feet. It would stare with its tiny head cocked to the left, looking somewhat annoyed, as if to say: 'I hope this is important. I was busy.'

"You should give him a name," Stanley Brahm said, opening the newspaper. "How would you feel if we only said 'Hey kid – kid, kid!' all the time?"

Billy's father had been coming in late for dinner all week, smelling like wood chips and varnish and tangy sweat. He'd normally get home by 5:30, but was taking advantage of the longer daylight for some secret project by the back garden. If Billy listened hard when he ate lunch on the patio with his mother, he could hear the faint *tip-tap* and *zip-zoop* of hammers and handsaws beyond the meadow.

"Don't encourage him, Stanley," Elizabeth said, taking her husband's dinner plate out of the oven. She popped the cap off a bottle of home-brewed beer and handed it to him. "We still haven't decided whether it will be staying."

Billy knew that the only way to keep the cat was to get his parents involved with it – to make the connection *personal*. Naming together was a good first step.

"What do you think would be a good name?" Billy said. He remembered asking Mrs. Thomas how she was able to come up with names for all of her cats. "*It's not my job to name them,*" she had said. "*It's my job to listen, and hear what they want to be called.*"

"Did I ever tell you I had a dog when I was your age?" his father said. "A big golden retriever. When it was a puppy, it would run around the yard, tear up the grass and flowerbeds, and try to dig holes clean through to China."

"Which is why we *don't* have a dog," his mother said from the kitchen, clinking the dishes in the sink.

"Be that as it may, dear, my Dad took one look at that pup going crazy in the yard and said, '*That right there is a dog that wants to go places. That's a travelin' dog.*'

Stanley went over to the bookshelf, and pulled out a large black atlas. "My Dad made me flip through one of these with my eyes closed, and then point to a random spot on a page. The closest place to my finger? That wound up being the dog's name – Jasper."

"What happened to him, dad?" Billy asked.

His father took the last swig of beer, and fiddled with the soggy label that was peeling off the bottle. "We moved a few years later and had to give him away. Found him a good home, though. Yep. I'm sure he had a good life."

Stanley Brahm tousled his son's hair, and gave the cat a quick scratch behind the ears. Billy and the cat both watched his father leave the room. When he was gone the cat licked a front paw, and then rubbed it across the top of his head where he'd been touched.

Billy flipped open the atlas, closed his eyes, and did what his father had described. He flipped the pages and jabbed his finger down at least fifty times – *Vancouver, Saskatoon, Orillia* – but none of them sounded right. They sounded like boring names of all the places he'd never see.

"Okay kiddo, time for bed," his father poked his head into the room. "Get a good sleep. Your mother says you've been moving around more. If you're feeling up to it, we'll go out to the garden tomorrow. Might have something waiting back there for you."

"What?" Billy said. "What is it?"

His mother came in the room and shoo'ed the cat from the bed. She fluffed up his pillow, straightened the blankets, and then tucked Billy snugly within them.

"Gimme-gimme never gets, don't you know your manners yet?" she said with a kiss goodnight on the cheek. The kiss smelled of dish-soap, and wine, and of the baking chocolate he knew was hidden on the top shelf of the spice cabinet. "Goodnight," she said, and clicked the light off as they left the room.

"G'night," he said.

When they had gone upstairs, Billy pulled himself free from the coffin of blankets and patted the mattress. He felt a soft and silent impact as the cat leapt onto the cot and padded across the bed. It stepped onto his belly, proceeded up to his chest, and sat.

The boy could only see its outline and the glints of moonlight reflected in its eyes, big and round and black in the darkened room. The cat leaned forward and pressed its wet nose against the boy's lips, tickling his chin with its whiskers.

Billy had read the myths. In the middle ages, some thought felines were demons that preyed on small children. The creatures would crouch on their victims' chests as they slept, and then steal their breath. If they stole enough, they'd have the child's soul.

The boy knew that was nonsense. He'd had better sleeps and no bad dreams since the cat arrived. So, the next day, before going to see any 'surprise' his parents had planned, Billy would reward his new friend.

He would take him to his favourite place in the world.

The boxy green tractor bumped and bounced and sputtered up the dry dirt road.

Billy sat in a wooden trailer pulled behind it, gripping its raised edge with one hand and cradling the cat against his chest with the other. The cat's head bobbed along with the trailer's motion, its gaze transfixed by Billy's crutches clattering back and forth beside his outstretched legs.

His father was driving, and would look over his shoulder every few meters to check on Billy, though he didn't speak. His mother had already walked up to the garden, straw baskets in hand, still tense from the morning's argument.

Billy had washed and dressed himself early, and keenly declared his intentions for the day. That's when everything went sour.

"You're not going *there* today," his mother had said, snatching the cereal bowls from the table. "Your father has been slaving on something for you, so that's where you're going."

"That's not *fair*," Billy had said, adding some edge to his whine. "It's my first day really outside, and we're heading back there anyway. I don't understand what the big deal is."

"No back-talk. That's final," his mother had said, folding the dishtowels for the third time that morning.

"Just a little while," Billy had pleaded. "I just want to take him there to play..."

"That's *enough*. If you keep this up, you can forget any talk of 'playing' this summer, or certainly of having a pet. In fact, I think you're getting far too attached to something we haven't said you could *keep*."

Billy lowered his head then, and his hands had curled into fists. He wasn't going to lash out, even if a part of him desperately wanted to. Instead, he was digging his nails into his palms.

He was trying his hardest not to cry.

"Oh, don't be so dramatic," his mother had tossed some paper towels on the table in front of him.

Billy swallowed hard, took the squares of paper in his trembling hands, and tore them up instead.

"How dare you waste those," she had said, hurling the scraps into the bin. "You have no respect for the value of things, young man, or of people's time and effort. No respect at *all*."

He gulped at the air then, the first few tears striking the formica tabletop in muted splatters. His next instinct was to bury his face in his armpit, and convulse with each muffled sob.

"It's not a big deal, Liz," his father had said, quiet at the table until that moment. He drummed his calloused fingers on the table's edge, and spun a chipped teacup in clockwise circles by the handle.

"A united front, Stanley," his mother had said, her face matching the shade of the cherry dishtowels. "We have to be a *united front*.

That's what all the books say. Otherwise, they never learn who's in charge."

Billy pushed back from the table then, and hopped to the living room without his crutches. He collapsed face-first into his pillow, clamping it around his head. The cat had been sleeping on the bed, and leapt back with the impact, wide-eyed and confused.

Billy couldn't hear much with the pillow against both ears but he knew his parents were fighting. It frightened him when they fought, and made him worry for the future. But, in the boy's heart, he also knew that today the risks were justified.

It was the only way, Billy thought, as the shouting grew and his pillowcase went damp. *It was the only way to get what I wanted.*

The tractor shifted gears and jerked to a stop.

Even at a snail's pace, it was just a quarter of a kilometer up the trail to their garden plot. This equated to a few minutes of laboured chugging up the hill.

But for Billy, who had been through so much the past few weeks? The last visit here felt like a lifetime ago.

His father killed the engine and walked around to unhinge the back flap. Billy scooted out with crutches in one hand, and a wriggling feline in the other.

"Let me take him." His father pried the cat from Billy's hand so the boy could stand on the crutches.

"Okay," said Billy, getting his balance and turning to head up the path. "But don't put him down 'til we're inside."

Billy's father held up the cat in front of his face, and watched it swipe at the empty air. "You know he's probably just gonna bolt back to the house, right? That's where the food is. That's what I'd do."

"He's not like you," Billy said, already halfway up the path.

Stanley put one hand under the cat's back feet and gave its chest a squeeze to keep it from wriggling free. It kicked and struggled as he walked up the path, but otherwise protested in silence. It finally surrendered and went limp as they met Billy at the path's end.

"Let me get the latch," his father said, and he pulled at the rusted gate. It swung open with a grinding, metallic squeal that echoed down the hill and into the valley. "Jeez, if anything wakes 'em up, it'll be that—"

"They're not *sleeping*, Dad," the boy said, annoyed. "They're dead."

Billy's parents never understood his love for the old cemetery. From the time he began walking outside, he had been drawn to this stark, hedged square that crowned the lone hill on the back of their property.

The township hadn't sent someone to maintain it in years and the lack of care was showing. The fence around its perimeter was more rust than black iron, and wild vines choked the life out of the bare, blackened trees that marked its corners. The scattered tombstones were cracked or crumbling outright, and the markings on them — the dates and symbols and solemn epitaphs — had mostly faded beyond recognition.

"Well, if anything pops out of the ground, gimme a holler," his father said, plunking the cat in the dry grass. "I'll be back in a bit, after I've helped your mother with the carrots. Don't wander off."

The boy didn't smile or acknowledge his father's weak attempt at humour for cripples. But it didn't bother him either. Billy Brahm was right where he wanted to be.

His father shut the gate behind him. If he was trying to keep his little friend from leaving, he shouldn't have been concerned.

The cat's eyes widened and pupils narrowed. It slinked through the tall clover and tufts of wild grass, stalking a black-and-orange flutter.

A monarch butterfly circled just out of reach, and landed on the arm of an old stone cross.

The sun was high in the sky, poking through rifts of billowing summer cloud. Billy planted his crutches into the dry earth, breathed in the warm air, and pushed past a row of headstones.

The more 'recent' ones – from 1900 onward – were simple in design. They had curved tops, smooth edges, and clear names and dates chiseled into their faces.

As he moved towards the far corner, the stones became older and more ornate. Markers were topped with carvings – like angels, hands holding books, doves with sprigs of ivy – and held engraved verse on their faces.

They told short tales of family, and travel, and sorrow.

SIR WENDELL SMYTHE

WITH WIFE MARY AND TWO SONS

DECEMBER 2nd, 1826

BUILDER OF BRIDGES, MAKER OF TOWNS

TAKEN BY SICKNESS IN THE NEW WORLD

And another:

FATHER GEORGE TINKER

GIVEN TO THE GROUND

JULY 10th, 1773

HE BROUGHT THE WORD TO HEATHENS

HE IS SURELY SEATED AT GOD'S TABLE

The further back he went, the harder the writing was to decipher. As a curious young detective, Billy had spent many afternoons with charcoal and tracing paper making impressions of the stones, and had graves dating back to the early 1700's. He liked to imagine all of them as adventurers braving the open seas, overcoming hardship and loss, excited to begin new lives in another time and place.

Back by the thorny hedge, two large slabs laid flat on raised mounds. They were rectangles of stone, and probably the oldest markers in the cemetery. This is where he usually came to rest, atop one of them. Their ridged faces were worn smooth from wind and rain, so Billy could lay down with his hands behind his head and look up – past the prickly hedge, and through the twisted branches of the bald maple that leaned over it – to the realm that loomed above.

Billy would see all sorts of things again and again in the puffs of white and grey. Helmed knights with swords raised. Winged beasts belching smoke. Ghostly galleons, tossed on waves of cloud. Billy could marvel for hours as the shapes grew, and twisted, and smooshed together before dissolving in an ocean of brilliant blue.

But on this day, Billy saw something new – a *face.*

Tips of wayward cloud trailed, and started to resemble tufted ears and curved teeth. Narrow, jet-trail wisps formed clear lines protruding from either side. Darker rifts of cloud lingered in arcing parallel, like stripes. And two large gaps at the top, oval and empty, seemed like mournful eyes watching him from another world.

The boy lost himself in its gaze. And, as he began to drift, a sleeping memory stirred in him and spoke in a cold whisper.

'Find the one who hears...through the Veil of Tears...with the fang o' the Great Cat's Maw.'

MrrROW.

Billy, jarred by the sound, sat up.

The cat was pacing back and forth at the foot of the slab, rubbing itself against its edge. His black tail was pointing up, quivering as he paced. He peered over the edge of the stone, and spoke again.

Mrrowww.

The sound was soft and inquisitive, and lilted up at the end like a question. It was the first time that the cat had shared its voice, and to the boy it was as beautiful as any sound he had ever heard.

"So you *can* talk," Billy leaned forward on the stone.

T-t-t-r-r-rowwww. The cat trilled in answer, and then blinked before ducking behind the slab.

"What are you doing?" Billy said, crawling over to the grave's edge.

He saw the cat pawing on the side of the mound. It had found a large anthill, and the troops were swarming around the entrance. There were hundreds of them, armoured frames pulsing in unison, like a beating heart sending black veins into the dirt.

"No," Billy hoisted the cat up and away from the ants. "Don't do that. They'll bite you." Billy cradled it in one arm and wagged a finger in its face.

The cat's tail thumped against the stone, unimpressed. Billy tried to hold it still, but the cat lashed out a paw and dug its claws into his scolding finger.

"Owww!" he yipped, shoving the cat from his arms and over the side of the grave into the tall grass. It shook itself as a wet dog would before bobbing its head as it licked at its shoulder.

"What was that for?" Billy sucked on his finger and checked to see if any blood was drawn.

MRRR-rrrrr.

The cat's voice was throaty and low, and it wouldn't meet Billy's gaze. Mrs. Thomas had taught him what that meant, yet this time the boy didn't need to be standing in the way of a hungry cat's dinner bowl to get the message. It was a warning.

"Fine," said Billy, sliding off the stone and picking up his crutches, "but don't come to me when you're covered in bites."

He huffed as he strode, the old wood squeaking each time the rubber tips struck the ground. When Billy reached the entrance and called to his father, he thought he heard the cat's mewing, muffled by the squeal of the gate.

A chill raced up the boy's spine, and the hairs on his forearms stood on end. He turned around, half-expecting to see the cat bounding towards him, but it was gone. He called out to it, but the only reply came from whistling wind.

Billy ambled down the slope, climbed into the trailer, and laid down on the dusty tarp. The face in the clouds had vanished too, swallowed by waves of grey. They rolled over the world like a stormy sea, and seemed to be getting darker by the minute.

As his mind drifted back into the sky, the trees began to creak and sway. The wind danced in the willows by the cemetery on the hill, and Billy listened.

He heard something then, like a whisper beneath the world, or an echo from the corners of his darkest dream. Two pained words.

'Nooooo...morrrrre.'

A dog barked in the distance. Another chill shot through the boy, and his leg began to ache.

V

Of Forts and Falling

AS THE TRACTOR RUMBLED past the vegetable garden, Billy waved to his mother. She paused for a truce in her battle with deep-planted carrots and called out to him.

"Close your eyes!" she hollered, covering her face with dusty garden gloves.

Billy played along, and did the same. It wasn't anywhere near Christmas, and he'd already wrecked his birthday presents in the accident, so he wasn't expecting much of anything. Maybe they made him his own garden plot – a clever bit of blackmail that would assure productive (and pickled) contributions in the future.

After a few more minutes of bumps and turns, the engine coughed and the tractor lurched to a stop.

"Can I look now?" Billy said.

"Just a minute," Stanley stepped down from the driver's seat and opened the trailer door.

Billy felt himself slide out of the trailer and then his father's arms reach under to lift him, one supporting his legs and the other his back. As he was carried a few steps into the breeze, Billy caught a whiff of sweat and earth and drugstore aftershave – Stanley Brahm's scents of summer.

The footsteps came to a halt.

"How about *now*?" Billy said.

"Nawwww...you wouldn't like it," his father said, clamping his own hand over Billy's face.

"Oh, come on!" Billy twisted in his father's arms, freeing his face for a look.

At first, because he was facing down, all he saw was the sandpit. But, as he turned, he could see thick wooden posts sticking out of it. And beams between the posts. And overlapping planks attached to the beams to form a floor, four walls, and a flat roof.

It was a fort.

"Oh my God," Billy said, staring slack-jawed at the structure. "*You* made this?"

"First, watch the language. We're not religious," his father chided. "Second, what do you think I was doing last weekend, and after work all week?"

"Golfing?"

"A bit beyond our budget this summer," his father said. "But it was a golfing buddy that gave us all the wood. That's what they call 'networking'. Meanwhile, this'll give you something to do while you heal up, instead of being stuck in the house."

"It's amazing," Billy said, and he meant it. "I can come out here by myself?"

"That's the idea. Instead of wearing a groove in the carpet, you can get some exercise gimping up here." He patted Billy's cast and set him down on his feet, leaning against the tractor. "That way, your mother doesn't have to drive the tractor, which is—"

"A waste of *gas*," Billy hobbled towards the ladder that led up to the entrance. It was more step-like, with wide boards spaced between two angled struts. It would allow him to climb up without his crutches, even with a backpack on.

"I know, I know," his father said, "She can be a stickler, but saving money helps to pay for these..."

He reached into a burlap sack in the tractor's cab, pulled out two navy blue bricks of plastic, and gave one to Billy. The boy was quick to realize what he held in his hands.

"Walkie-talkies!" Billy said, playing with the buttons and dials until the receiver made a *squawwwk*. "I wanted these for my birthday."

"We know. You told us. Many times." His father slid open the battery panels and checked the connections. "We ordered them a couple of months ago from the hardware store but they came in late. Sorry, kiddo – these things happen."

"That's okay," Billy said, feeling a tad ashamed. Following his spaghetti-and-meatball birthday dinner, when he had blown out the candles on the homemade double-chocolate cake, and right after ripping open two presents wrapped in that week's newspaper? The boy hadn't been shy in asking *'Where are the rest?'*

"So, it's pretty basic stuff," his father twiddled the knobs on his walkie. "Just tune to this channel, turn the volume up about three-quarters, and press the big red button when you want to talk. Got it?"

"Got it," Billy pressed the button a few times to hear the static pop on both boxes. "*Testing, testing, 1, 2, 3—*"

"Roger. Testing. Repeat after me," his father pressed his mouth against the mic panel. "*I am a fart-face, fart-face, fart-face, over.*"

"C'mon, Dad," Billy moaned, "it's not like I'm *six*." He thumbed down the volume, and clipped the walkie-talkie to the front pocket of his jean shorts.

"Not so long ago then," his father said, clipping his to the front of his fraying overalls. "You're all set. I tested their range already, and they reach the garden and the house. So, let me just help you climb up and—"

"I can do it," Billy pushed him aside, and crawled up step by step.

"Alright," his father climbed back on the tractor, "I'll be in the garden."

"Hey Dad...?" Billy said, approaching the top.

"Mmhmm?"

"If you see the cat, tell him where I am."

"Right." His father stepped on the gas pedal, and fired up the engine.

From the top of the ladder, Billy watched the tractor putter back down the trail towards the garden. It wasn't that far away, but it was over a ridge and around a treed bend. A minute later his father was out of sight. But Billy was amazed by what he *could* see. Seated on the planked floor of the fort, he had a view all the way across the valley.

Billy scanned the vast dairy pastures a few properties over and spotted the river meandering through them. It veered to the east and was capped by a modern dam that was one of the town's few tourist attractions. In the other direction, he could just make out the shape of the old radio tower that marked the industrial edge of town. Off to the north, the sea of clouds had washed over the hilltops, parting only to make room for a lonely peak.

Billy lifted up his legs and spun on his bottom to look inside the fort. His father had cut a window in the ply-board sheet that made the far wall. He crawled across the floor, ignoring the splinters collecting in his palms and bare knee, and stuck his head out the window.

The pit didn't seem *that* far down. If his leg hadn't been broken, Billy would've been tempted to leap out with a barbaric cry. He pictured himself scrambling across the sand, cardboard tube-sword drawn, ready for battle in some forgotten kingdom. He'd rally warriors to his side. Lead armies through the desert. Defend the realm against the greatest Evil the world had ever known.

Billy didn't hear them at first. He didn't sense them hovering overhead, moving closer with each breath that he took. He didn't know until something pinched the back of his neck, just below the hairline.

There was a pain. It was fast and sharp and stabbing. And it *burned*.

He fell sideways to the floor, catching his hand on an exposed nail. The metal went deep, opening a gash on his palm and spilling blood down his wrist. The boy groaned, and slapped at the back of his neck with his good hand. He felt something *crunch*. He squeezed it hard between his fingers and threw it out the window.

That's when he heard it – the *buzzing*. To this day, Billy Brahm would swear on his life that it spoke to him.

'*Cursed...cursed...curssssssed.*'

He rolled onto his back, and saw the things dart and circle around the ceiling. He watched their ranks swell in the air around him, filling it with their angry, alien drone. They hovered there, sharp and black and terrible.

And then the wasps attacked.

The swarm started on Billy's head. They were swift and merciless, jabbing into the boy's cheeks and forehead then stinging his scalp as he tried to swat the first wave back.

When he rolled across the floor and flailed his arms around his head, they struck at his bare arms and leg. When he tucked into a ball and tried to cover up they pierced the thin fabric of his shirt, savaging his back with stings.

Mrrreeeowww.

Billy heard the yowl and squinted through his fingers to see what made it. In the heart of the swarm, he spied a whirling and furious shape – a *shadow* – striking at the air and sending bits of bug raining to the floor.

The wasps regrouped, and swept down to strike at the boy's hands. Billy wanted to scream but was afraid to open his mouth. Tears threatened to burst from his eyes. But then he heard it again. Closer. Louder. Unmistakable.

MMRRRAHHWWWWWW.

The cat.

He stood on hind legs in the fort's entrance, swatting at the cloud of wasps circling his head. The ones who dared to descend and sting him were quickly torn from his body and bitten in half.

The horrible scene slowed in Billy's mind. For a moment, as he watched his friend hiss and shriek and crush the winged devils in his jaws, the boy's fear ebbed. His hands stopped shaking, and he reached for the walkie-talkie dangling at his waist.

"Help–" he stammered, fumbling at the thing with swollen, bloody palms. He jammed at the red button again and again. "*HELP US!*"

Billy crawled into the heart of the angry swarm and swept the cat up in his arms. It hissed, and clawed, and even bit him on the shoulder in a feral rage.

But Billy didn't feel it. He was drunk with panic, save for the only thought in his young head that made any sense. With a crown of wasps stabbing at his eyes and ears, he loped across the planks with the cat clutched to his chest...

And then he leapt out the window.

The world went quiet. A cool breeze kissed Billy's face as he fell. He saw the sand dune rushing up to meet him and opened his arms. He felt four strong paws push off from his chest, and watched the spotted blur twist away from him.

He'll land on his feet, Billy thought. *He's a cat, after all.*

The boy almost smiled as he crashed into the sand, and then the world went dark.

Billy felt the cold, and knew he was in the bathtub.

He gasped, inhaling the sharp stench of vinegar. His cast was propped over the edge of the tub. It didn't look damaged. Billy could see that the toes poking out of it were caked in sand.

He tried to wiggle them, but they wouldn't move.

"It's okay," his mother said, looking anything but calm as she dabbed baking soda on the welts on his face. "A doctor's on the way. You need to stay in here so we can bring the swelling down."

The baking soda fizzed as the vinegary water splashed on it. He remembered the third-grade Science Fair, the one where he made a soda-and-vinegar volcano. It had won him a pretty red ribbon. Now he was covered in tiny, blistering volcanoes of the same colour.

"Where is he...?" Billy groaned, touching his face. He was shocked at the number of the lumps that he felt, and pictured his face like one of his father's golf balls, but with the dimples pushed outward instead.

"Where is who?" she pulled Billy's hand down from his face. "Don't touch them, it will only make it worse. That's what the doctor said. Forty-three stings, Billy. *Forty-three*. How could this happen?"

"I didn't do anything," Billy felt faint at his mother's words. "I was just sitting in the fort and they attacked me. But the cat...it tried to help—"

"Stop the nonsense," his mother snapped. "And why on Earth would you be so stupid as to jump out the window?"

"I was scared," Billy said, shivering in the tub. "I'm cold. Where *is* he...?"

"Stanley!" his mother turned off the tap and poured in more vinegar. "You should call them again."

"Hold your horses," his father said from the front room. "He's just pulling in the driveway now."

"I hate this," his mother dabbed a square of toilet paper at the corners of her eyes. "I hate that this keeps *happening*." She patted his hand as she spoke, and kept on patting as his father and a thin man with bushy eyebrows joined them in the bathroom.

The doctor and his parents began to speak. Their voices were faint, and seemed to melt into each other. Billy felt flushed and weak as he listened. It felt like he was about to boil, and disappear in the steam.

"He has a bad fever."

"How could you not see a nest?"

"He's lucky. People have died..."

"I swear it wasn't there yesterday."

"His toes...is the leg getting worse?"

"The fever should break in his sleep."

"The leg can't get much worse."

"You...are...CURSED."

Billy was pulled from the tub and then moved to the cot. He was forced to drink something cold and salty. A feverish ache burned through his body. The wasps' venom had dug past his skin, and slithered into his veins.

"Please..." Billy moaned. Someone placed a cold towel over his face, dimming the world even further. *"Where is he?"*

"Shhhhh," a voice said, far away in the dark. *"Sleep, child. Wish yourself good dreams..."*

The words lingered as he lost consciousness, and somehow the boy heeded them. His last thought was a wish, and that wish was for a dream.

That's when it happened.

That's when it came to him.

That's when Billy Brahm stepped through the Veil, and saw the other side.

V I

Of Stones and Shadow

THE TREES WERE DENSE, and the giant leaves obscured any sunlight. Yet the jungle glowed somehow, its greenness filling each of his breaths with a vibrant force. There was magic in this place. He knew this.

Billy Brahm also knew that he was dreaming. He was completely aware that he was still on the cot in the living room, covered in wasp stings and dabs of baking soda, and fighting a bad fever. That was his reality.

But this place felt more *real* than anything the boy had ever experienced in his young life.

He pushed his way through the jungle, damp earth yielding beneath bare feet. Each step sent shivers up his legs like faint shocks of electricity. The feeling grew as he walked, the energy washing over and through him in a ceaseless, tingling tide.

Billy touched the trees and leaves and glistening vines along his path, and the sensation continued. He passed beneath huge flowers hanging like violet lanterns in a leafy cathedral, their scent making him swoon with a warm, penetrating sweetness.

There was a sound. It seemed to come from all sides, but was strongest just in front of him. It grew as the boy pushed onward, and began emanating from the trees, the plants, the ground, and even the air itself.

Humming.

The hum enveloped Billy's face. It compelled him forward through the twisting trees and tangled roots, until a curtain of massive leaves blocked his path. He blew on a leaf and it shivered, thin as paper, a veined page in some emerald book that waited to be turned.

He grasped the edge of one to pull it aside, and felt the hum move into his hand and ripple up his arm. As the leaf yielded to him, a brightness beyond filled his eyes. The hum grew, and spilled into his chest.

Music.

That was the only way to describe what the boy felt then. The most beautiful music imaginable was being played inside of him, filling him with a feeling he had known so rarely in the waking world. Peace. As he stepped into the brightness tears welled in his eyes, but it wasn't from pain. Or from fear. Or even from the sadness that he knew so well.

Billy Brahm cried for the breathless wonder that lay before him.

The jungle grotto gleamed from every surface. Every blade of grass, and flower petal, and bare stone, and drop of water *shone* like a million diamonds spinning in the sun.

At first, Billy shielded his eyes for fear that he would go blind. But then he listened to the music swelling in his chest. He surrendered to the song being hummed by all things in this sacred place. The boy relaxed then, and he remembered.

This is a dream, Billy thought. *This is MY dream.*

He stepped onto the cool grass. The grotto was like a valley the size of his school playground, sheltered on all sides by dense jungle and bleached walls of stone. Looking up, the trees and cliffs seemed to stretch forever, as they often do in a dream. The dome of sky was clear and sapphire, with points of light that turned and twinkled within it like daytime constellations.

He walked along the sloping ground, the grass whispering against his heels and toes. From all sides of the clearing the earth dipped down towards the middle, forming a verdant bowl of grass, wildflowers, and rich brown earth. A sparkling waterfall cascaded down the ivory stone face of the far wall, filling the space with a mist that refracted the light, making tiny rainbows flicker in the air.

The water flowed down the sloped earth and into a pool in the center. The pool was made of interlocking stones in two shades, forming alternating peaks of light and dark on its raised edge and outer facade. This was a distinct structure, and the only thing within the space that seemed crafted by another's hand. The boy knew that there was something important here – something old, and powerful, and beyond the dream itself.

Billy stepped towards the pool and knelt down by its edge. The hum hammered in his belly and chest now, and began to climb into his throat. He gripped the stone rim and leaned forward. The hum rose, and Billy felt as if he were about to vomit.

He opened his mouth over the pool's still water. He tried to breathe, but the vibration within him wrestled with the air and won. It slid from his throat, flattened his tongue, and rattled his teeth as it was born into the air.

RRRRRAAAAAAAAAAAAHHHHHH.

The boy was helpless as it came, as it pushed its way through him and made the air itself shake. Every cell in his body trembled with the same awesome frequency. Billy felt as if a light was beneath his skin, growing so bright that it would burst him into a thousand shining pieces.

He could see the waves of sound moving through the air, making it warp and shimmer before striking the surface of the pool. The hum hit the water like a stone being dropped from a height and made perfect circles ripple out from the middle, each one colliding with a splash against the pool's edge. The pool began to brighten, and soon all of the water in the grotto – in the stream, in the mists, and in the great waterfall – was aglow like iron in a fire.

Billy's fingers dug into the stone as his chest began to heave. His mouth and eyes were strained wide, and tears gleamed on his cheeks. The hum grew deafening, the light blinding, and the boy feared that what began as a dream could very well be the end of him.

The hum became a scream of angels. The waterfall, brilliant as a bolt of lightning in a summer storm, was cleaved in two. Its shimmering flow parted and something emerged from the darkness behind it, and into the light.

The hum ceased. The grotto dimmed.

Billy gasped, collapsing on the stony rim of the pool. His hands dangled in the water. The few lingering ripples rushed past his fingertips, cool and silent.

The figure in the distance moved forward. As it stepped, smooth stones rose to meet its feet. They pushed the stream aside, giving the illusion that the thing was gliding towards him.

Through the mists, Billy could see that it had the shape of a man, though larger. Much larger. As it neared, the boy thought that, once upon him, the thing could conceivably blot out the sky.

Billy lifted himself from the pool's edge and sat perfectly still, watching it approach. His fear was fading, and with each breath he took it was being replaced by something else entirely.

Awe.

The figure stood at the side of the pool, towering and motionless. It was clad in a robe of radiant scarlet, fringed in golden bands of thread. The threads appeared to *move* when he looked at them long enough, shifting and twisting and worming across the red fabric. Long, wide sleeves hung low at its sides hiding its hands from view. A wide-peaked hood did the same for its face, obscuring it in shadow.

Billy watched this mysterious being cloaked in red. He watched as it stood before him in this fantastic place. He watched as the air around it hummed with power. He watched, transfixed by its strangeness, and by its majesty.

Billy watched it for so long, he almost forgot that he was dreaming. That was when he remembered to blink.

And that is when it spoke to him.

"Why are you here?" the being said. The words boomed and rolled together in a cavernous growl. The surface of the pool trembled, and the sound washed over Billy like warm ocean froth.

"I'm dreaming," said the boy.

"Are you?" it said, raising a robed arm and pointing at the pool.

The words pounded in Billy's head, and he understood what he was being asked to do. He stood slowly, hands pressed against the pool's edge, and gazed into it.

At first he could only see water, and the dark-light pattern of interlocking stones that contained it. He looked harder, and the reflection on its surface came into focus. Billy saw the jungle's edge, and the high cliff, and the water spilling down in the distance. He saw the great robed being, mirrored upside-down in the water, its arm still raised and pointing.

Billy narrowed his gaze to focus on the pool's centre, and saw the sky. The blue dome high above had turned black in the reflection, but the points of light still shone within it. He watched them move and shift and realign, until the last three slid into place, gleaming along their familiar curve.

Billy knew what it was. He knew it from the real world and from his dreams – the constellation *Orion*.

The stars flared, and storm clouds converged upon them. Forks of lightning blazed through the vision's sky, and flooded the pool with light. In a flash, the water churned into a raging sea. The skies shrieked, the seas groaned, and three black mountains rose on the horizon. And there in the heart of the storm, flung about like a child's toy by wind and wave, was where Billy first saw it...

A sailing ship.

Lightning crashed, and the scene burned away. The boy squinted but wouldn't avert his gaze. He knew there was more hiding in the pool's depths. There was something else waiting for him and him alone.

The pool's bottom disappeared, and bubbles began to rise from the blackness. They clung to the surface and linked together, changing shape and colour to make a moving image in the water. A *scene*.

The vision formed, bright and clear in the pool. The boy's heart sank when he understood.

Billy saw *himself*, lying on the cot in his home. There was light creeping through the blinds and casting long shadows across the living room. There was a small towel folded on his forehead, and water dripping from his ears. There were gruesome bumps on his face and neck and arms.

The boy had never seen himself like this, for no normal mirror could reveal what was being shown to him. He was being laid bare, and the secret shame that he carried was written on every curve and bone and pore of him.

Billy Brahm wasn't special. He was just a sad little boy that was too strange, and too weak, and too frightened to be loved. Or, perhaps, to even be alive.

A single tear fell from his eyes, dripping from his chin and into the pool. A tiny wave skimmed across its surface, rippling the vision.

Something changed then. A blur of white and black leapt into the scene from the shadows. It settled at the foot of the boy's bed.

The cat.

"He's back," Billy was tearful, reaching out to touch it. "He came back."

"*You are sick,*" the robed being still loomed by the pool's edge. The words hung in the air, heavy and grave.

"I'll get better," said Billy, hearing the doubt in his own voice, "won't I?"

"*You have help,*" the thing said, "*but not enough.*"

Billy watched the cat sniff along the plaster and stop at the spot where his leg had broken. It shook its head in disgust, yawned, and then draped its paws over the cast and rested its body against it.

The cat's eyes closed. And then, as if leaking through the walls of the dream, Billy could hear purring.

"What's happening?" the boy said, scared and confused.

"*The blood knows. The blood...and the stones.*"

"I...I don't understand," Billy said.

The cat pulled away from the cast and crept up the edge of the bed. It stopped by the boy's hand and sat. It was the same hand that Billy had injured in the fort. It was bandaged, and a spot of blood had leaked through the gauze.

"Blood..." Billy watched the cat lift a paw, and place it on the wound.

"*And stones,*" the being said, its words crossing the pool and ringing in the boy's ears. "*Then you will see. Then you will know.*"

Billy lifted his hand from the pool's edge – the same hand wounded in the waking world – and concentrated.

He closed his eyes, and felt himself lying in the bed. He felt the cloth on his brow, and the heavy blankets on his body. He felt the throbbing heat of the wasp stings, and the gentle touch of the cat's paw pressed against his palm. And then, with a twinge of pain, he felt the cut.

A spot of blood appeared on his hand.

"Yes," the being said. "*Now you will see.*"

Billy smeared the blood on the pool's stone rim, staining it. The streaks of red shivered and bubbled on the rock, shrunk to crimson beads, and disappeared.

"*Now you will know.*"

The pool exploded in flame.

Fire engulfed the boy, blazing on all sides. It burned, but had no heat. He stood there in shock, trying to fathom what he was seeing. It was all around him. Inescapable.

The vision from the pool was projected clear as life on walls of flame. The boy was still lying in bed. There were still blankets, and wasp stings, and dust drifting in rays of sunlight. But the plaster cast was gone.

In its place was his bare leg. The limb was shriveled and blackened. It was plagued with sores that oozed and wept. And through the fire, he could smell it. It was the same terrible smell from his nightmare underground.

Death.

Billy wanted to drop to his knees. He wanted to wail and flee from the awful sight. But he didn't. He couldn't. For, as he gazed into the flames, someone appeared at his bedside.

Who is that? he thought. *My father? A neighbour? Another doctor...?*

A sudden breeze blew the curtains open. A swath of sunlight filled the room. And that's when Billy saw it.

It wasn't a *man* sitting on his bed, clad in a dark cloak. It wasn't a *person* pressing a clawed hand against his. It wasn't a *human* closing its golden eyes, bowing its whiskered face, and thrumming a soulful purr.

"That's...that can't be *real*," Billy stammered.

The walls of flame collapsed. Waves swept through the pool and the scene reverted to its original form, sinking slowly into the water.

The boy was still in a fevered sleep.

His leg was still in a cast.

And the cat – and nothing more than a cat – was curled in a ball at the foot of his bed.

"*You have seen it,*" the being said, lowering its robed arm.

"This is just a *dream*," Billy said, overwhelmed. "I need to wake up now."

"*You are cursed,*" the being turned and took a step around the pool towards him. "*You need help. As do We.*"

"What are you?" Billy said, taking a step backward.

"*FIND me,*" it said, menacing strides bringing it even closer to the boy.

"What ARE you?" Billy said, retreating.

"*In the dream, OUR dream, We will be drawn to it. To the KEY. But We are asleep. You must find it. We must AWAKEN!*" The thing closed in, and reached out a robed arm.

Billy panicked and turned to flee. He had only taken a step before colliding with a muscled wall. It was draped in a blood-red robe, and there was nowhere left to run.

"Please," Billy quivered, "don't hurt me."

"*We will HEAL you, child. Lift the CURSE*," it said, raising its arms, "*but there is a PRICE.*"

"No," Billy cried, "This is just another bad dream. I don't know where to find any *key*...not for you, or for the man with the rats...I just want to wake up!"

"*So...the Enemy moves...gathers at the Gate*," the being's voice softened with a hint of despair. "*Please...help Us. Find the KEY. Find my SHADOW.*"

"I'm sorry," Billy said, moved by a wave of helplessness and curiosity. "I wouldn't even know where to start."

The sleeves of the robe slid back as the being raised its arms. Striped paws with cracked yellow talons pinched either side of the hood fringed in gold, and drew it back.

"*Look for my FACE.*"

Huge, inhuman eyes gaped back at him, fierce points of onyx afloat in radiant blueness. Beneath them was a cavernous and beastly mouth, lined with ivory blades that caged a tongue the breadth of the boy's head.

Billy lifted his hand, suddenly possessed by the mad urge to reach into its jaws. He yearned to *know* the thing. To understand what stood before him like a man, yet wore the face of a tiger.

Trembling, the boy touched a tooth, the longest on the bottom row. It shone, brilliant and blinding like the sun. There was a deafening roar, and then darkness.

Billy lurched up in bed gasping and wild-eyed.

The house was quiet, save for the ticking of their grandfather clock. Morning light spilled through the blinds in the living room. The cat twitched by his feet, wiggled an ear, and continued to purr.

'Find the one who hears through the Veil of Tears with the fang o' the Great Cat's Maw...'

The boy sat there, head fuzzy and awash in whispers. He squeezed his hands, as if clinging to what he had seen for fear that it would slip away.

The cut on his palm had re-opened and the gauze was drenched. Crimson droplets fell from Billy's hand as he squeezed, spattering across his thigh.

The dry plaster drank up the blood, much like the stones had done in his dream.

VII

Of Vets and Visions

THE FAMILY CAR SPED THROUGH THE COUNTRYSIDE, its beige curves rolling beneath sheets of grey draped high above.

The Brahms may have lived in a small town, but today they were definitely headed for the *country*. They passed by endless fields of cattle and corn, acres of tilled brown earth, and orchards that stretched up the valley to meet the horizon.

Stanley whistled as he drove, calling out the names of any 'foreign' license plates he spotted. Elizabeth, anxious and claustrophobic, kept adjusting the air conditioning. Billy had wanted to lower the windows so he could stick out his hand and surf the passing air, but his mother was quick to nix the urge.

"You never know. He could get spooked and jump out the window. Who'd be sorry then, hmmm?" she had said.

But Billy knew his mother wasn't really being cautious. She just didn't like the smell of manure.

A week had passed since the wasp attack and the boy was feeling a bit better, all things considered. The swelling had gone down, with only small crusts lingering to mark the sting sites on his torso, arms, and bare leg.

But the venom and the stress had conspired to make his psoriasis flare back up. Billy wore a long-sleeved plaid shirt to hide the silvery spots, and had asked to cut the right leg off one of his pairs of jeans to conceal it.

"I'm not going to destroy a perfectly good pair of pants because you're self-conscious," she had said. "No one will even notice. Not everything's about *you*."

Billy held a cardboard box in his lap, and teased his fingers in the holes that Mrs. Thomas had cut in the sides. He felt a paw swat at them, and wee teeth gnaw playfully.

Enid had visited after the incident (with pie, of course), and listened to Billy reenact everything that happened in the fort. His parents stood close by, nodding politely and making the odd remark about his 'vivid and dramatic imagination'.

"What's done is done," Enid had said. "You were looking out for your little friend. The least I can do is the same."

The old woman had insisted on making the appointment with the animal doctor, despite Elizabeth's protests – wasp stings were bad enough for a small boy, and the cat had suffered several of his own. When Enid assured them that it would be free ('*He owes me a favour or two from all the repeat business.*'), Billy's mother had acquiesced.

That's when the boy told Mrs. Thomas about his dream.

His mother had been quick to usher Enid out the front door then, with a promise to pick up her homemade cat-carrier later in the day. She had heard more than enough about her son's strange dreams, and questions about his leg, and foolishness about talking cats. The only things she wanted to hear next, after sending the old lady on her way, were the sweet sounds of country music and the popping of a cork.

Billy felt the cat scurry in circles inside the box. It chased after his fingers, and tried to poke its nose out one of the larger holes. Billy tickled the moist pink flesh as it sniffed at the air.

The cat gave his finger a lick with its sandy tongue, retreated, and then pushed up through the cardboard flaps. Its head bobbed up and down with the rhythm of the car, and it turned to watch the green and grey world blur by the window.

"Put him back inside and close the lid right now!" his mother scolded. "If he gets loose and crawls under the pedals, we could have an accident."

"He won't do that," Billy said. "He's just taking a look."

"Don't argue," she said. "Tell him, Stanley."

"Well, your mother has a point," his father hesitated, "but I guess it doesn't matter now—"

"*Stanley*—" she said. Her voice made the cat's ears press back against its head.

"*What*, Liz'? I'm just saying that we're pretty much there."

They passed a row of gnarled trees that marked the boundaries of a chicken and goat farm. Beyond that was a timber fence that snaked up the hillside.

His father signaled a turn and eased the nose of the car into two grooves of mud. They narrowly missed a rusty mailbox with a horse painted on it, marking the driveway's entrance.

"Oh dear, she could've warned us to wear rubber boots," Elizabeth said.

There were puddles and patches of dirt along the sides of the long driveway, leading to a ragged red house and barn. As they drove further back, the rusted corpses of several vehicles were in various stages of digestion by the overgrown lawn.

"Interesting way to live," his mother said, bristling a little with every bump and lurch.

"I don't know...I kinda like it. Rustic," his father said.

"I'd say condemned. How could someone *live* here?"

As the car pulled to a stop in front of the barn, Billy's mother scanned the property. The grass was patchy and uncut, and clumps of dandelions and other weeds were left to grow wild. There was no proper flower garden to speak of, and no clear path leading from the house to the barn. From the rusted pickup parked diagonally across the lane, to the tools and farm implements left scattered on the ground, everything seemed so *haphazard*.

Most disturbing to her were the bowls and bowls of coloured plastic strewn about the property. It was like a pet-food minefield, which meant a high likelihood of even nastier explosions underfoot.

His father turned off the car and beeped the horn twice. There was barking, followed by several *moos*, clucks and quacks, some bleats, and a whinny.

Stanley pointed up at the sign above the barn door: 'ALL CREATURES GREAT AND SMALL'.

"This must be the place."

"Yes, Einstein, a master detective," Elizabeth said.

"Einstein was a *scientist*," Billy said. His mother removed her glasses and massaged the bridge of her nose.

The cacophony of animal noises continued, making the cat anxious in his cardboard prison. It growled, and scratched at the walls of the box. A pack of barking dogs bounded around the corner of the barn, and Billy heard the cat hiss. He tried to calm it by making eye contact through the breathing holes, but the cat swiped at him whenever he got close.

"We need to make them quiet. He's scared," Billy said.

"It's not our place," his mother said. "I'm sure they're perfectly nice creatures."

"Perfectly nice," his father said.

"I just hope he cleans up after this menagerie. *Can you imagine all the poop...?*" she whispered, tucking her brown polyester pant-legs into tall white socks.

"There he is," Stanley said, quick to get out of the car and greet the fellow who loped around the corner.

Mr. Jessome was a tall man. Even with a bit of a hunch, he stood nearly two meters high (not counting the swoop of wavy black hair). There were streaks of silver in his close-cropped beard, his nose was long and hawkish, and his ears were anything but small.

Yet he had an effortless charm to his smile and a twinkling in his eyes that convinced most folks that he was handsome. Even with the limp.

Billy's mother seemed to agree. She checked her face and hair in the side mirror, opened her door, and exited the car with her best attempt at grace.

The dogs bounded around Mr. Jessome's legs as he approached. He sported a wooden cane, and tried to shoo them away with it as he shook the Brahms' hands. That only made the dogs bark more. The sound from inside the box on the boy's lap was graduating from a hiss to a yowl.

Exasperated, Billy opened his door and called out, "Could you *please* make them stop? They're scaring my cat."

"Don't be rude," his mother shot a withering glance, then resumed smiling at the handsome vet. "He's young, and still has a lot to learn."

"Seems pretty sharp to me," Mr. Jessome said, bending down to pick up a stick.

He waved it in front of the barking pack and tossed it high and far into his backyard. The dogs watched it tumble through the air until it struck the grass, then dashed off to fetch it.

"That's tall grass with lot of old sticks," he said, putting his cane against the ground and stepping towards the car. "It should buy us a minute of peace." He pulled open the passenger door and bent down to shake hands with the boy.

"Hello," Billy said shyly, doing his best to shake the man's hand properly.

"And hello to you, young man," Mr. Jessome said. He spotted Billy's cast and crutches. "Do you need some help out?"

"It's probably best if you stay in the car, son," Stanley said.

"Yes," Elizabeth said, "this yard isn't as level as the one at home, and you *know* how clumsy you can be. I'm sure the nice man will take good care of the cat and the whole thing will be quick and painless."

"That may be true," the vet said, "but I could use a little help in there. Besides, us *gimps* have to stick together."

Mr. Jessome lifted his left pant-leg and whacked his shin with the walking stick. Billy watched, spellbound, as the wooden wolf's head that topped the vet's cane rapped against a plastic limb.

An urgent *mewing* broke the spell. Billy whispered into the box and passed it carefully to the vet. Then he grabbed his crutches and slid out of the car on his own.

"How did yours happen?" Billy asked the man, Elizabeth reddened at her son's boldness.

"Motorcycle accident. Yours?"

"Hit by a car," Billy said.

"That's right, you're the one that made the papers," Mr. Jessome said. "Cool, so, when does the cast come off?"

"We're not rushing things," his mother interjected.

"I'm supposed to have an X-ray in a month or so. I want it off then," Billy said.

"Try not to count your chickens, son," his father said.

"These things can take time. We have to be *realistic*," his mother countered, wringing her hands.

"If I needed realism, I'd be an accountant," Jessome quipped. He popped open the top of the box, picked the cat up by the scruff, and held it in front of his face. It seemed content to dangle there, relaxing in the man's hand as he muttered something unintelligible.

The cat blinked, and sniffed at the unfamiliar air.

"Instead, I'm Dr. Doolittle," the vet said. "I spend my days talking to and, yes, *counting* my chickens. There are worse fates." He plopped the cat back in the box, closed the lid, and put it under his arm. "Let me show you around before we take care of your little friend."

The backyard was spread out over several acres, with wooden fences and poplar trees marking the borders. There were large pens, some wood and some metal mesh, for the various livestock. The more domesticated animals like dogs, cats, and even pigs had free rein. Billy spotted them roaming through the wild grass, digging under brambles, climbing trees, and splashing in the mud.

It was an animal Shangri-la, and all within the shadow of the cloud-capped mountain that loomed westward.

The pack of distracted dogs had finished fighting over the stick, and was bounding back towards their master. Billy tried bracing himself with the crutches, but the ground was soft and the charging canines – two Black Labradors, a grey husky, a Golden Retriever, and a Portuguese water dog – weren't exactly puppies. They yipped and barked and leapt around the guests, eyes crazed and tongues lolling with slobber.

"Sorry about this...you just gotta show 'em who's boss," Jessome said, waving his cane.

The dogs kept barking. Billy heard the cat hiss from inside the box and moved to comfort it. One of the Labs leapt and nearly knocked him over when it pawed at the boy's chest.

The vet called out over his shoulder, "*Sweetie! Could you give us a hand?*"

A loud whistle sliced the air.

"*Down!*" a voice said, commanding. "*To ME!*"

There was another whistle. The dogs dropped to all fours, trotted past the vet and the Brahms, and hopped over a row of bushes in the direction of the sound.

Mr. Jessome followed them with the boy hobbling close behind. Billy's father held out an arm and his mother – being extra careful where she stepped – circled around the wall of brush after them.

They stepped into a small clearing. The ground there was all patchy grass and raked earth, and standing in the middle was the skeleton of a large cage. It had cedar beams and chain-link fencing for walls, and a thatched grass roof.

The dogs were sitting in front of it in a sloppy circle, panting and begging for cookies being thrown from inside the cage. Billy recognized the thrower as soon as he spotted the faded denim and shaggy blonde hair.

"Like I said," Mr. Jessome beamed, "you just have to show 'em who the boss is."

Lynn Jessome went to Billy's school. She was a year older than him, and had a kind of brash confidence that the boy admired. At recess and lunch she could be found joking with the older kids, throwing hockey cards, or even playing full-contact Red Rover and British Bulldog.

And now, with the wooden planks strewn around the cage and a bucket of nails by her feet, it would appear that the girl was also handy with a hammer.

"Hey Dad," Lynn said, brushing the hair from her eyes and petting a German Shepherd laying by her feet.

She held a bone-shaped cookie near the dog's mouth and it nearly swallowed her hand. She laughed, wiped the drool on her jeans, rolled up the bag of cookies, stuffed it in her coat, and stepped out of the cage.

"Looking good," Mr. Jessome said, inspecting the cage and nodding to the Brahms. "This is my daughter, Lynn. Lynn, meet the Brahms."

"Nice to meet ya," Lynn said, extending her hand. She noticed Mrs. Brahm's discomfort. "Don't worry...my Dad says that dogs have way less germs in their mouths than we do."

"That's...good to know," Elizabeth said, suppressing the urge to ask for directions to the nearest bar of soap.

"I know you," Lynn said, stepping over to Billy. "You're the smart kid. Gonna be in my class next year, huh?"

It was true. Billy's teachers had suggested skipping him ahead another grade. Despite his worries about fitting in, his parents had agreed.

"Yeah, I'm Billy," the boy said, leaning on one crutch so he could shake her hand.

Her grip was firm, and she was bigger than him in every way. Her hands were rough, and her nails were caked with dirt. She had rips in her jeans and little smears of mud on her cheeks. When she smiled, he noticed the gap between her two front teeth. She had a blunt nose that turned up a little, and silver-blue eyes that seemed to sparkle even under the cloudy sky.

"Cool. You can do my homework, and I'll make sure you don't get messed with too much." She punched him in the shoulder, which made him wobble and wince.

"My, my," Elizabeth said, admiring the cage, "you're very *capable*. It's too bad Billy's not comfortable with tools. His father could certainly use the help. But, as you can see, he's our little *calamity*."

"I saw you in the paper. Hit by a car? That's cool," said Lynn, checking out his cast. "Can I sign it?"

"Sure...maybe later...I guess," Billy said, not knowing whether he was blushing from his mother's comment, or from the sudden attention.

"What are *these*?" Lynn said, kneeling to better see the marks on his leg that he had hoped to hide.

"Ummm, I was stung by wasps...and my skin...it's sensitive," Billy stammered.

"Coooool," she said, poking at one. "A few more of these? You'd look like a cheetah or something!"

"Well...I like running," the boy blushed.

"And speaking of *fast cats*," the vet said, noticing Mrs. Brahm whispering and pointing at her watch, "we have a patient to attend to."

Mr. Jessome lowered the box, and lifted the flaps so his daughter could take a peek.

"Cute," said Lynn, "What's its name?"

"I don't know yet," said Billy.

"Why not?"

"Because...because he hasn't told me what it *is* yet," Billy said, his face changing shade from pink to 'fire engine'.

His mother sighed, and his father gave a forced chuckle. But the girl didn't flinch at Billy's explanation. She just smiled and scratched the cat behind the ears, watching it sniff at her hand and denim cuffs, learning the scents of dirt and dog and girl.

"Cats are coy like that," Mr. Jessome said, folding up the box.

"That's why dogs are better," Lynn said. "They don't care what you name 'em, and they do what you tell 'em because they think you're leader of the pack."

"That's why *cats* are better," Billy said, defensive. "I read that when they bond with us, they see us as their prized possession. They choose *us*, instead of obeying because they have to."

"Nah, they just know a sucker when they smell one," Lynn walked back inside the cage. She crouched down by the German Shepherd, took its face in her hands, and let it lick her cheeks. "This is Seamus – and *that's* love."

"That's *gross*," Billy said.

"You're such a *girl*," she laughed.

"Well...you're such a...*boy*," Billy said.

"You're both *fine* the way you are," the vet said, his voice deepening to signal the conversation's end. "All creatures great and small, eh? Let's head back to my office."

The group turned to leave and Billy gave Lynn a half-hearted wave. The girl watched him adjust his crutches, press forward a bit too far, and almost slip on a clump of clover. She couldn't help but snicker and roll her eyes.

"Hey," she called to him. "Are you going to Tommy Clayton's party next week?"

"No," Billy said, regaining his balance, "I wasn't invited."

His mother, just a few steps ahead, turned to interject. "That's right. Little Tommy's turning twelve. I'm sure he'd *love* to have you there. I'll just give his mother a call when we get home."

Billy sighed, lowered his head, and plodded after them. Lynn watched him leave, and reached down to pat her dog on the belly.

Seamus sniffed, and caught a whiff of the cat. He licked her hand, drowning any trace of the smell in rivers of spit.

Mr. Jessome's 'office' turned out to be little more than a room in the back of his barn. It was in the far corner, behind stacks of firewood and next to a big, lumpy something covered in a dusty black tarp.

The area was walled off on three sides and lined with red metal cabinets. There were posters and pictures pinned on the walls showing the anatomies of different animals, photos of people with their livestock and pets, and newspaper clippings of blue-ribbon winners from the county fair.

"It's that season again," Jessome said, pointing to one of the pictures of a prize hog. "Busy time of year, what with everyone trying to prove who's best through their pets."

A shiny metal table on black wheels sat in the centre of the room. The vet made muddy foot-and-cane prints on the cracked tiles as he walked over to it, set the box down, and waved the Brahms in.

"Okay, Billy," he said, taking the cat out of the box. "Do you think you can help me out? Just lean against the table, and hold him in place."

"Are you sure he–?" Mrs. Brahm fretted.

"I can do it," Billy said. He propped his crutches against a cabinet, hopped over to the table, and steadied the cat on the cold metal. "See."

"I knew you could," the vet smiled. He rifled through a cabinet, and placed some implements on a plastic tray. "So, this is your first cat?"

"Yup," said Billy.

"Yes, *sir*," said his mother.

"Don't sweat the formalities here, Mrs. Brahm. I'm no saint. Just a country boy with all kinds of shit on his shoes."

Billy's eyes bulged at the curse word. He turned to his parents, who seemed keen to pretend that it never happened.

"It's our first *pet*," his mother said.

"Really?" Jessome said, shuffling through another drawer. "Most boys your age want a dog. Maybe even a snake."

"There will certainly be no *snakes* in our house," Elizabeth said. "And I find dogs tend to be loud, and too messy for our tastes, right dear?"

"We didn't really *plan* on getting a pet," Stanley said, scratching at the stubble on the side of his jaw. "It just kind of happened."

Mr. Jessome brought the tray over to the table and placed it on the far end. The cat tensed its shoulders at the clanging sound, and considered leaping from the boy's grasp. Billy stroked the back of its neck, and nuzzled its forehead with his nose.

"A famous man once said that life's what happens while you're busy making plans," the vet said, grabbing a small flashlight from the tray. "And Billy was right out there. From my experience, you don't make a cat your pet. You don't *make* it do anything. As you say, Mr. Brahm, it just kinda happens."

The vet gave the cat's cheeks a scratch, and then folded its ears open like pea pods. He shone the light inside them, made a *cluck-cluck* sound, and nodded. Then he placed his hand over the cat's face, gripped it by its upper jaw, and pulled its mouth open.

"No ear mites or buildup, you handsome devil," he said to the cat, shining the light around its mouth. "Nice teeth and gums, too. If cats had toothpaste commercials, you'd be rolling in catnip." He released its jaw and gave it a quick scratch under the chin.

Billy felt it squirm and tightened his grip around its belly and hind legs. It didn't look angry or frightened, but no one would mistake this for a cat that was having a good time.

"So, you got him from Enid." The vet grabbed a pair of claw clippers from the tray. "She's a *special* one, eh?"

"Yes...you can't help but wonder, you know, about her state of mind?' Billy's mother chose her words carefully. "A house that big, with all those cats...I don't understand why she doesn't just sell and a get a cozy flat in town."

"That old house has a *pull*," Jessome said. He pressed each of the cat's paws between his thumb and forefinger, pushing the claws out from their fleshy sheaths. "It sure does for the cats. According to her, most of them don't get brought there," he said, as he inspected and trimmed. "They just show up."

"Oh really?" Mrs. Brahm said, the doubt in her tone wearing a thin disguise.

"There's more in Heaven and Earth, as the bard says," Jessome squinted, trimming the last of the claws. "Though I bet part of the answer is just people dropping off bags of kittens in the night–"

"That's mean," Billy stroked the cat's back, and watched its black tail sway over the table's edge.

"You're right. But there's worse." The vet's face soured. "People can be cruel. All they have to do is bring 'em in here and I'll give 'em a snip. Less strays. Less suffering all around."

"Maybe they think they can't afford it, or they live too far out to make the trek?" his mother said, crossing her arms.

"It's just some gas, Mrs. Brahm. I'll fix 'em for free. Is it that hard to make an effort for a living thing? How much time and money do people put into turkeys and hams each Christmas?"

"Well, I...I'm sure they haven't given it much thought."

Mr. Jessome reached for the tray and lifted up a syringe. It was the biggest Billy had ever seen – bigger than the one they used on him in the emergency room – and filled with a pale yellow fluid. The vet pinched the cat by the scruff and wiggled the folds of skin as he inserted the needle. The cat's mouth opened and its eyes widened, but it didn't make a sound.

"*Thought.* You see, there's the rub," Jessome said, pushing down slowly on the syringe. "Animals are smarter than most of us *think,* and yet we still treat them horribly overall. Take cats, for instance," he paused the injection, massaging the skin around the puncture. "Did you know that there are studies showing that the average domestic feline has more brain activity than we ever imagined? We're talking problem solving, long-term memory, even vocabulary. This is real science that, in theory, says you're adopting the mental equivalent of a three year-old boy."

"Oh, now that's just—" Mrs. Brahm blurted.

"Wait...what do you mean 'vocabulary'? Like, meows?" Mr. Brahm said, scratching his earlobe and reassessing the furry lump on the table.

"Much more than that," said the vet. He removed the needle, and had Billy hold a piece of cotton against the wound. "Cats have tons of ways they communicate. Meowing, sure. Vocal trills, hissing, and growling. We all know that crap. But combine those 'voices' with how open the eyes are, with combinations of posture and tail position, and with the scent signals from glands in the cheeks and back end? Those are *messages.* They're talking all the time. We just don't know how to listen yet."

"That's...an interesting *theory.*" Mrs. Brahm tapped her foot on the tiles as the vet grabbed a compact scale from the top of one of the cabinets.

"What about purring?" Billy asked.

"Ah, everyone knows that means a happy kitty," said his father.

"Sometimes," Mr. Jessome placed the scale on the table, and took a moment to calibrate. "But not always. I've read of cats purring to keep warm. Purring to stay cool. Hell, I've had cats brought in here on death's door – abused or burned or hit by a car – and making sounds like a motorboat. Did you purr when you got hit, son?"

"No, sir," Billy said.

"Neither did I...neither did I," Jessome limped as he placed the cat on the scale. "There's something else going on with that. If you ever figure it out, you be sure to let me know, okay?"

"Okay," Billy moved to the scale, and stared into the cat's golden eyes.

"Six-point-two kilos," said the vet, scribbling the number on a lined form. "Not fat, not skinny – just right. Try to give him a mix of wet and dry food. Too much of one can rot the teeth, and too much of the other is hard on the bowels."

"Isn't the cheap kibble good enough?" Mrs. Brahm said, doing invisible calculations.

"You can cancel my allowance," Billy pressed his forehead against the cat's. It sniffed his brow, and rubbed its cheeks against his.

"That's a good kid you got there," Jessome said. "Both of them."

He ticked off a few more boxes on the form, stapled it to a blue folder, and popped it in one of the cabinets.

"I'll keep the info on file here for his next visit. The shot I gave him will reduce any inflammation or lingering infection from the stings. I can also send you off with a vial of flea potion – you just dribble it between his shoulder blades so he can't lick it off. Oh, and a tube of hairball medication, just in case."

"Hairballs. I hadn't thought of that," Elizabeth blanched, imagining a sea of bile and wet fur flooding the dusty rose perfection of her bedroom carpet.

"Don't worry, Mrs. Brahm. He's a shorthair, and an outdoor cat with grass to eat. On the off-chance he does get one, he'll take care of it outside. Cats prefer to be alone when they're sick."

"Sounds pretty low-maintenance, Liz," Stanley patted her on the back with one hand, while shaking the vet's with the other.

"They're great pets," said the vet, "and your timing couldn't be better. With all the rain this spring, there's talk of rats leaving the city and migrating south."

"Rats? But our garden—" Elizabeth Brahm started putting the cat to work in her mind. She watched it nuzzle her son as she spoke, but had failed to see both of them twitch when the vet had first uttered the word.

"No worries, then. You've got your very own tiger on the prowl," said Jessome. "Any other questions before you head out?"

A nightmare of rats. A dream of tigers.

"I have a question," Billy said. He pursed his lips and held his breath, well aware of how weird he was going to sound when he asked it.

"Shoot," said the vet.

"We *really* should be going, honey. Grilled cheese and soup night, remember?" His mother turned towards the door and signaled her brood to follow.

"It's not a problem, Mrs. Brahm," said the vet. "I want to hear it. Ask me."

Billy exhaled and placed his hands on the tabletop for balance. He lowered his head to the cat's level. And then he slowly blinked at it.

The cat twitched its whiskers, and blinked back.

"Can cats come into your dreams?"

"Oh, *silly Billy*," his mother groaned.

"Come on, son. Let's not waste the nice man's time." His father picked up the cat and tried to put it back in the box. The cat had other ideas, wedging a paw against three cardboard corners in protest.

"Interesting question," Mr. Jessome said, helping Stanley get the cat inside. "I'm no expert, but there are thoughts on the subject."

"Really?" the boy asked.

"Really," said the vet. He gently closed the box on the cat's head before it could escape. "For a long, long time, people have thought cats were magic in some way, good and bad. Since before the witch trials. Or before the plague. Before kings and emperors used them to predict disasters, which I personally think there might be some science to–"

"Of course you would," Billy's mother sighed just out of earshot.

"There are old wives-tales. Stories of shamans casting 'dream spells', with cats as their guides. Further back are the cat legends of Asia. And the Buddhist cat parables. And don't forget the myths from Egypt. They worshipped cats, y'know."

"I know," Billy said, "I've read all about it!"

"But that's all they are son. Myths."

Mr. and Mrs. Brahm gave Mr. Jessome an appreciative nod, and he handed them the box.

Disheartened, Billy hobbled over to grab his crutches from against the cabinet. He turned to leave, but the vet bent down in his path.

"That said? There *is* something about the whole matter I do find pretty neat."

Billy wiped his nose on his sleeve, and the vet brushed the hair from his eyes.

"Well, those scientists? The ones who figured out how smart cats are? They found something else. And they found it while the cats were sleeping."

"What?"

"They found that the same stuff happens in their heads when they sleep. They make the same type of brainwaves. The ones that only happen when we *dream*."

"Wow..." said Billy, his mind splintering in a thousand directions.

"Mmhmm," the vet returned to his full, intimidating height. "And, as I'm sure you know, cats love to sleep. Up to sixteen hours a day. That, my friends, is a lot of dreaming."

"Oh, to be a cat in the next life," Elizabeth said, leaning over the box. "Spoiled rotten, lazing in sunbeams, and all the rats you can eat.

Sounds like heaven. Meanwhile, the rest of us have to live in the real world." She stepped out the door, waving as she left. "Thank you for your help, Mr. Jessome. Time to go, Billy."

"Okay," Billy said, pushing his way across the room.

"A grilled cheese waits for no man," said the vet, soaping his hands over a stained white basin. "Nice to meet you, Billy Brahm."

"You too, Mr. Jessome," Billy said, stopping by the exit.

"Anything else I can do ya' for?" Jessome said, rubbing his hands into a lather.

"I was just thinking. About how much you said they sleep. Around sixteen hours, right?"

"Yup."

"Which means that they're awake for eight or so?"

"Yup," the vet said, picking at his fingernails.

Billy shifted on the crutches and turned. As he stood there, half in the room and half in the barn, it was as if he was being carved in two – split down the middle by light, and by shadow.

"So, it's like the *opposite* of us then," Billy said.

Mr. Jessome stopped scrubbing and turned to face the boy. Water trickled through his fingers, soaking the front of his pants and the floor around his feet.

"I never thought of it that way before," said the vet, drying his hands on his shirt. "That's clever, Billy. Very clever."

"Thanks," Billy said, before turning on his crutches and plodding off into the dark of the barn.

VIII

Of Paws and Pencils

THE NEXT WEEK WAS SLOW TO PASS, and not without its share of discomfort.

Billy's leg throbbed when he stood, ached when he moved around the house, and his toes looked like overripe grapes ready to burst from the tip of his cast.

At the very least, the boy was happy to be off the medication that dulled his wits and free of the lumpy cot downstairs. He was back in his own room, surrounded by his own things, and able to sleep in his own bed.

Not that he was sleeping much. Whether due to the lack of meds, or the mounting concerns swirling in his young head, Billy was restless.

Any sleep that he got was shallow and brief, with dreams being even more elusive. He'd awaken pained and confused, with the lingering sense that he was forgetting something.

Meanwhile, the cat remained close. Billy watched intently as it sniffed its way around his room, exploring its new territory.

At first, it poked its head in the closet, skulked under the bed, and rubbed its cheeks against the legs of the pine wardrobe. Then it got more daring, hopping into the laundry basket, batting toy soldiers around on the floor, and finally leaping up onto the windowsill.

There it would sit for hours and gaze out the window. The boy imagined that it yearned for the same things beyond the glass – the tall grass, the rolling meadow, and the graveyard on the hill.

Billy's mother delivered sandwiches and milk and cookies like clockwork. She would ask if he wanted to join them out in the garden, or play some backgammon with his father, or even come down to watch some TV.

After a few days of little interest and too many plates of half-eaten food, she came to his room armed with pad of paper and a handful of sharpened pencils.

"If you're going to laze around all day, the least you can do is be creative about it." She propped him up with some pillows, and put a pencil in his hand.

"I hate drawing," Billy said, "I'm no good at it."

"Well, if you practice, you might *get* good at it. But if you don't even try, you'll stay exactly where you are."

"I know where I am," Billy said. "I'm a cripple. I'll be stuck like this forever."

His mother pursed her lips, removed her glasses, and massaged the bridge of her nose. Then she sat on the bed, put the glasses back on, and laid her hand on his.

"Forever's a long time," she said. Her voice was soft, and cracked a little as she spoke. "Nothing lasts forever. Everything changes. That's life."

"But it still *hurts* so much," he scowled. "When will it get better? How long until I can run again?"

His mother lowered her head, nostrils flaring as she huffed. She was remembering. Remembering the first days her son stood on his own. Remembering him trundle across the kitchen to meet her open arms. Remembering him run down the driveway to catch his first bus to school.

"You shouldn't worry so much," she said, squeezing his hand. "That's a job for grown-ups." She put the notepad in his lap, and pointed to the cat on the windowsill. "Focus on something *good*. Then the worries will disappear."

She picked up his plates and glasses, and started to close the door behind her as she left the room.

"What if the cat wants to leave?" he said.

"He'll be fine here for a bit," she turned to say. "Besides, a true artist needs a captive subject."

She closed the door gently, and Billy heard the muffled thumps as she went down the stairs.

"*Kitty...heeeere kitty...wss-wss-wss,*" Billy called, and the cat spun its head and looked back at him.

The glare of afternoon sun made its pupils shrink to needles floating in jars of oily gold. The light shone through the cat's ears, making the skin inside glow warm and pink. Its whiskers were trembling threads of silver. Its nose looked broader, the nostrils darker, the skin rough and ridged like a lion's.

Its hind legs tensed, muscles rippling beneath swaths of fur. Its black tail swished down along the wall under the sill and curled like a hook at the tip, as if trying to catch the shadows below.

But the cat didn't come to him, not with Billy's first call or the two that followed. It merely stood, arched its back, yawned, turned around in an impossibly small circle, and sat back down in the exact same spot.

So, Billy started to sketch.

He drew a rough rectangle for the window, and pinched curves for the drapes that hung on either side. The cat began as a slender shape – a pear that quickly grew triangle ears, stiff whiskers, and an upside-down question mark for a tail.

Billy angled the pencil to shade in spots of black fur, finishing with the tail and the tips of the ears. He used the eraser to clean the edges and smudges, and even penciled in the treetops outside.

The boy looked at the finished picture. *Too many mistakes*, he thought. *It's not right.* He felt the telltale knots of frustration in his gut – the ones that always came when he failed to make things right.

Billy slashed at the page with his pencil, tore it out of the pad, and tossed the crumpled sketch at the bin by his dresser. The paper ball bounced off the bin's rim and hit the floor.

The cat whipped its head around, spotting the ball. It leapt down from the sill and swatted it under the bed. Billy could hear it scurrying around underneath him.

He pictured the paper ball as a mouse, and the cat toying with its doomed prey. The last thing the poor creature would ever feel would be the hot and bloody slide into the belly of the beast.

The beast.

Billy put the pencil to a fresh sheet of paper and started drawing. He didn't think, and didn't question, and didn't pause to find fault. He drew. And, as he did, the vision returned to him.

It was clear again, as if he had just woken from it. Clearer, like he was still fast asleep.

He sketched the eyes first, rimmed in black, with marks like teardrops running down the sides of its nose. Then came the face, broad and full, with dotted cheeks and high, tufted ears. Then he shaded the muzzle, and made dark slices fan out from its nose.

The mouth came last, gaping and fearsome, a fat tongue flattened behind monstrous teeth. The fangs looked smooth and sharp and deadly with one that glinted at the tip, as if piercing a star.

There it was – the tiger – a paper phantom staring back at him from the depths of a fevered dream. And that's when the boy remembered its ominous words.

'You are sick.'

Billy slumped and lowered the sketchpad. Sitting behind it, in the space between his knees, was the cat. It sat there, still and silent, and looked him square in the eyes.

"If I don't find him," Billy pointed at the sketch, "I'll lose it, won't I?"

The cat tilted its head, puzzled.

"This," the boy slapped at his thigh with troubled eyes. "This!"

The cat turned towards the cast, and pawed at the Billy's knee. It lingered there, opening its mouth and poking out its tongue as it sniffed. It then proceeded to sniff down the length of Billy's shin.

The cat stopped, yawned, and curled in a tight ball below the boy's knees.

"I'm going to lose my leg," Billy said, trembling as his face and hands went numb.

The cat made the tiniest *mew*, closed its eyes, and began to purr.

I X

Of Foes and Felines

THE NEXT MORNING, after another night of restless sleep, Billy's mother insisted that he join them for breakfast downstairs.

Billy hopped down the hall, slid down the stairs on his bottom, and had his father carry him to the kitchen table. He was feeling tired and cranky, and the worries hovered around his head like a cloud of gnats that couldn't be swatted away.

Even homemade blueberry pancakes with crispy bacon and maple syrup couldn't lift the boy's spirits. He just pushed the food around the plate while his parents played a game of cribbage and drank their morning tea. When they were distracted (teasing each other over who was next to get 'skunked'), Billy would sneak bits of bacon off the table.

The cat was an ideal accomplice – it quickly snatched the bits, gulped them down its gullet, and continued to weave between the three sets of legs without pause or suspicion.

"So, I have some news," Billy's mother said.

Historically, when she announced 'news', what she actually meant was '*I have something I want you to do*'.

"I spoke with Mrs. Clayton, and everything's been sorted. You'll be going to Tommy's party on Saturday. Isn't that nice?"

Billy stared at the rivers of buttery syrup on his plate. They threatened to spill off its edge and flood the wastelands of the scuffed green formica.

"Sure," he said.

"There will be games, and a BBQ, and cake and ice cream, of course. I hear they even hired entertainment. Goodness, they certainly know how to spend, don't they?" she said, spraying crumbs from an unflattering mouthful of toast.

"Mmhmm," Stanley said, surveying the cards in his hand. "They even have an in-ground pool now. Should be fun."

"*Great*," Billy said.

Elizabeth furrowed her brow at her husband's slip – their son wouldn't be swimming anytime soon with a cast made of plaster.

"You won't need to bring a present. Instead, we can spend the afternoon making him a card. That should more than suffice, considering last year's misunderstanding."

The boy remembered all too well.

Billy had spent most of the previous year trying to join the bigger kids at recess. It was an obsession.

He lined up for tetherball and nearly won a few rounds, despite his size and a tendency to bruise. In 500-up, he almost caught a long fly heading for the back fence, had he only remembered to open his glove before catching.

But what the boy really wanted was to *run*.

Billy wanted a chance to race with the older boys on the school field. On those days, right before the recess bell, Billy ran like a wild thing. His eyes grew wide and his feet possessed, gangly arms flapping in the wind. Sometimes, he didn't finish dead last. Sometimes, he very nearly won. Running was his chance to prove that he could hold his own – that he *belonged* – which would someday make up for every mean word, and every smashed lunch, and every smooshed face in yellowed snow.

It was on one of those days, after one of the last races of the school year, that Tommy Clayton approached him. He was inviting Billy to his birthday party.

"It'll be the coolest," Tommy said. He chomped on a wad of grape gum, nodding to his playground posse. *"And it'll only cost you ten bucks to get in, plus a present."*

Billy was overjoyed.

That night, while his parents slept, he put his ceramic piggybank under a pillow. He knew his mother would never give him money *and* help him buy a present, so this was a necessary evil. The boy sat on it, bouncing until it broke open.

That weekend, Billy took his first bus ride into town. He went with Mrs. Thomas – under the guise of helping her carry cat litter – and popped into the dollar store. And there, with six months of allowance in hand, he bought Tommy Clayton a red, white, and blue baseball mitt with a matching plastic ball.

Billy hid it in his backpack, and snuck tape and newspaper up to his room. After three ripped and misshapen failures, he was finally able to wrap up the glove in pages from the Sunday comics.

The following Saturday, his father drove him all the way out to the Clayton's place. They pulled up the long driveway, and Billy felt a rush of excitement as he hopped out to ring the doorbell.

In his hands were the wrapped glove and an envelope. Inside the envelope was a five-dollar bill, along with five more dollars in quarters, dimes, and nickels.

The door opened, and a thin woman welcomed him with an awkward smile. Billy remembered being dazzled by her huge teeth, the pearls hanging on the tanned skin around her neck, and a plume of stiff yellow hair.

She spoke in singsong tones, saying something about Tommy and his friends leaving for a camping trip the night before. She patted him on the head, took the glove and the envelope, and smiled as she closed the door.

Billy was quiet. When he got home, he told his parents that he must've heard Tommy wrong.

'*It's no big deal,*' he said.

His mother insisted on getting to the bottom of things despite his protests. A week later, they were driving back to the Clayton's house for a 'play date'.

Billy's parents sat with Tommy's on their sprawling deck. They spoke of polite and parental things.

Tommy shook Billy's hand and apologized in front of everyone – apparently, his real birthday wasn't until July. He handed Billy a crisp ten-dollar bill, and asked if he wanted to kick the soccer ball around.

"*Play nice, boys,*" his mother said. "*We'll be watching.*"

Tommy placed his arm around Billy's shoulders and flashed them all a huge grin. Then he led him back to the property's edge. As they walked, Tommy's grip began to tighten.

"*It's toast, you know,*" Tommy said, tilting his mouth near Billy's ear. "*Me, Trevor, and Michael poured gas on it. Then we made a fuse out of toilet paper and lit the end. You should'a seen it pop in the air when the flame hit. BOOM!*"

Tommy kept walking, hand tight on Billy's shoulder, and moved towards a circle of raised bricks. As they got closer, Billy saw the black streaks on the bricks, and the mound of ash piled in the middle.

It was a fire pit. In its ashes, a charred glob – a burnt, misshapen thing that had once been red, and white, and blue.

"*That's what happens to cheap shit,*" Tommy said, digging into Billy's shoulder. "*And if you tell mommy and daddy on me? That's not all that's gonna burn.*"

For the next hour, Billy kicked the ball back and forth with Tommy without saying a word. After that, they joined their parents on the deck for cheeseburgers and potato salad. An hour later, he shook Mr. and Mrs. Clayton's hands, thanked them for their hospitality, and left.

It was only that night, taking his Sunday bath, that Billy let himself feel it. He sank into the steaming water, beneath shifting mountains of bubbles and froth, and screamed where no one could hear.

BEEP-BEEEEEEEEP.

"And there's the other news, right on time."

Billy watched his unfinished plate being cleared, and his mother brush the leftovers into the garbage beneath the sink. Recognizing the sound, he limped to the bathroom to wash his hands and face. He even brushed his teeth without being asked, and used a splash of water to part his hair to the side.

Ms. Savage waved through her window and parked on the side of the road by their driveway. She was a pretty woman with a radiant smile and bobbed, coppery hair. The driver door concealed a sturdy frame (Billy's mother referred to her as 'womanly'), but her vehicle made her look tiny by comparison.

The Bookmobile was a converted motor home – or RV, as his father called it – that had been gutted, refurbished, and turned into a library on wheels. The outside had a silvery shell, with cartoon characters painted on each side. There was a unicorn with a fire-breathing dragon on one side, and a bearded pirate with a rocket ship on the other.

On the back was a bright rainbow with a pot of gold. Underneath it were the words: *READING LEADS TO UNTOLD TREASURES.*

"Hello there, handsome!" Ms. Savage leaned out of her window and turned off the engine. "Sorry I couldn't come sooner, but I was on vacation. When your mom told me what happened? You couldn't keep me away."

Billy's father led him around the other side of the Bookmobile, checking for traffic. The boy waved at the old Thomas house, even though Enid was nowhere to be seen – he liked to think that she was still watching from behind her dusty windows.

Stanley Brahm boosted his son up through the folding door and took away his crutches. The space would be too narrow to use them, and Billy wouldn't have far to hop. The room could hold only so many books, and there were folding chairs to rest in. Besides, Billy liked the idea of Ms. Savage bringing books to him – she was a cool lady, and her recommendations had always been good ones.

"Give a honk when he's done," his father said, smoothing a lick of hair over his exposed scalp. "We'll just be puttering around in the back."

"No worries," she said, helping Billy into a chair. "We've got all the time in the world for this one."

The 'we' Ms. Savage referred to was herself and her cat, Lucy. Lucy was a plump tortoiseshell that had been a fixture of the Bookmobile for as long as Billy could remember. She used to pace back and forth on the carpet, brushing against the heels of readers, hopping into laps, and mewing when she felt ignored. These days, however, you'd tend to find her curled up on one of the lower shelves like a fat, furry book that had been bound in charcoal and rust. Today was no different.

Billy looked around the cramped space, and saw Lucy open her wee green eyes in the back. Despite his calls, she didn't move from her spot on the second shelf except to raise her head and sniff the air. Her whiskers drooped, and her orange muzzle trembled as she sniffed. As she lowered her head into her black-and-brown paws, she opened her mouth and gave a faint meow.

"Getting old, poor girl," Ms Savage wiped sweat from her rosy cheeks with a t-shirt sleeve. "Happens to the best of us. Might need to visit the lady 'cross the road one of these days. These wheels just wouldn't be the same without a cat in 'em."

"I have a cat now," Billy said. "They let me have one, after the accident."

"Aren't you lucky, and in more ways than one!" she said. "Could've been worse, kiddo, the way folks tear down this road. So, when do you lose the chick-magnet?" She winked, and pointed at the boy's cast.

Billy wiggled his leg and felt a twinge of pain below his knee. "Three weeks...maybe...I think."

"Piece of cake," she beamed, snapping her fingers. "Better give you my autograph before it's too late."

Ms. Savage fished for something in her pocket. Her face scrunched up as she sucked in her belly and battled with the snugness of her shorts.

"There it is," she huffed, pulling out a red pen. "Lucy and me gotta go on a diet one of these days, but she'll have none of it. Damn selfish, if you ask me."

Billy smiled as Ms. Savage knelt down by his leg and took the cap off the pen. She chose a spot on his lower thigh, and wrote in tiny script:

"Tragedy delights by affording

a Shadow of the pleasure

which exists in pain."

~ PB SHELLEY ~

"Do you understand what that's trying to say?" Ms. Savage peered up at Billy with pensive hazel eyes.

"I think–" he said, letting the words glide and hover before descending to his tongue, "I think it means that when something bad happens, it can still remind you of something good?"

"Pretty much," she smiled, brushing strands of hair off his forehead. "I always knew you were more than just a pretty face."

Billy blushed. As Ms. Savage tugged at the bottom of her shirt, tightening it across her ample chest, he couldn't help but stare. If he were a bolder boy (or an older one), he might've asked for a hug, but Billy was neither of those things.

"So, what are you in the mood for today?" she said, leaning against the nearest shelf. "Adventure? Fantasy? Something scary? You've gone through a lot of it, but we've still got some hidden gems in here."

Billy hadn't been a big reader. With his penchant for TV and comics, his mother had worried that all the 'drivel' would conspire and turn his brain to oatmeal. But Ms. Savage knew that there was a type of book for everyone, especially dreamers like him. So, she introduced the boy to magic rings and epic quests, to boy kings and ghastly beasts, and to hidden worlds just waiting for the right person, at the right time, to find them.

But Billy didn't want any of that today – not with the ache in his leg and a mystery to solve.

"Do you have anything on *tigers*?" he asked.

"Tigers, hmm? Fiction or non-fiction?" she said.

"Non-fiction. Something with pictures. But facts, too."

"Okay. I should have something," she moved across the space to another shelf, "but you could just use a computer for that, couldn't you?"

"I like books better," he said.

This wasn't necessarily true, but the only computer in Billy's house was behind the spare room's locked door. He was allowed a few hours on it each week, but every click was monitored for fear that he might talk to strangers or stumble on something 'inappropriate'. With a book, Billy could at least keep his thoughts and findings to himself.

"A man after my own heart," said Ms. Savage.

She scanned along the rows and pulled out a glossy hardcover. It had a photo of a tiger on the front. She held it up, awaiting the boy's approval: *"The A-Z of Big Cats"*.

"Sure," Billy said, and she placed it on a stool by the door.

"Alright, ya' got two more," she said, mopping the sweat from her brow. Billy saw the damp spots under her arms and trailing down her back, and felt a pang of guilt – with enough time, the Bookmobile could probably cook a person in the peak of summer.

You'd just have to be patient, Billy thought. *And mean.*

"Ummm, do you have anything on *dreams*?" he asked.

"Dreams? Hmmm. Same question."

"Non-fiction."

"Been having some weird ones after the hospital, huh? That's pretty normal," Ms. Savage said as she tucked amber locks of hair behind her ears and combed a shelf. "My sister went in for an operation, and told me that after it she kept dreaming that all her teeth were falling out. And she wasn't even sick!"

"Then why was she in the hospital?" Billy said.

"Self-*improvement*. Let's leave it at that," she smirked, squatting down in front of a different shelf. It looked like her thighs would burst her shorts at the seams, as curly blue worms crawled beneath the skin on the backs of her calves. "Here's one," she said, sliding out a slim paperback, "'*The Secret Language of Dreams*'. Looks neat."

She read the synopsis and held up the book. The cover had a sleeping woman's face sketched in black-and-white, surrounded by watercolour paintings. Billy could make out a snake, a mountain, a butterfly, a knife, and a black cat.

"Looks good," Billy said, and the sweat-soaked librarian trudged over to add it to the pile.

"*Phew*," Ms. Savage said, standing by the open door and fanning her face with an oversized book of crossword puzzles. "You've got one more, kiddo. Do the big lady a solid and make it quick, okay? I'm in my own gravy here."

Billy looked around the room, hoping for inspiration. He couldn't think of anything else that might help, aside from the latest edition of '*How to Lift a Curse in Five Easy Steps*' – the one that came with pictures of tigers, and a money-back guarantee.

"Any ideas, Lucy?" Billy said to the cat.

The question was rhetorical, but to the boy's surprise Lucy yawned a big yawn, mewed, and opened her eyes. She looked sharp and alert as she sniffed at the air, and turned her gaze towards the door.

"Hey there, fella," said Ms. Savage, stepping back from the entrance. "Wanna come up and introduce yourself? It's been too long since a girl in this rig had a suitor."

Billy spun around to the door and saw a cat – *his* cat – creep into the Bookmobile. It sat near the edge of the carpet, and met Lucy's gaze.

"What's his name?" the woman said.

Billy didn't answer. He was tired of the question, and too fascinated by what was happening.

Lucy opened her mouth and gave a brief, delicate trill. Billy's cat swished its tail twice, and then lowered its body to the ground.

"Your little guy plays well with others, right?" Ms. Savage bent down to stroke the visitor's fur. Billy's cat flinched, but remained focused on the elder feline.

"He's fine," Billy said, though he wasn't *completely* sure. He held his breath as Lucy unfolded herself, stretched her limbs, and slid down from her spot on the shelf.

"Someone's in the mood to flirt," Ms. Savage said. She took a step back inside, in case a peacekeeper was needed.

Lucy waddled to the middle of the carpet. She crouched on her paws and meowed again, her voice soft and curious.

Billy's cat took a cautious step towards her, belly on the ground, and stopped less than a meter away. His eyes narrowed, and his black lips pulled back to bare a row of pointed teeth.

"Okay, that's enough there, stud," the woman said. Her foot was raised, and the boy knew she was about to stomp it down and shoo his cat away.

"Wait!" Billy said, sitting up in his chair.

Both cats turned at the sound of his voice, swished their tails, and turned back to face one another. Billy's cat took three quick steps to cross the gap between them, and then lowered his head in front of her.

Lucy sniffed the top of his skull, the tips of his ears, and the sides of his cheeks. She gave a weak, warbling *mew*. With half-open eyes, both cats leaned in and touched noses.

"Would you look at that," Ms. Savage said, scratching her head. "The old girl's still got it."

The cats' mouths opened and their noses remained touching, as if sharing breath. Even with the RV's fan running and the sound of cars speeding by on the highway, Billy could've sworn he heard the two cats purring.

Lucy sat up and blinked. She swiveled her head around the room, scanning along each of the shelves. When her sights came to rest on the far corner of the room, she twisted her frame to face it.

And then, to the shock of all who were present (cat included), she moved. In truth, what Lucy did would be best described as *bolting*. And climbing. And leaping. In a blur of black and orange and brown, she had scaled the farthest bookcase and was now perched on top of it.

"*Oh my God,*" Ms. Savage gasped, grabbing a stool and sliding it to a spot beneath her cat. "She...she's never done something like that."

Billy watched Ms. Savage climb onto the stool and take a moment to find her balance. The colour had drained from the woman's skin and her back was drenched with sweat. As she reached for Lucy, he could see her hands trembling.

Lucy, on the other hand, looked fine. She was calm and content, shifting only to peer down at her human friend and blink at the feline one on the carpet below. As Ms. Savage reached for the cat the stool wobbled under her weight. Billy pushed out of his chair and stood on his left leg, ready to offer some help.

"It's okay," she gritted her teeth, steadying herself. "She's sitting on a book. Alright, you little bugger...you just stay still. I'm gonna slide you both out. Nice and slow...that's it. Think of this as your first elevator ride. See? Not so bad, is it? Good girl. And we didn't even have to call the fire department. Though that could've been our best shot at filling this place with eligible bachelors, eh?"

Ms. Savage stepped down from the stool and carefully lowered the book and cat to the carpet. Lucy paused to look left and right, stepped off the book, and crawled back into her sleeping nook without so much as a chirp of gratitude.

"Cats," said Ms. Savage, wiping her face in relief. "You saw that, right? They're crazy! You love 'em, and you'd climb a mountain for 'em, but sometimes you can't help but feel like you're not in on the joke. Like they're all getting together somewhere – probably while we're sleeping – and having a laugh at our expense."

Billy considered sharing some theories of his own when he looked around the room. His cat was gone.

"I think I'm starting to get what you mean," Billy said.

He hopped over to Ms. Savage and leaned against her arm. Be it instinct or cat-inspired curiosity, he wanted to see the book that helped bring Lucy down to safety.

"I don't know how interesting this would be to you," the woman said, brushing some dust off the cover. "In fact, I'm not even sure why I *have* this – a tad outside the Bookmobile's demographic, don't you think?"

Billy read the title, and traced his fingers across the cover. The tome was the shade of charred leather with ridged, ruby lettering bordered by flecks of gold leaf.

BLOOD AND STONES

An Illustrated Guide

to the Colonial History

of the Eastern Shore

The boy heard the words in his head, and remembered. He *knew* them. They had been spoken before. Released from the maw of a great beast. Growled by an impossible thing that beckoned from his dreams.

Blood...and Stones.

"I'll take it," Billy hopped to the front of the Bookmobile, and honked the horn three times.

That night, the boy dreamed.

It was after a macaroni and cheese dinner and a family game of cards. It was after he cleaned his ears and brushed his teeth. It was after his father turned out the light, and the glow-in-the-dark wallpaper encircled him with its ghostly fleet.

Billy dreamed.

He stood on the bow of a sailing ship. He could hear the timbered hull creak, and the rustling of sails in the wind behind him.

The sky was black except for stars. And the water was so smooth, and so dark, that it mirrored every star in that sky's perfect blackness. The boy felt like an astronaut, hurtling through space.

"*They point the WAY,*" a voice crackled behind him.

Billy looked up and spotted the points of Orion, shining brighter than the rest. He followed the arc of its belt down to the horizon. Three monstrous peaks loomed in the distance.

"When do we get there?" Billy said, but only in his mind.

He could hear footsteps dragging on the deck, heavy and close. And something else by his ear. Breathing.

"*When the cold winds blow and the waters flow upon the distant shore,*" it hissed. "*Then We'll be home. But the GATE is locked. Help USsss, and We will help YOUuuu.*"

Billy felt something touch his shoulder and scuttle across it. It dug into his flesh. The boy was too afraid to look. Too afraid to know.

"I'm cursed," the boy cringed, feeling the puffs of hot, fetid breath against his skin. "How can I help anyone if I'm *cursed?*"

The stars blinked out. The world went dark. But then a thousand burning eyes, fearsome and foul, opened in the sky and the sea.

"*We can LIFT it,*" said the voice, gurgled and sticky in his ear, like a thing that wouldn't stop squirming. "*A key for a KEY.*"

"I've told you...I don't know where it is!" Unable to resist, the boy slowly turned his head toward the voice. "How do I *find* it?"

Billy saw the rotting hand clenched on his shoulder. He saw the mass of maggots spilling from a muddy sleeve. They crawled up his neck, onto his face, and into his mouth and eyes.

The world burst into fire.

"*A friend knowwws,*" the Grey Man said, empty and dead like a hole in the world. "*We will send you a FRIEND.*"

The dream collapsed beneath the boy, awash in smoke and ruin. Billy wailed as he fell, reaching out in all directions for something to cling to. He swam the empty sky and flew the lifeless sea, lost in the endless void of both.

And then he felt himself forget.

X

Of Grudges and Gifts

SATURDAY AFTERNOON CAME and everything was amazing at the Clayton's.

The long driveway was freshly paved. Every blade of grass was trimmed on the lawn. There were bunches of red balloons tied to all of the trees. The air was thick with the scent of BBQ and sunscreen. A throng of happy bodies giggled and splashed in the new swimming pool behind the house. And there wasn't a cloud in the sky. It was as if Tommy's parents had ordered the perfect day from the perfect birthday catalogue.

Which made sense, because they were perfect people.

Mrs. Clayton – with her crisp white sundress, flawless hair and makeup, and a smile that hurt your eyes if you stared directly into it – delivered tray after tray of the tastiest lemonade ever to grace a tongue.

Meanwhile, Mr. Clayton – with his even tan, snug white shirt, and a full head of slick blonde hair – flipped the juiciest burgers and hot dogs on a grill the size of most people's beds.

Billy arrived late. He had asked his father to drive him there earlier, but his mother's logic had won out.

"If you go early, you'll be expected to stay until the end," she had said. "You're still too weak to spend a whole day out, so we'd have to make two trips. But if you go later, then we can run some errands across the river, you can eat an early dinner, and we'll swing back to pick you up when everyone's starting to leave."

It made sense. But to Billy, it meant being stuck in the heat of midday with little shade and no way to swim. It also meant looking every part the cripple to the greatest number of kids possible, as they celebrated the one who hated him the most.

Tommy Clayton avoided him at first, and Billy was content to go unnoticed in his grassy purgatory away from the pool. But, inevitably, kids started coming over to get a look at the boy who got run over and somehow lived to tell the tale.

And Billy told it. Many times. It got a bit grosser, and a bit bloodier, and a bit scarier with each telling. Eventually, a blue marker got passed around, and the crowd of kids lined up to sign his cast.

First was Kirk Leggett – a bucktoothed 11-year-old whose dad owned the general store, giving him the biggest hockey card collection in the county – and Joey Small, who kids called 'Carrots' because he was freckled and rake-thin with a pointy wedge of ginger hair. They both made loopy scribbles on Billy's cast, mimicking the signatures they'd seen their parents do at the bank.

There was Jenny Lee — a cute girl whose folks owned the town's only Chinese restaurant — who doodled a smiley face on roller-skates. And then Heather Hallsy — a stocky girl with thick eyebrows and pearish nose — drew a frowning bear that had dropped his ice cream.

Even Mikey Durlick and Trevor Spool — Tommy's knuckle-dragging lunch-hour lackeys — wanted in. Mikey took his time drawing a bug-eyed rabbit with floppy ears and oversized feet. And Trevor, perhaps foreshadowing a career in juvenile crime, sketched a skull-and-crossbones. It had sunglasses on, and was smoking a cigarette.

"Hey *buddy*," someone crooned from behind Billy's rickety lawn chair.

The crowd parted, scattering back to the pool as Mrs. Clayton approached with her smirking son. Tommy Clayton had really grown in the last year. The sinews in his arms and bare chest flexed as he pushed aside the sun umbrella, and made room for his oversized head.

"We're so glad to have you here", Mrs. Clayton said. "Your mother was absolutely right to get in touch. It wouldn't be the same without you, would it Thomas?" Her smile got so big, and so wide, that it looked like her face might break. But Billy felt a chill from the frost in her stare, and knew it was meant for him.

"Yeah," Tommy said through clenched teeth, "wouldn't be the same."

"Ummm...here's the card I made you," Billy said. He held up the piece of folded construction paper, glitter, and macaroni-and-glue he had whipped together the day before.

"Thanks." Tommy snatched it, held it up by his shoulder, and waited for his mother to take the thing away.

"That's *lovely*," Mrs. Clayton said, sparkling bits of macaroni spilling to the ground when she opened it. "I'll just go and put this with all the presents on the table. Will you boys be needing anything?"

"Nope," Tommy said, stepping forward and blotting out the sun. "We're good here, right buddy?"

"Thank you very much, Mrs. Clayton," Billy strained, attempting to sit taller in his wobbling chair.

"Well, you're *welcome* very much," she parroted, and turned to make a perfect line of perfect steps in her perfect shoes back to their perfect pool. Tommy watched her leave, his face darkening the further away she got.

"Uhhh...happy birthday, Tommy," Billy said.

"Happy *birth*-day, Tommy. Thank you very *much*, Mrs. Clayton," the boy mocked. "Such a kiss-ass."

Tommy moved closer to the chair, cracking his knuckles as he stepped. Billy swallowed hard and felt the temperature drop again, even though it was a scorching 33C in the shade.

"Maybe we should break the other one," Tommy said, crouching down by Billy's good leg. "Wouldn't need a car. It's just a stick. A *diseased* stick."

Tommy flicked a scale of silvery skin off Billy's knee, exposing the raw redness underneath. Billy felt ugly and exposed, but knew that if he called for help it would only make things worse.

"Are you gonna cry?" whispered Tommy, leaning close.

Billy couldn't hide his trembling or his quivering lip. All he could do was brace himself.

My life was smashed a month ago, Billy thought. *How much worse can it get?*

"Come on. It's my birthday. *Cry*," Tommy said, poking his finger into Billy's ribs. "If you don't, I'm gonna get you *and* your stupid mom."

Billy bit his lip and tried to twist away, but that just made Tommy push harder. His eyes pooled with tears, threatening to fall.

"Do it," Tommy grinned. "*Do it.*"

"Do *what*?" said a voice behind him.

The sound made Tommy yelp in surprise and roll back on the grass. Squinting through the high sun's glare he saw a pair of frayed denim shorts, a black tank top, and a long blonde ponytail.

"You're late," Tommy said, flicking blades of grass from his hands.

"Not my fault." said Lynn Jessome, holding out her hand to him. "My Dad was getting your present ready."

"Oh yeah? What did you get me, babe?" Tommy grabbed her hand and gave it a tug, hoping to pull her to the ground.

"Pfffft, *nothing*," she snorted. She let go of him and laughed as he fell hard on his butt. "It's from *your* dad. Mine just helped him. Retard."

Billy snorted, but covered his mouth when Tommy shot him an icy glare and cracked his knuckles again.

"Back off, jerkwad," Lynn said, circling to Billy's side. "Otherwise, I'll tell my Dad to take it back."

"You can't," Tommy whined. "My Dad *paid* for it."

"So? My Dad doesn't care about money."

"Yeah, 'cause he's a loser," Tommy shook his head. "Whatever. I wasn't gonna hurt the puss' anyway."

He grabbed the blue marker that had been dropped in the grass, and knelt by Billy's plastered ankle. He knocked on it twice, making Billy flinch.

"*Such* a puss'," Tommy said, uncapping the pen. "Remember the early birthday last year, buddy? Burn baby, *burn!* Good times."

Billy watched him as Tommy drew the shape of logs and a roaring fire. His jaw tensed and his teeth gnashed together as a single tear ran down his flushed cheek.

"That's enough," Lynn said, putting her hand on Billy's shoulder. "Stop it."

"Chill out," said Tommy. He blew on the ink to dry it, and appreciated his handiwork. "It won't be on there for long. You get this thing off soon, right?

"In...in a couple of weeks." Billy sniffled and wiped at his eyes, wondering what Tommy would say next. He knew, in the end, it wouldn't be anything good.

"Couple of weeks," Tommy patted the cast, capped the pen, and stood. "And then they'll hack it off and turn it into food for the cat lady."

"Tommy!" Lynn snapped, a vein popping on the side of her neck.

"Don't worry, buddy. Her dad's been through it all before. Maybe he's got a spare one lying around."

"You think that's *funny*?" Lynn took a step forward.

"*Hilarious*," Tommy said, puffing out his chest.

Billy grabbed her hand, rediscovering the calloused fingers and strong grip from their first hello. Her palm was warm, and a bit damp. Lynn looked down, gave his hand a squeeze, and slid free of his grip.

"My Dad might have a fake leg," she said, pointing a finger in Tommy's smug face, "but at least he's not *made* of plastic." Lynn turned to face the deck and called out to Tommy's parents. "Mr. Clayton! Mrs. Clayton! Everything looks *amazing*."

Lynn waved with a cupped hand and made her smile as exaggerated as possible. Tommy's parents turned their heads, grinned from ear-to-ear, and waved back in unison.

"Now *that* is hilarious," Lynn said.

Tommy opened his mouth to speak, but words didn't come. When he cracked his knuckles yet again, Lynn just rolled her eyes and walked back to Billy's side.

"*Whatever,*" Tommy said, flinging the marker to the grass by Billy's feet.

The birthday boy spit in his hands, rubbed them together, and ran his fingers through his hair until it was styled just right. Then he jogged up to the deck, hopped on the railing, and announced that it was time for everyone to watch him open his presents.

"Jerk," Lynn said, as the others gathered around Tommy on the deck.

"Yeah," Billy said, grimacing at the cheers as Tommy tore into his gifts, "but he's right."

"Bullsh...*crap*," Lynn said, catching her tongue mid-swear. "That's just bull crap. What do you think that lug-nut is right about?"

"That I'm a..." Billy paused, wrestling with a word that he hated to say.

"That you're a 'puss'?" Lynn asked, sitting on the grass near his feet. "You know what that means, right?"

"It's...I...I'm not supposed to *say*," he stammered, bursts of scarlet blooming in his cheeks.

"I don't know what *you're* thinking, but my Dad says it's short for cat – *pussy cat.*"

"Yeah, but–"

"So that's just his stupid way of saying that you're scared, or whatever. But you know all about cats, right?" Lynn pulled the tie from her ponytail, and shook her hair loose into a shaggy mane.

"Kinda," Billy said, watching the glint in her eyes, and the tip of her nose crinkle as she spoke.

"They might seem easy to spook, but put Tommy Clayton in a pit with a tiger, and see who poops first."

"Yeah..." Billy said, slumping in his chair. Her words conjured the thing he had drawn – the beast from his dreams – and with it, his woes.

"But...?" she nudged his chair with her sneaker.

"I think Tommy's right. About my leg. About what's going to happen to it."

"What?" Lynn gasped, one hand to her mouth and the other slapping down on Billy's bare knee. "What's wrong? What did the doctor say?"

"Nothing," Billy sighed, "but my parents have been acting weird ever since I got home from the hospital. Whenever I ask about my leg, my Mom gets all emotional and changes the subject. And then, well..."

"And *what?* Tell me."

"I've been having dreams," Billy said, low and grim.

"Okayyy. What *kind* of dreams?" Lynn popped a block of pink gum in her mouth, raising an eyebrow as she chewed.

Billy took a deep breath and looked at her with pleading eyes. It was a look that said he was about to share his biggest secret. They were eyes that begged for her to listen and to try and understand, because no one else would.

"The world's on fire," Billy said, words tumbling from his nervous lips. "It's falling apart. And then all the stars go out. That's when the bad man comes – the Grey Man, and his rats – and they attack me. He wants a *key.* Then there's a cat, but it's *more* than a cat, and it saves me. Then I'm somewhere else – a special place – and they say I'm *cursed,* but they can help."

"The rats?" Lynn asked, scrunching her face and doing her best to follow.

"The cats...well, a *tiger,*" Billy said, frantic. "But it's not a tiger. And I have to find the key to wake the tiger up and fix me. But there's a *price,* and they didn't say what it was. Something is coming. The dreams are getting worse. I don't know what to do. I just turned ten, and then the accident–" the boy stammered and lifted a forearm across his eyes, sponging up tears with his sleeve. "I don't want to *lose* it."

"Whoa," Lynn said, patting him on the knee. She pursed her lips as she exhaled, making a sound like a horse after a hard race.

"You think I'm crazy, don't you?" Billy said.

"Well, you're not exactly *normal*," Lynn arched an eyebrow and popped a cherry bubble. "But my dad says that 'normal' people can't be trusted."

There was shouting from the deck, followed by the *THUP-THUP-THUP* of a paintball gun being fired. Everyone had leapt into the pool, and Tommy stood on the diving board. With a red bandana wrapped around his forehead, he proceeded to play his own version of *fish-in-a-barrel*.

"See what I mean?" Lynn said, rolling her eyes.

Billy watched Tommy run around the pool and fire wads of red-and-yellow paint into the air. His mother squealed and clapped from her chair on the deck, and his father gave a hearty thumbs-up from behind the hood of the smoking grill.

"The dreams were right," Billy said. He pointed to his toes, which had matured from plump grapes to swollen cherry tomatoes. "They said it would get worse."

Lynn whistled long and low as she examined his toes up close, but didn't seem too bothered by the sight. Instead, she picked up the marker from the grass, twisted off the cap, and hunted for an open spot on the cast.

"You should relax," she said, grabbing his foot and swinging it into her lap. Billy's chair almost tipped, forcing him to cling to its arms to keep from falling out. "Sorry...I need to get at this one good spot."

"Great. I'm relaxed already."

"Shhhh!" she said, leaning in and drawing on the outside of his ankle. "I'm serious. My Dad says that all the problems in life come from stress. And stress comes from thinking about things that have *already* happened, or worrying about things that haven't happened *yet*. We can't change either of those, so all we can do is chill and be right here, right now."

"Sounds like a hippie," Billy said, trying to peek at what she was drawing.

Lynn pushed him back in his chair and cupped her hand to hide her work. "And where'd you hear that from, wise-ass?"

"My mom," he said, watching the Claytons hand Tommy another stack of presents at poolside. "She says that the smart people run the world, while the hippies are busy playing. She says that it's smart to worry – that a 'stitch in time saves nine', and 'an ounce of prevention is worth a pound of cure'. Oh, and 'the busy ant will have no regrets come winter, while the lazy grasshopper starves.'"

"Wow, your mom's a party," Lynn said, making detailed strokes with the pen. "But you're not like her."

"How do you know?"

"Because you like animals more than people. And that's because animals are real, and honest, and never waste their time worrying. They just want to *live*. And maybe show us how to be happy."

"Let me guess – your Dad said that, right?"

"Yup," Lynn said, admiring her work.

"And what does your Mom say?" Billy said. He watched a bead of sweat trickle down her cheek as she dried the sketch with a stream of breath.

"Nothing anymore," she said, gathering her hair and tying it back into a high ponytail. "She's dead."

The flood of embarrassment made Billy nauseous, and he dropped his gaze to the ground. A second later, a stiff punch in the arm sobered him up.

"Don't be all *weird*," Lynn said, unclenching her fist. "It was a long time ago. Crap happens. Maybe I'll tell you about it someday over a root beer float."

She stood and wiped her hands on her shorts. Blades of grass still clung to her legs like tiny green stripes on a blonde jungle cat.

"I like orange soda," Billy shifted his leg over, craning to see what she had sketched. "If you add vanilla ice cream, it tastes like a Creamsicle."

"You *are* crazy." She lobbed the pen in an easy arc so he could catch it against his chest.

"What did you draw?" Billy squinted through the glare from the cast, which was now propped in the sunlight. "A dog? Seriously?"

"It's those big brown eyes of yours," Lynn said, leaning down to pinch his cheek. "I couldn't help myself."

"Hey!" Billy pushed her hand away, though only half-heartedly. "You're gonna leave more marks than the car did. And what'd you say over its head? I can't read your chicken scratch."

"Just the truth – *Dogs rule. Cats drool.*"

"That's not true. They drool way more than cats. Everyone knows that!"

"Whatever you say, puppy-dog," Lynn stuck out her tongue.

There was loud barking from inside the house. The barks became *yips,* and a bunch of guests fled from poolside, laughing and shrieking and looking over their shoulders. Tommy ran after them until he reached the concrete's edge. He was holding a long red leash, pulled taught by the pointy-eared monster at its end.

"That's right!" Tommy said, straining to keep his new Doberman's tether in his hands. "You can run but you can't hide. Not anymore – because *Storm* is coming for you!"

"Awesome," Lynn rolled her eyes so far back that she looked like a pre-teen zombie. "Listen, I'd better go and make sure he doesn't get his arm bit off. Or make sure that he *does*. Haven't decided yet."

"Wait," Billy said, his expression a mix of serious and sad. "Don't tell anyone what I told you. Okay?"

"Cross my heart, hope to die," she said, making an 'X' in the air in front of her chest.

"Stick a needle in your eye?" Billy pointed at his eye.

"That's pretty badass for a puppy-dog."

"I'm serious. Swear!" Billy said, anxious.

"Fine!" Lynn pulled down an eyelid, and brought a finger dangerously close to her eyeball.

"And don't call me 'puppy-dog'!"

"He's no *puppy*," Tommy shouted, chasing after his new pet. The dog charged past Lynn and jerked to a stop at the end of its leash, just a few feet from Billy. Frightened, Billy leaned the chair away from it at a precarious angle. "Like I said, you're a *puss*'!" Tommy yanked on the leash, which made the dog bark and bare its fangs. "Get his scent, Storm. Someday you'll hunt him."

The dog growled, straining at its spiked collar. It snapped at the air and scraped its paws against the grass and dirt, inching closer.

Billy turned to Tommy then. All he could do was hope that this boy – this rich, strong, and handsome boy who had so many friends, a perfect home, and more gifts than he'd have in a lifetime of birthdays – would show him mercy.

Tommy Clayton saw the hope in Billy's eyes. He saw the boy's fear, and sadness, and desperation. He saw it all, if only for a glimmer, and it made him smile. And through that smile, Tommy mouthed a single word – '*BURN*'.

And then he let go of the leash.

Billy shut his eyes and covered his face with his hands. He pushed his broken leg forward, hoping the dog would attack it first. If it got through the plaster to the leg itself, it didn't matter as much – the boy was already preparing himself for the worst.

"*HEEL!*"

Billy swatted at the air, bracing for the first bite, when a loud *whine* made him peek through his guard. And that's when he saw Tommy

Clayton's Doberman – the dog named Storm – trot to Lynn's side, sit down on the grass, and beg for a treat.

"Aw, c'mon," Tommy said, dragging his feet across the lawn and holding out his hand for the leash. "Give him back!"

Lynn scooped up the leash and retracted it on its plastic wheel, shortening the lead. Then she knelt down, rubbed the dog's chest, and balanced a bone-shaped cookie on its nose.

"Stop it! You're gonna make him all *nice,*" Tommy pulled at his own hair.

"That won't happen," Lynn said, rubbing Storm's chest and giving his slender paw a shake. "Dogs learn from their owners."

"I wasn't gonna hurt him," Tommy glared over at Billy. "I was just scaring the puss'."

"I'm not a 'puss' *or* a 'puppy'," Billy said, his heart slowing, and the panic draining from his bones.

"*Burrrrn,*" Tommy chanted.

"Shut up!" Billy said.

"Stop it, both of you!" Lynn wagged a finger at them. "Tommy, let's go. I'll teach you how to treat your new and *only* friend, and we are gonna leave Billy alone. And Billy? You're not a puppy *or* a puss for the rest of the day. Alright?"

"Fine," Billy crossed his arms, and slumped in his chair.

"*Whatever,*" Tommy snatched the leash from her, "but it's my birthday and my dog, so eat it. Losers."

Tommy ran in front of the dog and unspooled the leash. He called to it but it looked confused – it turned its head back and forth between its 'master', and the girl who had just given him treats and chest rubs.

Lynn winked at Billy and snapped her fingers. Tommy slapped a palm to his forehead and made exasperated groans as Lynn and Storm trotted past him, their noses raised ever so slightly in the air.

Billy watched the three of them disappear into the orchard. He imagined them running and laughing together between the perfect rows of trees. He pictured them clambering up knobby trunks and branches, feasting on sour apples, and finding the best hiding spots in the treetops.

The worries returned. Billy looked down at his leg – at the drawings, and jokes, and scribbles on its plaster sheath – and wondered what his life would be like a month from now.

She's wrong. I can't relax, Billy thought. *Not yet. That would be like giving up.*

The boy wasn't ready to quit. Not yet. All he needed was a clue. A sign. Something *real* that he could hold in his hands.

"*Burger, buddy?*" a voice said, shaking Billy from his thoughts.

Mr. Clayton was holding a paper plate with a charred lump of meat squished between two pieces of white bread. "Just cleaning up the grill. Thought you might want the last one."

"Thank you, Mr. Clayton," Billy took the plate, and wondered what could be salvaged from the grilled wreckage.

"You're welcome, buddy."

"It's Billy."

"*Billy—*" the man said. He looked at the golden face of his designer watch, caught his reflection in it, and smoothed his hair back. "Right. That's great. Really *great*. Listen, buddy – what say you pack that burger back, and then help me out with a quick relocation."

"Okay. But, uhh, I'm not sure how much help I'll be," Billy stammered, nodding to his leg. He grabbed the burger in both hands and took a big bite, dribbling mustard and ketchup down his wrists.

"Not a problem, buddy."

"*Billy.*"

"Right. We're just gonna pick you up and move you over by the garden. Great spot. 'Chill', as the kids say. So when your folks get back, it's a just a short hop to the driveway. In and out like a ninja. Sound good?"

"Mmmm, I–" Billy said, mouth stuffed with burger.

"Great. Let's make it happen. Five minutes. Won't be long 'til the sun goes down."

"What happens then?" Billy said, wiping a blob of pickle relish from his chin.

Mr. Clayton pointed to the road that snaked through the valley. Three black trucks were cresting the closest ridge, painting trails of smoke on the grassy hills behind them.

"That's when the show starts, buddy."

X I

Of Mice and Magic

HIS MOTHER HAD SAID THE PARTY would have 'entertainment'. She wasn't wrong.

Billy had been relocated to a grassy mound near the back of the Claytons' flower garden, which offered a fair view of what was in store. For the next few hours, workers in black shirts and buttoned overalls unloaded long crates, metal poles, platforms and lights, piling them on the lawn by the pool. When they started to assemble everything, it quickly became clear as to why he'd been moved – the Claytons needed *all* of the space for a backyard carnival.

There were brightly painted game booths, where a good toss or throw or swinging magnet on a fishing line would win a stuffed animal. There were sandy pits with rubber horseshoes, and pop-up bowling alleys with plastic balls and pins. There was a tent with vintage arcade games and pinball machines. There was even a strongman tower, with an oversized bell that rung if you hit the bottom hard enough.

In the middle of it all was a makeshift stage. It was made of interlocking black boxes with tall poles sticking up from the sides. A shiny red banner hung between them, shouting 'HAPPY BIRTHDAY TOMMY!!!' in big block letters. And beneath the banner – in the centre of the stage – sat a high-backed golden chair.

The Claytons had spared no expense for their son's birthday. Billy tried not to sigh as two pretty helpers in sparkling tights led Tommy out of the orchard in a blindfold. He tried not to cringe as the guests *oooh'ed* and *ahhh'ed* as they followed Tommy up the lawn, his purebred dog prancing around his feet. He tried not to groan when the birthday boy was seated in his princely throne onstage and Mrs. Clayton waved to the crowd, hushing them with a jeweled finger to her thin, ruby lips.

Billy tried.

But when Mr. Clayton gave the signal for the lights?

When the pretty ladies peeled back the blindfold?

When the music blared, and the crowd cheered, and Tommy leapt to the front of the stage with his arms raised in triumph?

It was hard *not* to be jealous. And it only got worse – or *better*, if you happened to be the lucky boy in question.

As night fell, the acrobats appeared. They flipped and tumbled and cart-wheeled like limbed comets shooting across the lawn, orbiting the stage. Then came the jugglers flinging huge knives (or was it small swords?) around Tommy's head, as he clapped and hollered to the crowd.

There was even a fire-eater! He was a gargoyle of a man, and it was hard to see what parts of him weren't tattooed or pierced with rings and bolts and bits of metal you'd likely find in a kitchen drawer. He swigged from a bottle and held a lit torch near his mouth. And when he blew jets of flame into the air, Tommy stood on his chair and cheered. It was the only time he looked at Billy the whole night, grinning wide as the fire plumed in front of him.

The clowns and the stilt-walkers in outrageously tall hats came last. The painted fools stumbled and fumbled and fell in front of the stage, tripping the walkers and sending them reeling. They teetered and swayed and almost fell across the stage, before dumping hatfuls of glitter and confetti on Tommy's head.

The jangling music crescendoed, and all the performers turned to the stage to applaud. Tommy stood in a spotlight, bowing and soaking in the cheers as the bits of paper drifted in the air around him.

In the dark, with the lights aimed at the stage, it was as if something had shaken the world between its hands. Billy's tired eyes saw the luckiest boy in the world, happy and adored inside a brilliant globe of snow.

The crowd milled about and started to thin as the first parents arrived to collect their children. Billy felt sleepy. Nobody had taken notice of his exile save for Lynn; she was kind enough to bring him a piece of cake, and a half-melted scoop of ice cream.

"Double chocolate," she'd said, the smears of icing on her chin a dead giveaway. "*Triple* chocolate, if you count the ice cream *and* the cake."

She hadn't stayed long. Tommy had barged through the crowd soon after, yelled '*Fireworks!*', and pulled her back into the fray. Before Billy could even touch his plate, a pair of ravenous jaws had clamped down and devoured the whole lot. Storm sneered a chocolate sneer and trotted after his master, gobs of ice cream trailing on the grass.

BOOM...FZZZZT...BA-BOOM...FZZZZZT...PA-POWWWW!

Billy's father had bought fireworks for holidays before. Billy had been thrilled by ten-ball roman candles, sparkling mini-volcanoes, and whizzing cyclones nailed to the bird-feeder post. But now he knew better.

The sky above the house was showered in red and gold, and exploded with balls of silver. The flashes lit up the whole valley, and the booms echoed over the hills. The brightness trumped the stars themselves, forming new constellations of burning blossoms, glittering trees, and fiery swords that sparked as they clashed in the cloudless night.

The yard was soon filled with a sweet-smelling smoke. It hovered by the deck, covered the pool, and crept across the lawn. Billy heard laughter, and watched the children running back and forth in the haze, slipping through it like phantoms and shades.

High above, the last rockets soared to their zenith, and two balls of ruby light pulsed in the blackness. Billy waited for them to pop, or to fall and fade. But they just hung there in the sky. Burning. Waiting.

A strange shape lurked in the gloom that engulfed the yard. It stepped from the smoke, and tapped a finger on the biggest, most-swollen toe poking from the boy's cast.

"Ow!" Billy jumped in his chair, waving the smoke away from his face. "Who is that?"

The figure stepped closer. It pressed white-gloved palms together in front of its chest, and smiled.

It was a clown. At least the face – ashen paint with coal-black lips and eyebrows – made it *look* like a clown. But it wasn't a 'normal' clown, if there ever was such a thing. It looked more like a *pirate*.

The clown wore high black boots, buffed and polished, with square silver buckles above the toe. Its long black coat skimmed the ground, silver buttons the size of saucers running up the front. A frilly white shirt bulged between the coat's lapels, and frillier cuffs spilled from wide sleeves. A powder-white wig sat on its head, draping thick curls over its shoulders. On top of the wig was a three-sided cap, folded and brimmed like a puffy black pastry.

The clown spun a hand at the wrist with a dramatic flourish, lifted the cap, and bowed to Billy. At the bottom of the bow it lifted its still-smiling head, and looked at him.

Its eyes had been obscured by smoke and shadow until now. Dark irises consumed most of the whites in its eyes, making them look completely black. Billy wondered whether the clown wore special lenses to make them do that, or if he (or she) was born that way. The world was full of strange things, after all.

As he pondered this, Billy felt something touch his left ear.

"Hey!" he said, pulling away from the clown's hand.

The white glove twisted with another flourish, and opened to reveal a large coin. It was gold, like the ones Billy had seen in movies with pirates and chests of buried treasure.

"I know how you did that," Billy said, sitting tall and crossing his arms. "It was in your palm the whole time."

The clown frowned, its painted lips dipping down on either side of its pointed chin. It put the coin in its drooping coat pocket, dug around inside, and pulled out an egg.

"I know what you're going to do," Billy said.

The clown lifted the egg beside its ear and shook it. He listened to it for a moment, and made a surprised face.

"Go on," Billy said, leaning back.

As the smoke billowed around its shoulders, the clown pushed the egg into its ear. Its eyes went wide as its hand pressed flat against the side of its head. The clown coughed, and spat an egg from its mouth into its palm.

"Ha," Billy smirked.

The clown repeated the trick in the other ear, straining to produce the second egg.

The boy remained unimpressed. "The eggs were already in your mouth. You put the others up your sleeve as you pushed."

With a grimace, the clown removed its hat and tossed the egg high in the air. It caught the egg in the hat and turned it over. No egg. But when it tapped on top of the hat, something white fell to the grass. And it *squeaked.*

Billy tensed as the clown picked up a small white rat by the tail, and then waved it in front of his face. Its pink eyes bulged at him, and its pointy teeth gnawed at the air by his nose.

"The hat has a false bottom with two compartments. You caught the egg in one, and tapped the other side to drop the rat," Billy said, shielding his face with a hand. "Now take it away."

The clown arched both painted brows high on its forehead, as if to ask, '*Are you sure?*'

"Please," Billy said, scrunching up his face. "Get rid of it."

The clown gave the smallest of bows, titled its head back, and opened its mouth. Billy stared in shock as the clown dangled the rat above it, the poor thing squirming and squealing between blackened lips. And then, eyes closed, the clown dropped the rat in whole.

"What are you doing?" Billy said, appalled.

The clown rubbed its belly and pretended to chew. Then it made an exaggerated swallow. The clown's eyes popped open, and it bent its knees to squat.

"No, no–" Billy said, preparing himself for something altogether unpleasant.

The clown's eyes bugged out, its face strained, and it turned to lift the tails of its coat. There on the ground, scurrying in teeny circles, were four baby rats.

The clown opened its mouth and moved around its stained tongue. There was nothing in its dark gullet except rotting teeth and strings of spit.

"How'd you do that?" Billy asked.

The chalk-skinned magician winked, scooped up the rats in its hat, and put the hat back on its head.

The boy was curious now. The other tricks were kids' stuff – he had learned them all when he was seven, and tried performing them for a third-grade Show and Tell. When he was mocked and heckled, he swore off magic forever.

Illusions don't help anyone, his mother had said at the time. *They only exist to prove you're a fool.*

The clown pulled a shiny white block from its breast pocket, held it up with both hands, and fanned it open.

"Not cards," Billy shook his head. "I get enough of that at home."

The trickster raised a long finger to its black lips, and the lights around its body changed. It now had a golden halo, and the smoke curled around the edges of its coat like yellow vines. Billy spied shadows frolicking in the smoke behind it, moving as if wading through molasses.

The clown stepped forward and held the deck out to him. Billy took one of the oversized cards and looked at it.

It was blank.

"Nothing," he said, holding it up and showing the mime both sides. "It's white on both sides."

The clown narrowed its eyes and shuffled the deck. He fanned it open once more, and showed both sides to Billy.

"They're all blank," he said, scratching the card's smooth surface with a fingernail.

The colours in the smoke changed, and the scene was aglow like a jack-o-lantern. The clown put a gloved finger to its waxen temple and looked up, as if deep in thought.

It snapped its fingers and pointed at the air – *Eureka!* – and lunged forward to kneel by Billy's leg. The clown put the deck on the ground, lifted the top card, and slid it along the boy's cast. Finding a spot, it pressed the card into the plaster and rubbed its knuckles against it.

"What are you doing?" Billy said, growing tired of the show. People were leaving, his parents were late, and his tummy was growling with thoughts of all the chocolate he wasn't eating.

The clown grinned wide, and its eyes went even wider. It peeled the card from Billy's cast and held it up for him to see.

It was the picture of a golfer – the one that his father had drawn on his cast – recreated in every detail, right there on the card.

And it was *moving*.

"How...?" Billy murmured.

The clown slapped the card against the plaster. It went blank again.

"Wow!"

The clown smiled, pressed another card against the cast, and rubbed the back of it. When it was peeled away, Billy saw Mikey Durlick's sketch; the floppy-eared rabbit wiggled its nose, and began tapping its foot to the rhythm of the carnival music.

"That's...that's *amazing*," Billy said, reaching for the card.

The clown snatched it back and shook its head. Then it slapped the card on the cast, and the rabbit disappeared.

"One more time. Please," Billy said, transfixed by the trick. He'd watch more closely this time and figure out how it was done.

The conjurer drew another card and pressed it firmly against the cast, this time on Tommy's bonfire.

"You can *really* make that one disappear, if you want."

The clown's eyes narrowed as the card peeled back. Billy watched the edge of it, and saw nothing but empty white plaster as the card was lifted. The magician snapped its fingers, and held the card close to the boy's face.

Billy watched as the inky blue flames swayed and burned. He could almost hear the popping, and the crackling, and the sizzling of it. He could almost smell the burning wood. He could almost feel his face get warm, then hot, then too hot, until the card burst into sparks and ash before his eyes.

The smoke in the air became thicker and darker, and the lights turned a murky scarlet. Billy looked for people in the haze, but they had all disappeared.

The clown leaned in close with a finger raised to its lips, and Billy saw its eyes change. The irises shrank and vanished, swallowed on all sides by the whites. Only the black pupils remained, trapped in a pair of frozen voids.

'Shhhhhhh,' it said, but the boy heard the voice only in his mind. It sounded like someone squeezing a bag filled with shards of broken glass.

"What *are* you?" Billy said, a chill shooting through him.

The clown drew a card and held it aloft. There were red letters on its face, scripted in the style of old-fashioned quill and ink.

FRIEND.

"What do you want?" Billy whispered, his breath fast and shallow. A memory stirred in him. Voices on a boat. Whispers in a nightmare.

The clown looked sad, and caressed the boy's face with its gloved hand. Billy closed his eyes at its cold touch, and prayed that he was dreaming.

He felt three hard taps against his cast, like *knocking.* A sudden lightness swept through him, and he knew that something had changed. The magician's hand tugged gently at his face, and Billy opened his eyes.

The cast was gone. His leg was healed, smooth and healthy. There wasn't even a scar.

"*Oh my God,*" Billy hugged the clown, who smelled of smoke and overripe fruit. "You fixed it! But *how*–?" The clown pushed Billy back and shook its head, pointing down at the boy's leg.

His heart sank – the cast was still there.

"Why?" Billy sobbed, pressing his face into his hands. Hot tears streamed between his fingers. "What's *happening* to me?

The clown reached into its breast pocket and pulled out a silken handkerchief, white like the gloves that it wore. Bits of silk dabbed at Billy's eyes and wiped at his cheeks. Then the silk slid down his torso, along the length Billy's leg, and pressed against his shin.

"No more *tricks,*" Billy begged. "I can't take it anymore."

Gloved hands pushed against the plaster, and then snapped the silk into the air. The clown unfurled it, revealing the thing now upon it – the first thing that had been drawn on the boy's cast.

The symbol of the *cat.*

"So?" Billy said, woeful and confused. "What am I supposed to do with that?"

The clown flipped the handkerchief.

FIND IT.

"Find *what?*" Billy bristled. "There it is, on my leg. What do you *want* from me?"

The clown tilted its head, peered down its powdered nose, and flipped the square of silk.

THE KEY.

The clown looked at the message and then looked at Billy. Then it raised an eyebrow, and stared at the thing Mrs. Thomas had drawn on Billy's leg.

"*That's* what they want?" Billy said, pointing to the symbol. The clown pulled its thin black lips into a chilling smile.

"That's just a drawing, but...is it a drawing *of* something? Something *real*?" Billy asked, fragile and urgent.

The clown leaned closer, pupils shrinking to pinpricks of onyx. It nodded, slow and deliberate.

"So...how? How do I *find* it?" Billy said.

The smoke swirled around them. The lights pulsed in rhythm with the echoing calliope that looped over and over in the boy's ears.

The harlequin folded the handkerchief in half, then again, and held the folded silk in its hands beneath Billy's face. As they both watched, the flap of silk unfolded – turning like a page – and a final message appeared.

BOOK.

Billy saw the word, and sucked cool air between his teeth. The thought turned and turned in his mind, as he recalled the past month in meticulous detail. He bit his lip, and squeezed his fingers, and tried his utmost to sound brave as he spoke.

"If I help you...how will you help *me*?"

The trickster swept a hand along the length of Billy's leg, and pointed to the playing card still sitting in the boy's lap. Billy flicked the top edge of the card, pinched the corner, and flipped it over.

Azure eyes opened, and stared into him. Striped jaws gaped wide, as if to swallow him. Curved fangs gnashed together, as if trying to chew him to bits.

It was the face of a tiger, come to life on the card. It was the same one Billy had drawn – the same one from his dream.

"You know how to find it?"

The smile disappeared. Another nod.

"Where? Where is it?"

The clown stood, and the lights changed again. It drifted away from the boy, shrinking into a luminous tunnel in the smoke. It became like a shadow, its form stretching and warping, distorted by the haze. It made a final flourish with an alabaster hand, and waved a finger back and forth in refusal.

Billy stood. Dreadful pains shot through the length of him, but the boy lurched forward to give chase. He hobbled across the grass, flailed in the smoke, and called out to the stranger.

"Please," he said, stumbling in the haze, "tell me how to find it!"

The shadow bowed, and vanished in a burst of light.

Billy pushed forward and kept calling out. But there was no answer in the dizzying sea of smoke and bursts of light. He could only hear the music now, rising and rising, faster and faster, hammering through his skull.

The boy stumbled, falling through waves of mist and music and the kaleidoscope of lights. The ground receded from him, and he remembered the dream where it seemed he had fallen forever.

"*Billy...*" came a voice at the vision's edge.

He felt something prod his shoulder, and then something else caress his face.

"*C'mon Billy,*" it said, less gentle and more urgent. "*Time to wake up now.*"

His limbs jerked, and he felt himself hit the ground. When Billy opened his eyes, he was splayed out on the grass beside his lawn chair. His father was crouched beside him.

"Probably not the smartest idea," his father said, hoisting the boy in one arm and the crutches under his other. "Sleepwalking with a busted wheel."

"*Sleepwalk?*" Billy croaked, shaking the cobwebs from his head. "What time is it?"

"Time to go home. Sorry we're late, but there was a night market in town. Summertime. And you know how your Mom likes a deal."

"Yeah," Billy wiped the sleep from his eyes.

As he loped beside his father, the pains in his hip and shin burned away any lingering trace of the dream. He looked around the yard — except for a few stragglers most of the kids had already left, and the carnival crew was packing up.

"Thanks for coming, buddy," Mr. Clayton half-saluted from the deck as the Brahms crossed the lawn.

"It's still *Billy*," the boy said, grumpy and annoyed.

"Be *nice*," his father said, giving his shoulder a squeeze and waving to the hosts.

The remaining guests were also on the balcony, gathered around the birthday boy. They watched him wrestle with his dog, and dig through an obscene pile of presents.

"Thank you, Mr. and Mrs. Clayton," Billy said, grinding his teeth as the words squeezed out. "I...I had a really good time."

"*I had a reallllly good time*," mocked Tommy from just out of sight. Storm yipped in reply, and there were snorts and giggles from the deck. Even Mrs. Clayton made some bubbles in her pink martini.

"Quite the party animal you got there, Stan. Looks like the apple *can* fall far from the tree, eh?"

Stanley Brahm chuckled, and gave the handsome man a neighbourly thumbs-up. Mrs. Clayton lowered the glass from her lips and whispered something in her husband's ear. Mr. Clayton looked down at Billy as he hopped to the edge of the driveway, and spoke just loud enough for father and son to hear.

"Well that explains it then. Those rejects *never* turn out right."

Billy looked back over his shoulder as the man's words hung in the night like the stink of rotten eggs. Mr. and Mrs. Clayton were clinking glasses, and back to watching their son hold court on the deck. The only person who broke from the pack to say goodbye was Lynn, who leaned against the railing and waved.

Billy didn't wave back. He just pointed a finger at his own eye and then at the girl. Lynn sighed and rolled her eyes, made an 'X' across her heart with her right hand, and held the left one up with the palm facing him.

In Billy's mind, it was official – she made a *promise*. With witnesses. And, for the time being at least, it was a promise that was being kept.

"You should take a look, Liz," Stanley said to Elizabeth as he pushed the shopping bags aside and slid Billy into the back seat. "They sure went to town on that party. Talk about whole hog."

"How nice for them," Elizabeth said, surveying the carnival workers as they hauled crates across the lawn and loaded them into their trucks. "It's going to do a number on their grass. All those people and machines. The trucks are parked right in the front yard! That's bound to affect the property value, no matter how nice the view is."

"Mmhmm," Stanley started the car and flicked on the radio. Elizabeth lowered the volume, and pressed her ear against the window as their car reversed down the long driveway.

"What's that?" she said. "Barking?"

"Tommy got a dog. A Doberman," Billy muttered. His voice was weak from the backseat, and his mind was elsewhere. "He named it Storm."

"Well, that settles it," his mother turned up her nose. "Dogs are proven to lower a home's value, what with the noise and the digging and all the...poop. And to get a breed notorious for violence? I have no idea what they were *thinking*."

Stanley tweaked the radio knob, and the twang of classic rock 'n' roll filled the car.

"Tommy wanted one," Billy said, "so they gave it to him. That's why."

His mother turned in her seat. "Well, like the song says, you can't always get what you want."

"Whatever," Billy stared out the window as they pulled onto the highway.

The Clayton's house shrank behind them. From up the road, it looked like a model kit that needed glue and paint and instructions. The carnival trucks were like the die-cast miniatures he'd send careening down strips of plastic track on the basement steps. The workers looked like ants, filing in and out of the trucks, tireless and mindless.

"But sometimes you *can*," said his mother, "and what I want is you in your seatbelt, mister."

"Fine," Billy sighed and rolled his eyes, safe in the knowledge that it was too dark to see his face. He reached under and around himself, searching for the clasp.

There was something in his back pocket. It was flat and thin. The edge of it was sticking out from the denim flap in his shorts, and he grunted as he tugged to pull it free.

"What are you doing back there?" his mother said, looking in the passenger vanity mirror with her glasses in her hand. "Don't make a production out of it – just put the belt on."

"Just a second," Billy said, frustrated. He finally pulled the thing free, squinting to read in the low light.

It was a flyer, printed on heavy stock paper:

THE LAWRENCE COUNTY FAIR
Returns AUGUST 22-25 to
The Middleton Fairgrounds
RIDES —- GAMES —- PRIZES
Fun for the whole family!!!

"What is that?" Elizabeth said, snatching the card.

"Wait! I wasn't done—" Billy leaned between the seats.

"Yes, you are. Now sit back and put on that belt, unless you want your *father's* belt instead. Understand?"

Billy surrendered and snapped the seatbelt on, even with the idle threat. His father had only spanked him once in his life, and the boy had cried longer and louder than the Brahms thought possible. It would only be worse now with the shape his leg was in, so Billy planned on milking the small window of parental leniency for all it was worth.

"That's right, the *fair*," his mother said, donning her glasses and turning on the cabin light to read the card. "Summer's over already. Where does the time go?"

"It gets faster as you age, at least for some of us," his father said, earning him a playful smack on the arm with the card.

"See, Billy," she looked back over her shoulder, "Tommy's parents spent all that money trying to impress people, but you'll get the *real* thing for only $10."

"Plus the horse poop," Stanley quipped, resulting in another smack.

"Oh, my goodness," Elizabeth flipped over the card. "Now there's something I bet wasn't at the party."

She passed the card back to Billy, and his throat closed tight. He had to put the card in his lap because his hands shook too much for him to read it:

AUGUST 22/23 — TWO DAYS ONLY

LIVE IN CAPTIVITY

GET A PICTURE TAKEN WITH 'SNOWY'

— THE WHITE TIGER —

ONLY $50!!!

"Maybe if you're good, we'll take you there after your doctor's visit. It's not that far from the clinic, and we can save on gas," his mother said.

"Ummm, shouldn't we maybe go to the fair first? You know, in case it's bad–" his father peered in the rearview mirror, lines of concern etched around his eyes in the glare of oncoming traffic.

"The *weather*...right...the roads could be a problem if there's a storm," she said, her voice jumping up half an octave. "Well, we'll figure something out. Still have to confirm the appointment. Still have time to prepare." She gave a cheery hum in time with the radio, and shut off the interior light.

As Billy brushed his fingers against the lines and letters on the card's waxy surface, he saw his mother's hand join his father's on the gearshift, and remain there for the rest of the drive home.

At bedtime, Billy opened the window in his room and called to the cat. The plum-sized June-bugs buzzed by the eavestrough, and blinking fireflies did loops and figure eights over the blackberry bushes. But there was no sign of his feline friend in or outside the house. The boy resigned himself to a lonely session of research.

He had a real clue now, and the flyer for the county fair gave him hope that this wasn't just a case of too many cheeseburgers and a dash of sunstroke. Something *was* happening. If the clown's message was right, then the next puzzle piece was in one of three books at his bedside.

In the '*Big Cats*' book, Billy searched for information on white tigers. He learned that their Latin name was *Panthera Tigris Tigris*, that they were exceedingly rare, larger than all other tigers, and some – the true 'albinos' – didn't even have stripes. Apparently, there were many legends surrounding them, the most enduring one being from Chinese mythology. It said that a white tiger was seen as 'The Guardian of the West', and only appeared when the world was on the verge of a lasting peace.

In the book on '*Dreams*', tigers seemed to represent a lot of different things. A tiger in your dreams could mean strength and courage, rage and hunger, or just the basic fear of being eaten. But one section stressed how some cultures believed that the big cat is an important symbol of health. According to the book, a tiger held the power to heal the dreamer from a great injury.

The boy saved '*Blood and Stones*' for last. It was a history book, so maybe it could help him sleep. The cramped blocks of text droned on about the first settlers in coma-inducing detail. There were notes on their countries of origin, the contents of their ships, and the family names on their registries. But there was drama to be found as well. He read accounts of fires and floods, of famine and of plague, and grisly tales of clashes with the natives over land, food, and religion.

Billy was getting tired, so he thumbed through the pen-and-ink illustrations the book featured every few pages. There were several recreations of architectural designs from the 17-1800s, complete with margin notes for the original builders and stonemasons. Billy found detailed sketches of old churches and schoolhouses, forts and other military outposts, and some of the more notable homes from the time.

He soldiered on through the pages, absorbing everything he could about thatched roofs, and retaining walls, and earthen cellars, and water wells, and bell-towers, and millwheels, and foundation stones from the 18th century. When he had had his fill and his eyelids grew leaden, he closed the book.

But before he did, he marked his spot.

Billy knew it was 'wrong' to bend back the top of a page and dog-ear a book (every parent, teacher, and librarian alive will be happy to remind you of that immutable truth), but he dog-eared it anyway. For him, sometimes the smallest rebellions felt like the biggest victories.

That's when it appeared, square in the middle of that triangle of folded paper. It was right there, same as the one on his leg, just like the clown-magician had asked for.

The symbol of the cat. The *key.*

Billy flipped the page and flattened out the fold he had made. The symbol was in the upper corner, and part of a sketched block of stone. That stone was itself part of a larger design – a foundation – for a home that was to be built in 1777.

On the opposing page were rough sketches – designs for a retaining wall and split cellar – along with handwritten notes. Billy read of a plan for a water well that would be fed from a neighbouring marsh, which was itself supplied by a nearby river.

There was one more faint sketch in the bottom corner, perhaps the roughest of the lot. It was for an arch made of stone, with the following note:

> *It is to be built betwixt the well and the north wing of the abode, oriented in such a way that would allow one – when standing beneath IT, upon the Solstice – to witness the sun's rising above the spot where they rest. The smallest of tributes, made to the first brave and Godly families of the New World.*

Billy closed the book, and got out of bed.

He limped to the window, ignoring the pain, and stared out at the horizon. Behind him stood a very old house. Beside it was an arch made of stone. And in direct view of it, crowning the closest hill?

A colonial cemetery.

It was time to cross the road again and meet with Mrs. Thomas. It was time to speak of more than apple pie and cats.

XII

Of Stealth and Sandwiches

BILLY HAD WAITED THREE DAYS to meet with Mrs. Thomas. She was busy in town on Sunday, and his mother didn't feel like helping him cross the road while his father was at work during the week.

"I'm not really in the mood to *socialize*," she had said. "Besides, didn't you have enough of people at the party? If you're not careful, you'll become an extrovert before you know it."

Billy's mother was an expert at turning the tables like this. With a quip and a sigh she could quickly deflect his requests, leaving him feeling selfish and flawed for having asked in the first place. She was a tough nut.

But now, he had a plan to crack her defenses.

He'd ask for snacks while she was ensconced in a crossword puzzle. He'd hide the batteries in the remote, and ask her to change the television channel by hand between commercials. He'd call out to the garden when she had just started to dig up the onions and cucumbers, and ask for 'assistance' in the bathroom. Not to mention the countless times he'd plead with her to look for the cat, which had shown little of itself since the party.

So it was on Wednesday morning – after three days of tactical strikes, and with his father honking as he rolled off to work – that his mother presented her terms for surrender.

"I gave Enid a call," she said. "She'd love to have you over for a late lunch."

Billy spent the rest of the morning washing up, packing his knapsack, and preparing. This visit was important. The boy was going to make doubly sure, no matter what happened, that he was ready for it.

"Did you bring the walkie-talkie?" his mother asked, taking his arm as they looked both ways down the empty highway. "I want you to check in, and give me some notice of when you plan to come back."

"Yes, Mom," Billy said.

The boy's gaze lingered on the road, and the shimmers of heat distorting it in the distance. He imagined the horizon transforming into a thunderous wave, crashing across the countryside. He pictured the northern mountain, lone and grey against the cloudless sky, exploding with forks of white-hot lightning. He heard a howling, a hissing, and a buzzing clamour over the fields, and nest in the weeping willows around him.

"Stop daydreaming!" His mother gave him a shake. "This is why you can't be trusted to do these things on your own. I swear...if your head wasn't screwed on tight enough, you'd let it fall right off."

She guided him across the road, which only took four long steps with the crutches. It took another five to her driveway, and eight more to the side of her house. Then Billy reached up, as he always did, and gave three sharp knocks on the screen door.

Soon enough, Elizabeth Brahm was helping Mrs. Thomas bring out the feast. Crusty-roll ham and cheese sandwiches. Carrot and celery sticks with creamy garlic dip. Sweet and spicy pickles and onions. Red potato salad with mustard and dill. Watermelon iced tea with fresh mint leaves. And homemade chocolate chunk cookies, the size of flattened softballs.

There wasn't a bare spot left atop the cracked stone table in the garden. This was probably the crafty old woman's plan from the beginning – all the more difficult for her 'children' to poach from.

"I'm going to leave you two to it," Billy's mother said, arms tight by her side, nervous with the feline parade around her feet.

"Please, Elizabeth," Mrs. Thomas scattered handfuls of kibble on the ground away from the table. "There's more than enough."

"No, no, I simply couldn't," his mother replied, inching back through the throng of cats and nearly tripping on a portly brown tabby. "I'm on track with my diet – half a grapefruit and a hard-boiled egg."

"How admirable. To the disciplined goes the reward," Enid beamed.

"So they say...so they say," Elizabeth sighed a small sigh. She bid her farewells, reminding her son not to be too much of a burden on their neighbour, and to check in with the radio in a few hours. With that, she was soon across the road to revel in spotless windows, scrubbed countertops, vacuumed carpets, and feline-free solitude.

"It's good to see you again, young man," Enid said, stroking the head of an old, sad-faced calico named Minou in her lap. "To what do I owe the pleasure of your company?"

Billy was tempted – by the scrumptious food, and the tranquil surroundings, and the joy in being back across the road – to forget his worries. But at this point it was impossible to ignore the nagging questions, the lingering dreams, and the growing ache in his shin. So, Billy lifted up his cast, rested it on top of a stone stool, and pointed to the thing that Mrs. Thomas had drawn upon it.

"Why did you draw this?" he asked.

Enid adjusted her glasses with a quizzical look. "Well, my goodness...I just figured you'd *like* a cat."

"I do. But why *this* one?" Billy traced the symbol's outline as the clown had done, a chill kissing his fingertips. "Why did you draw it like *that*?"

"I honestly couldn't tell you," she said, stumped.

Billy opened his backpack and pulled out the book: '*Blood and Stones*.' He opened the dusty tome, turned to the dog-eared page, and passed it to her. He nibbled on sandwiches, and sipped iced tea, and teased the curious tails of passing cats as the woman perused the pages.

"This is all quite remarkable, isn't it?" she said, astonished. "I *knew* there was something about this old house. My grandfather always said so. He used to say, '*This is a special place, and needs special people to tend it. Honour it. Don't let our ancestors' struggles be in vain.*'

"There was talk of colonials on both my mother's and father's side, but I never gave it much thought. I was just happy when father, bless his soul, passed the house to Robert and me. You see, Billy, I grew up here. I fell in love here. This is where my life blossomed. And it's also where the petals have fallen from the rose, if you'll pardon the phrase.

"So, when the real estate agents come by each year, offering fantastic sums for me to move to some cookie-cutter flat in town? Or worse, to some retirement hall reeking of powdered milk and tinned peas? I shoo them off. If this house was good enough for my grandparents, my parents, and my husband to spend their last days in? Well, then it's good enough for me."

Billy had re-filled his plate as she spoke, listening intently while dangling strips of ham under the table. Mrs. Thomas stood with care, easing old Minou down to the grass with trembling paws and a tired mew. The old woman made sluggish steps over to the stone arch, removed her glasses, and brushed the silver curls and dampness from her eyes. Minou followed a few steps behind, flopping in the grass by her feet. The sun broke through a patch of cloud as they both gazed at the cemetery atop the hill.

"You've lived here a long time," Billy said, washing down a chunk of bread with a swig of iced tea.

"I would be happy to do so longer, God willing," Enid said, the remnants of tears in the corners of her eyes. She turned back to look at the boy, smiling when she saw him sharing scraps of food with a tangle of twitching tails in a mass of mewing, multi-coloured fur. "Besides, who else would take care of my darlings?"

"I would." Billy reached into a nearby bag, and tossed a handful of crunchy cat food into the grass. The cats' heads moved as one, following the kibble's arc in the air. When it hit the ground, they scattered to devour it like a school of fish being chummed.

"I know you would, dear boy," she said, shuffling back to the table. "I might hold you to that someday."

"If the book's right, then this symbol is *here*. You must've seen it before, right? Somewhere in the house?"

"I may be getting on, but I'm not the dullest knife in the drawer. Trust me when I say to you that I have no recollection of that design. None whatsoever."

"From the sketch, it looks like it's somewhere in the cellar. Maybe we could take a look?" Billy said, pointing to the book as he gulped down the last of his second plate.

Enid shook her head. "I'm sorry, Billy, but you know my thoughts on the basement. I wouldn't want one of my babies getting trapped down there. Besides, all of these thoughts have conspired to tucker me out. I think I might head inside for a nap."

"But I don't want to leave," Billy pleaded. "I could help you clean up, and play with the cats."

"Won't your mother be expecting you soon?"

"She's happy I'm over here. Trust me."

Enid shared a knowing grin. "Fine. If you promise not to cross the road without calling her to escort you, then you're welcome to stay in the garden with your friends." Mrs. Thomas gathered the plates and picked up a tray. Some cats sniffed at her heels, while others ran to the door ahead of her. "Meanwhile, would you mind if I borrowed that book for a few days? I'm keen to read more when I'm...in a better frame of mind."

"Sure," Billy propped himself up on his crutches. With *Blood and Stones* under one arm, he hobbled to the side of the house. He passed it to her, and held the door open for her. "And I promise to call my Mom. But maybe I can come in for a bit, before I go?"

"Billy," Mrs. Thomas placed the tray down on the kitchen counter amidst a chorus of meows, "there are times in life when we all need to think of ourselves first. That may sound selfish, but it's not. It's just the right thing to do. And doing it will help us to help *others* better in the long run. When those moments come, you'll *know* it – you'll feel it in your bones – and nothing should stand in your way.

"So for me..? It's important, at *this* moment, that I have some time to myself and a little rest. Do you understand, my dear? Can you respect that?"

"Yes ma'am," Billy handed her the book, and moved away from the screen door. "Thank you very much for lunch."

"You're very welcome," she said. There were cats hopping through the plastic cat-flap at the base of the door, even though the door wasn't closed yet. Enid pointed to Billy's cast, as the cats vaulted over it like show-ponies. "And who knows? Maybe I'll remember where I saw that picture after a good nap."

"Who knows," Billy said, retreating to the table in the garden.

"Or...maybe I *did* see it in the house before. Just not while I was awake," the woman said, eyes twinkling. "Maybe...I saw it in my dreams."

Enid pressed her grooved palm against the mesh, gave him a pained smile, and closed the screen door.

'Maybe I saw it in my dreams.'

Her words fused with the sounds of chatting cats in the yard. They stayed with him as he pressed the tips of his crutches into the uncut grass, and hobbled over to the stone arch. They hovered in the air as he stood in the shadow of the stones, and followed the line of her gaze up to the dying trees, rusted gate, and cluster of graves on the hill.

'You'll feel it in your bones.'

Billy steadied himself against the column of stone, closed his eyes, and took a long, deep breath. He listened to the cats trilling, and the wind whistling, and a truck making shockwaves in its passing.

In a moment of stillness, he put his weight on his right foot. Daggers of pain stabbed at his leg, tremors and shocks ripping through his guts and chest, exploding in his head. White-hot tracers strobed behind his eyelids, and the boy bit down on his lip and held his breath to keep from screaming.

'And nothing should stand in your way.'

Billy lifted his foot and opened his eyes. With a gasp of relief, the air rushed from his nostrils and the world came flooding in. He slid the crutches under his arms and plodded back to the stone table, grinding his molars to dull the pain that now came with each step.

A pair of lean black cats hopped from the stool to the tabletop, making room for him to sit and unzip his pack. Everything was still in there, except for the book that Mrs. Thomas had borrowed.

Billy was ready. His mind was made. All he had to do now was wait.

The old lady was a heavy sleeper, which one would have to be in her situation. Her afternoon rests – 'kips', as she called them – usually lasted around an hour, and she was quick to drift off when she set herself to it.

Mrs. Thomas was long-since immune to the daily din of scratching posts, litter scuffing, and greedy eaters. At the same time, she had shown herself quick to waken at the first sign of more serious kitty commotions. But those were rare – the cats seemed to know her schedule, and tended to shift their furry gears midday to join her in sleep.

Billy grabbed the walkie-talkie from his bag and pressed the call button. The squawk of static made nearby cats spin perked ears and curious heads in his direction. Billy turned down the receiving volume, and pressed the button again.

"Are you there, Mom?"

There was a pregnant pause, with low fuzz coming through the receiver. The cats around his feet went back about their business of sniffing and stretching and rubbing their scent on the stools. The two black cats on the table took some cautious steps closer, lost interest, and began to groom each other.

"I'm here," belched the radio, his mother's voice distorted into a beefy baritone. "Can you hear me? Is this thing on?"

"You don't need to shout, Mom. I can hear you." Billy held the walkie close to his mouth. "I just wanted to check in. Everything's good."

"Good...that's good. When do you need me to come over?" she said, softening with a hint of a slur.

"Not for an hour or so. We're just...talking history and stuff. She's gone in to find some photo albums."

"Take your time dear, take your time," his mother said, a glassy *clink* in the background.

"I will. See you later," Billy said, turning the knob to 'OFF'. He put the radio back in his bag and zipped it shut.

That's one down, he thought. *But now the clock is ticking.*

Billy felt butterflies start to swarm in his stomach. For a distraction, he tested himself on the names and stories of the cats in the garden.

The near-identical pair on the table were called Harbour and Biddles. They squinted their mustardy eyes at each other, small for the width of their faces, and meticulously preened at their black fur. The only way to tell them apart was by their whiskers. Harbour's were short and plentiful, giving her the air of a young girl brimming with enthusiasm. Biddles had less, and the ones she did have were long and droopy, making her seem dour and suspicious. They'd been here since kitten-hood – superstitious adopters claimed to have enough bad luck in their lives without tempting fate with a black cat.

A striped grey tabby named Midge batted a paw at the swishing tail of a creamy long-hair named Mooch. A grizzled corn farmer had brought them in together two years earlier. He had said, '*If it were up to me, I'd give 'em one good meal and then the shotgun*'. Thankfully, the farmer had a softhearted wife – now the pair could be found rolling in the tall grass, and punishing Billy's shoelaces.

Near the door sat Nonny – a frisky white pouncer that had been dropped off anonymously – and Zen, the 'too chatty for a quiet house' Siamese with chocolate tips and marble-blue eyes. Meanwhile, the muscled ginger rump of Bart bounded up a birch tree after a sparrow, showing with tooth and claw that he was still 'too lively' for most meek Appleton households. And far below, Dorcus and Squidge stalked each other through the flowerbeds. They looked like cross-eyed panthers, distracted every few steps by their own ringed tails – visitors suspected inbreeding, and gave them a wide berth.

On the periphery – looking on with tired eyes from his vine-choked perch – was Smoke, a battle-scarred tom that still suffered from years of abuse. He looked a bit like an old lion with his tattered grey mane, but he coughed, and wheezed, and limped aside when younger cats – like the black-spotted Grendel, or the bob-tailed Loki – conspired to usurp his birdbath throne.

Billy watched and listened and waited. The cats began to mellow, and their numbers thinned. They were falling asleep in sunbeams, preening in pockets of shade, or slipping back inside through the cat-flap.

Billy rose and cocked his head towards the door. Even from that distance – a patch of lawn, a kitchen, and a living room away – he was convinced that he could hear faint music, and the steady snores that accompanied it.

"Maybe I saw it in my dreams."

Her words had stayed with him as he waited. They shrouded him as he slid the backpack over his shoulders and laid the crutches on the ground. They followed him as he limped back to the door, brushing the rubber-soled cast across the dirt, with the pains clawing up through his knee and hip. He grabbed the tarnished brass handle, twisting it with the softest of squeaks, and they whispered to him.

'In my dreams...'

He eased the door open and the words disappeared, smothered by another sound – an urgent cry that cut through the air like his father's saw through lumber.

It was the cat – *his* cat – loping across the road towards him.

"Shhh!" Billy warned, raising his hand. The cat stopped on the gravel shoulder, sniffed at the air, and meowed again. Its tail was raised, and vibrating.

"Go *home,*" he whispered, leaning his head away from the door. The other cats were stirring now, and a few had caught the scent of their old housemate on the breeze. Billy's cat tensed and crouched, springing across the ditch into the reeds and tall grass.

Bart leapt down from the tree with teeth bared. Dorcus and Squidge slithered from the flowerbed, bellies and ringed tails to the ground. Biddles and Harbour stirred from sleep and gave clipped, chirping mews. Midge and Mooch trotted across the driveway to take posts on either side of the arch. Smoke hissed at Grendel and Loki, and they shrank away from the birdbath to give the veteran a clear view of the invader.

Billy pulled at the door again, and the hinges squealed. The cats in the yard turned at the noise, and some took steps towards it.

They're going to rush the door. They'll run inside and make a racket. Then it was all for nothing, Billy thought, tugging again. The window of opportunity was fast slipping away, like the door handle in his clammy palm.

MMMMRRRRRROOOOOOWWWWW.

It all happened in a furry, spotted blur. Billy heard his cat yowl, throaty and mean, and saw it pounce through the reeds and onto the edge of the lawn. The fur bristled along its spine, its eyes bulged wild, and it slapped its tail back and forth on the carpet of green.

He's taunting them, the boy mused.

The old woman's cats tightened their circle, advancing in staggered, menacing steps. His cat lunged to the left and then bolted right by the rose bushes. The defenders followed, zigging and zagging as one, giving chase around the front of the house.

Billy didn't hear any howls, or growls, or screeches of feline combat. There was only silence in the yard, and silence in the house — save for the sounds of old music and muffled snores — so he pulled the door open.

Nothing came bounding through the cat-flap as he brought it shut. Billy tested the rubber sole of his cast on the checkered squares of linoleum. It didn't slip. This would afford him a straight line through the kitchen, while still putting most of the weight on his good leg.

Years before, Mrs. Thomas had taught him the old word for a group of cats — a *clowder* — and it seemed fitting now. Cat upon cat paced and lazed in the kitchen like low-hanging clouds, gathered near food and water bowls that covered nearly half the floor. They didn't pay Billy much attention — the boy wasn't bearing salmon treats or a bag of catnip, so he was considered a non-event.

A few of the friendlier ones — like Mimi the doe-eyed Ragdoll, and the portly Mr. Brown — brushed against his leg as he passed. He reached up to scratch the chin of Ivan the Russian Blue, squatting in his preferred spot atop the refrigerator. And Billy made sure to blow a kiss to Frosty — the weepy Persian with a missing eye — who always played peek-a-boo with him from the kitchen sink.

The boy stepped with his good leg into the middle of the main hallway and stretched his arms out. Wooden trim ran along both sides at waist-height, helping to steady him as the old oak floor groaned with each footfall. Billy had to be patient, and synchronize his steps with the songs and snores coming from the hall's far end.

Step by step, he pushed forward. Past Enid's sewing alcove, with the rocking chair and angled ceiling. Past the downstairs bathroom, with potted ivy climbing up the walls above a claw-footed bathtub. Past the narrow pantry, with cans and jars floor-to-ceiling, like a mouth crammed with too many teeth.

Black-and-white portraits lined the walls, trimmed in silver frames. As Billy crept down the hall it was like moving back through time – their clothes and hair, their gnarled features, and the generations of wise and wounded eyes.

The music stopped. Billy approached the end of the hall, and heard a soft clicking repeating over and over – *ca-chik-ca-CHIK...ca-chik-ca-CHIK...ca-chik-ca-CHIK.*

He slid his hand along the oak banister at the bottom of the staircase, gripping its pointed peak for balance. Billy put his weight on his good leg, and leaned into the living room.

Mrs. Thomas was still asleep. Her snores made her lips quiver and her mouth move slightly with each breath, as if speaking. Her eyelids fluttered and twitched. Thin blue veins branched up her neck, pushing through the pale skin around her temples. Lying there, contorted on her old green sofa, she didn't seem much like the sassy sage that Billy adored. This woman looked tired and frail.

She was covered in her beloved 'kitty quilt' (the one she was proud to say she had sewn herself), and surrounded by both the oldest and the smallest in her feline family. The cats slept in clusters by her feet, in her lap, and on yellow pillows around her head. *'Blood and Stones'* lay open across her chest, bony fingers curled around the book's spine.

Ca-chik-ca-CHIK...ca-chik-ca-CHIK.

The needle was skipping on her old record player. A marmalade kitten sat on the upright piano next to it, mesmerized by the spinning disc and the needle's wavering arm. The kitten seemed to sway in a beam of sunlight. A photograph of Enid's husband – taken decades earlier at the same piano – grinned from the wall above.

Billy shifted his bad foot to retreat from the room, and the floorboards creaked. Some cats stirred at the sound. They lifted their heads, noted the boy and his familiar scent, and returned to blissful slumber.

The kitten was startled, and hopped onto the piano keys. It scampered across the keyboard, trying to outrun the *plinks* and *plonks* that pursued it.

Billy held his breath. The old woman stirred, and the cats squirmed and twitched. The kitten leapt to the windowsill, ending its impromptu recital with a high F-sharp hanging in the room. Mrs. Thomas smacked her lips, grumbled something indecipherable, and turned onto her side.

The marmalade kitten walked the length of the sill, its raised tail brushing the undersides of mobiles that hung on bits of clear fishing line. A stained glass butterfly clattered its wings against the pane, and a rainbow hummingbird rocked in small arcs as the orange tail passed beneath it.

The kitten's ears twitched as it turned to look outside. Its tail quivered, and its head darted back and forth. Its tiny jaw opened and it gave a thin, staccato mew.

Ca-chik-ca-CHIK...ca-chik-ca-CHIK...

Billy took another step back, and the kitten pressed its face against the glass. He took another, and the air in the room went still, the note from the piano fading. He took a third, watching the kitten bob its head up and down.

The hairs stood on Billy's arms, and he shivered. The kitten turned, staring wide-eyed at the empty space above the piano. Its pupils narrowed, and its whiskers trembled.

Ca-chik-ca-CHIK...ca-chik-ca...THUD!

Something struck the windowpane. The kitten leapt back and tumbled to the carpet. It shook its dazed head, and scrambled beneath the couch where Mrs. Thomas and her cats, miraculously, still slept.

Billy's cat was perched on the outside ledge. Its tongue pressed forward, and it took in rapid breaths through its mouth. It scanned the room, fixing on the boy with a look that seemed to say: '*Hurry...I can't do this forever.*'

Billy held his breath and backed out of the room, the cat watching him as he left. He crept back to the stairs, adjusted the straps of his backpack, and tiptoed around the sloping banister. He inched past the hanging ferns and the shelves of dusty keepsakes – silver cat spoons and ceramic cat thimbles – and moved into the shadowed alcove beside the stairs.

Ca-chik-ca-CHIK...ca-chik-ca-CHIK...

Billy approached the basement door. Its panels blended with the wood along the side of the staircase. Its brass knob was cool to the touch, and squealed ever so slightly as he turned it. The boy eased the door open, and a gust of cold air breathed over him.

It's now or never, Billy thought.

And then he stepped down into the dark.

X I I I

Of Basements and Blood

BILLY'S LEG TWINGED as he slowly descended the first planks of wood that formed stairs down to the cellar. He tugged on a string dangling from a bare bulb that hung from cobwebbed beams. A wedge of dull light filled the passage, and the boy eased the door shut behind him.

The snoring and the skipping phonograph disappeared in the underground vacuum. The only sounds beneath the house were the dull thumps of his footsteps, and an unnerving whistling in his nose as he breathed. Reaching the bottom, he inhaled deeply and limped onto the cellar's earthen floor.

Grey shafts of light angled down through the narrow windows at garden level, enough to see the room with. To the left were cardboard boxes, which Billy had helped Mrs. Thomas to bring down and stack the previous summer. He had spent weeks watching her fill them with yellowed magazines, old clothes, and some of her dead husband's things.

'Can't part with it just yet,' she had said. 'Besides, basements are a good place to hide treasures, don't you think?'

The sump pump, furnace, and water heater were off to the right, where Billy needed to go. It was darker there and the ground sloped. He ran his fingers along the stone foundation on the front of the house to keep his bearings. The machines loomed on the far wall like misshapen monuments, and the boy imagined himself as a lone explorer on the verge of unearthing a long-lost tomb.

Billy reached the furnace, and leaned against its blocky metal shell. The steel groaned beneath the weight of his shoulder, echoing through the room as he removed his pack. He pulled out a flashlight from the front zip-pocket and clicked it on, sweeping the ring of blue-white light across the wall, around and behind the dusty contraptions.

If the drawing in the book was accurate, Billy thought, then this is the separating wall of a split cellar. There must be a way to get through.

There were glints of light from the machines, and nets of cobwebs strung between them. The stone wall glistened with moisture, olive and muddy brown veins snaking across its surface. Billy followed the wall and swept his beam along it, hobbling past the water tank. The light breached the darkest corner of the room, grazing the edge of something that Billy hadn't noticed before.

A short wooden bureau stood flush against the wall. It had three large drawers with black iron handles, and a flat desktop that protruded above them. Its caramel finish was rough and scratched, but Billy could still discern a pattern along its edges.

There were waves etched into the wood, curved and interlocking, rising up the bureau's sides and flowing onto the surface of the desk.

The waves met on the back face of the desktop, converging in a woven ring around an intricate carving of an old sailing ship.

I keep seeing this, he thought, running his fingers across its sails. *In my dreams.*

Billy removed his pack. He took out his sketchpad, tore off a sheet, and laid it across the carving. Then he took a piece of charcoal, and rubbed it back and forth across the paper as he had done so many times in the graveyard on the hill. He pressed hard, charcoal splintering in his fingers and smearing them black.

The desk wobbled under the pressure and tilted forward as he pushed down to finish the impression. Another gust of air struck his face, colder than the first, with a noxious smell. He put his weight on the wood and leaned the bureau away from the wall, shining his light behind it.

A hole.

Billy carefully placed his artwork between blank sheets of paper, and slid the sketchbook back in his bag. With the flashlight between his teeth, he gripped the sides of the desk and pulled it away from the wall. The thing was heavy and scraped across the dirt. Billy strained, digging his heels into the earth as the pain awakened below his knee. At last, there was just enough room for him to move behind it. He crouched on all fours with his backpack in one hand and flashlight in the other, crawled to the mouth of the opening, and shone the light inside.

Scritch-scritch-SCRITCH.

The sound came from behind him. He spun and shone the light, and saw something scratching at the closest basement window. The glass was too dirty to clearly see what it was, but it was small, and spotted, and persistent.

Not now, thought Billy. *I'm almost there.*

He turned back to the crawlspace, and took another look inside. From what he could make out it was empty – just mounds of dirt in all directions, like dunes in a desert.

Billy pulled the collar of his shirt up over his nose, but it did little to lessen the smell. His father had talked about sewers and septic lines before, and how vital it was to 'maintain them to code'. '*If they get blocked and overflow, it could fill a house with gas. That's a serious hazard,*' he had said.

But right now, as Billy prepared to crawl through the muck on a mad search for a miracle? He didn't care much about any of that – he just wanted to keep his lunch down.

Scritch-scritch-SCRITCH...RRRrroooowwwWWW.

The boy ignored the cat's plea for attention and pressed onward. The ache in his leg was bearable while crawling, as he just let it hang limp. Billy pulled himself along on his forearms and elbows, the flashlight's beam swinging in erratic arcs across the dirt slopes.

So far, so good, he thought. *I found the way in, and now I need to find the southwest corner of the foundation. That's where it was in the book.*

As he dragged himself forward, Billy recalled the many times his mother had chastised him for watching a show, or burying his head in a book. '*You're just counting the hours between sleeps,*' she had said. '*Wasting your precious days on dreams and fantasies.*'

Scritch-scritch-scriiiitch...

Billy heard the faint pawing from the other room as he felt something squish beneath his hands. He shone his light on the ground by his hands, and gagged at the sight.

Worms. Hundreds of worms. The earth was alive with them. They writhed and squirmed and tunneled in the mire. They crawled between his fingers, and wriggled up his wrists. The boy snorted in disgust, shook them off his hands, and kept moving. The stench was getting harder to bear, so he bit down on his shirt collar and sucked air in through clenched teeth, refocusing.

Have to find it...the symbol...the KEY.

Billy spotted a stone wall to his left, and shone his light along its length. The dirt was piled higher there, and spider webs were plentiful. He dug his elbows in hard and pulled forward, aiming towards the wall.

Scritch-scritch-scriiiitch...

It was getting harder to breathe. The space was growing dangerously narrow, and Billy's face was getting clogged with webbing. He thought he felt things scuttling on his scalp, and skittering across the back of his neck. When the flashlight finally revealed the southwest corner of the room, the boy wasn't sure whether he wanted to cry for joy, or vomit. He swallowed hard and charged ahead on his forearms, tearing through a stringy layer of webs and dead roots, and pulling parallel with the western wall.

As the flashlight's beam swung with his movements, Billy was unaware of the sudden drop in front of him. Lunging ahead, he tumbled down a steep slope, sliding headfirst into the corner column.

"Ow!" Billy said as his head struck the angled stones. The flashlight had fallen from his hand and lay flickering in the steep mound of earth. He brushed the dirt and webs and who-knows-what-else from his hair and face, caught his breath, and reached for the light.

Scritch-scritch-scriiiitch...

Billy froze. The sound hadn't come from the other side of the cellar. It was too loud. Too close.

Scriiiiiitch-scraaaaaatch-SCREEEEEEETCH.

He dove for the light and rolled on the slope, turning to shine the beam in the sound's direction. There was nothing there. The circle of light fell on his backpack, lying on the ground where the two walls of stone met.

Pffft...PFFFFFFFFFFFFFT...chuk-chuk-CHUK.

The radio, he thought. Billy scrambled down, moaning as he jarred his leg on solid earth. He brushed aside the worms and beetles crawling on the front flap, unzipped the pack, and pulled out the walkie-talkie.

It was still turned off.

"Plant them deep as the Watchers SLEEEEEEP," hissed a voice through the receiver.

"What? Hello?" Billy turned knobs and mashed buttons in disbelief.

"Dig, boyyy. DIG," it said.

"Who *is* this?" Billy said, but a part of him already knew.

"WE are coming..."

The radio shrieked with static, then went dead. Billy turned and pushed and pressed it again. Nothing. He dropped it in the dirt, moved the bag, and shone the light on the ground in the corner.

This is where the book said it would be, he thought. *God...maybe I just dreamt it all. Maybe I'm dreaming now.*

The boy put the flashlight between his teeth — spitting out bits of dirt and moving things he chose to ignore — and clawed at the earth with both hands. His heart pounded and he wrestled for breath around the metal tube in his mouth. A cold sweat dripped from his forehead, and ran in trickles and brooks down his spine.

The stink in the air worsened. Billy coughed and gagged as he dug, and almost choked on the light. The dirt lodged in clumps beneath his nails, and his fingertips wore raw. His leg throbbed and ached to the point of agony. He bit down hard on the flashlight, and felt one of his teeth chip against the spit-soaked metal.

Billy had cleared a wide arc of dirt when he finally reached something solid. He cupped his hands and scooped out the earth on top of it, then shone the light down.

It was a flat square of dark stone, with lines and ridges on its face. He tried to dig around its edges to get a grip but the ground wouldn't give. He took a screwdriver from his pack that he'd snuck from his father's shed and tried to pry at a corner. The stone held fast.

PFFFFFFFFFT-chuk-chuk...

The static sliced through the stillness.

"Billy? Billy! Did you try calling? Where are you?" It was his mother's voice.

Crap, Billy thought, scrambling out of the hole to kill the radio. *Time's up. She'll come looking for me any minute, and I have no idea how to get the damn thing out. Think. THINK. You're supposed to be some genius. Prove it!*

Billy took a deep breath and closed his eyes.

The Grey Man wanted the 'key'. The Tiger told me to find it. The clown at Tommy's had asked for it, too. It pointed at the symbol on my cast – the cat Mrs. Thomas had drawn – and pressed a card against it. And then...?

It made an impression of it.

Billy tore a sheet from his sketchbook and fumbled for the charcoal in the bottom of his bag. He hunched over the hole he had dug, laid the paper on top of the stone, and pressed the charcoal flat against the page.

Please, he thought. *Please work.*

The black block squeaked between his fingers as he dragged it back and forth across the page. Billy pushed harder, and rubbed faster, and through the sweat and grime stinging his eyes an image began to form. Ridges turned into lines. Lines connected to curves. The curves gave way to a shape. A symbol.

The *cat.*

Billy lifted his fingers from the page. Something was wrong. The squeaking sound of the charcoal hadn't stopped. It still echoed in the darkness. Getting louder. Coming from all sides.

He fumbled with the light, and turned it to the crest of the slope where he had first fallen in. The beam's glare seared his eyes with spots of dancing crimson. He mashed his lids together but no matter how much he blinked, the tiny balls of red wouldn't fade.

He squinted in the darkness and scanned the ridge of dirt with his light. And it was then, as the revelation struck him with a chilling sureness, that the radio surged with cackling static.

"FRIENDS."

They were *eyes* in the darkness. Rats' eyes.

Billy screamed as the first wave of vermin charged down the slope. He grabbed his pack and swung it in front of him, sending squealing bodies smashing into the wall. He backed into the corner as more scurried towards him, swinging careless and wild. He felt something cling to his leg, and bashed it with his fist before it could climb past his thigh. Another climbed on his bag, and paid the price as Billy hurled it against the cornerstones.

"Get back!" he yelled, grabbing one on his sleeve by the tail and flinging it into the pack. The sea of rats parted, watched their comrade hit the ground, and swept back in to hold their position. "Get BACK!"

Billy swung the bag and waved his light as he shouted, hoping to frighten them off. The rats scurried back and forth looking to flank the boy, inching closer and closer as they gnashed their pointed teeth. The boy felt his arms start to seize and become leaden in the mounting din of hisses and squeals.

There was a loud *THUMP* from beyond the room. Then another. And a *CRACK*. The rats shrank back in unison, lifted their heads, and twitched their whiskers.

Mrs. Thomas, Billy thought. *She's awake.*

"Help!" he yelled. "I'm downstairs!"

There was another thump, followed by the sound of breaking glass. Some of the rats stood on their hind legs and sucked at the air. Others ran in nervous circles, rubbing noses with their brethren. The rest scurried up the ridge, flattened their tails, and began to hiss and screech.

Billy watched them with a mix of dread and fascination, but in the madness of it all there was something that he missed – a black, oily thing the size of a small dog. It had lidless eyes, gnarled ears, and deep scars on its flanks. The thing was slinking along the front foundation wall, dragging its hairless tail through the muck as it prepared to strike from darkness.

The group on the ridge shrieked as one, cuing a violent symphony of growls, yowls, and gurgling whimpers. Billy held up the light and saw a tornado of vermin on the ridge, and the broken rat bodies being tossed down it. The ones near the boy's feet began burrowing into the ground, clambering up the walls, and fleeing in panicked packs over the far sides of the ridge.

They're being attacked, Billy thought. *Slaughtered.*

That's when the creature struck. It leapt up the foundation, dug its foul claws into the moss between the stones, and pounced on the boy. Before Billy had time to react, the monster had its jaws clamped down on his hand, drawing blood.

"Get off!" the boy screamed, flailing and shaking and trying to smash the thing against the stones. The rat was relentless, digging in its claws to hold fast, and then scurrying around Billy's wrist at the threat of another blow. It kept on biting, tearing at the sides and palm of his hand, and leaving gaping wounds in his flesh.

Billy wailed and toppled into the hole he had dug. He tried to trap the thing beneath him and squash it against the stone. But the thing squirmed free, and ran up his arm towards his neck.

Then there was *roar.* It was a primal, ferocious cry that rang in the boy's ears. The roar was answered with a defiant *hiss.* Then came the terrible shrieking, which at last ended with a sticky, sickening crunch.

Billy pressed against the stone with both hands and propped himself up. He held his breath, and peeked over the edge of the hole he had made. There in the beam from the fallen flashlight lay the black rat, lifeless in the dirt. And, clamped tight around its bloody throat, were the jaws of a cat.

Billy's cat.

"My friend," the boy whispered, tears streaming down his cheeks. "You really *are* my friend."

The cat released its hold on the rat's neck, lifted his head, and placed a paw on its dead body.

"I don't know if you understand me," Billy said. He picked up the pack and the radio, and wiped his bloody hand on his shirt. "But... *thank you.*"

Billy reached down and tugged at the corner of the page still pressed against the stone. It peeled off slow and sticky like a bandage, his blood having soaked clean through and leaving smears of scarlet on the slab. He laid the symbol flat between two fresh sheets of paper, and slid it carefully back inside his pack.

"Are you coming?" Billy asked the cat as he dragged himself up and over the ridge.

The cat didn't move. Its paw still rested on the black rat's corpse, and it stared at the hole that the boy had emerged from.

"Okay," Billy said, digging his elbows in for the return trip, "but try not to be gone so long this time."

He crawled a few meters with the flashlight in his mouth, and looked back over his shoulder. He was hoping for a glimpse of his saviour, but all he could see were long shadows on the stone wall, swaying in shimmering rays of red.

Another trick of the light, Billy surmised. He turned towards the exit, and dragged himself one last time through the worms and the bugs and the dirt.

He pulled free from the crawlspace with a grunt and a whimper. The numbing rush of shock and fear had waned, leaving him with an aching leg and sore, stinging hands.

The light sifting through the windows now gave the room the feel of a church. Billy hobbled over to the laundry basin, shut the flashlight off, and rinsed his hands. The old pipes shook and squealed with a gush of muddy water, and trails of brown and red orbited the drain.

Billy wiped his hands dry on his shirt, but the bites on his wrist and palm kept bleeding. All he could think to do was wrap it in a tea towel hanging by the basin, and hope the pressure would quell the flow before he got home.

Home, Billy thought. *Did mom really try to call me?* Everything from the crawlspace was still a spooky, surreal jumble in the boy's head. Billy couldn't hear any voices from upstairs. He hoped that the thick floors had let Mrs. Thomas sleep, and that his mother was still 'prioritizing' with a glass of wine and her soap operas across the road.

Billy lurched through the room and heard something tinkle and crunch under his foot. He looked up, and saw knives of glass stabbing in from all sides, framing a hole in the middle of the window. A cat-sized hole.

Billy kicked the shards aside. He knew there was no time to clean up properly – he had to get upstairs and back outside. He needed to be sitting at the garden table with his crutches when his mother came. He'd figure out a way to explain the rest. A good story. A simple one.

'I was playing with too many of cats at once and got bitten and scratched', Billy thought as his first excuse. *'Or...I saw our cat, and crawled after him through the rose bushes. I was stupid, and grabbed a bunch of thorns. I'm sorry.' Yes. That could work. She should believe that.*

Billy hopped up the stairs and pressed his ear against the door. Nothing. He flicked off the bulb, eased the door open, and tiptoed back into the hallway. A few cats padded by, with some others squabbling over kibble down the hall, but nothing else. The house was quiet.

Billy swooned with relief as he crossed the kitchen floor. As he passed the fridge, he held up his hand to Ivan and got a fuzzy high-five. As he hobbled by the sink, Frosty followed him with a lone, cautious eye, flinching at his scent. He turned the door handle, traces of dirt and blood clinging to the brass as he pushed the door open.

Billy basked in the heavenly bouquet of the garden, and the warm breeze wafting through it. He marveled at the butterflies on the trellis, flitting from rose to rose. He smiled as a plump cat nuzzled her kittens in the clover.

I did it, Billy thought as he stepped into the sun. *This is the best day ever.*

"William Brahm!"

The boy froze, and turned towards the voice. The two women stood in the driveway. Mrs. Thomas' face was creased with worry and disappointment. His mother's was worse, swollen and soaked with tears. He knew it was really bad because her quaking jowls had passed 'red outrage', and gone straight through to 'purple murder'.

"I can explain," Billy whimpered, stunned by how quickly the best day ever was about to become the worst.

XIV

Of Lies and Listening

'YOU'RE LYING.'

A lot can happen in a week. It had been seven days since Billy's mother had dragged him across the road by his ear. She had cleaned him up as best she could, called the boy's father home early from work, and made an emergency appointment at the clinic across the river.

Nothing was said on the ride into town. They marched Billy into Doctor Patel's office – the same doctor who had stitched the boy's lip six years earlier. The odd little man dabbed at Billy's wounds with iodine, and tried to calm the situation with his clipped, sing-song tone.

"Mrs. Brahm," he said, "I would not worry. Rabies is far less common than you think. Perhaps in my country? But not here, no. I would recommend to keep the area clean, and watch for the fever."

"'The fever'. You mean *a* fever? That's *not* good enough. We need to be sure. I want him tested," Elizabeth said, clutching at her purse. "How much will it cost?"

"I believe it is covered by your medical plan. But we will need to take quite a bit of blood."

"Please Mom, I'm fi—" Billy tried to say.

"Do it," his mother said, stone-faced.

A toothy nurse with a hairy mole on her upper lip jabbed a needle into Billy's arm. Elizabeth flinched, while Stanley sat on a stool in the corner and counted wooden tongue depressors in a glass jar. Billy felt faint and bit his lip, focusing instead on the doctor's tufted eyebrows.

"When will we get the results?" his mother asked.

"They will be ready in a week. We can forward them to Middleton, for the boy's appointment on Thursday," said the doctor, pushing a cotton ball against the spot where the syringe had entered.

"Fine."

Billy looked up from his arm, and scanned his parents' faces. *They already booked the appointment*, he thought. *They're scared of what's going to happen.*

His father spun on the stool and fiddled with a blood pressure gauge. His mother checked her watch, and tapped her foot on the tiles.

"Before going, could someone tell me how it happens that a boy in this town could find himself bitten by rats in this way? I must say...it is exceedingly strange." Doctor Patel peered over his thick lenses, and fastened a bandage snug across the cotton ball.

The three adults looked at Billy and waited for an answer, their faces running the gamut from curious, to confused, to livid. The boy stared down at the rusty splotches of iodine staining his hand and wrist, and imagined the terrible eyes of the creature that bit him staring back.

"I..." Billy stammered, "I was stupid."

The Brahms didn't speak on the ride home either. Not a word until Billy's mother slammed the front door, stood in the living room with her arms crossed, and nudged her husband with an elbow.

"Sit down," his father said, pointing to the couch.

Billy was slow to hobble across the room, taking his time to balance the crutches against the chair's arm, and gave an audible groan as he sat. In these situations, he had learned that it was crucial to go for maximum dramatic effect.

"What were you *thinking*?" his mother seethed, jabbing a finger towards his face. "How could you *do* something like this?"

"I don't know," Billy said, averting his gaze and scratching at fresh psoriasis on his thigh. The silvery scale flaked off, exposing red and weeping skin underneath.

"Don't play stupid with us!" his mother said, her neck turning the same shade as the spot on his thigh. "We *know* you're not stupid. What then? Are you saying that the school was wrong? That all the tests were wrong? That you have some learning disability we never knew about?"

"You say I'm stupid all the time," Billy mumbled, letting his jaw quiver, and the tears pool in his eyes.

"Oh, for God's sake...*we do not*," she said, exasperated. "Stanley, tell him what we mean!"

"I think," his father said, pausing to summon his paternal voice, "what we mean is that, sometimes, you make bad choices. We...well... we just don't understand."

"I don't want to *understand*," fumed his mother, "I want it to stop. All of it. This is not normal. These things do not happen with a *normal* child!"

Billy gulped at the air, buried his face in his hands, and let the tears fall. His father was about to kneel down in front of the couch, but his mother squeezed on his shoulder.

"*United front,*" she said through clenched teeth. "We can't give in to emotional blackmail."

His father sighed, rolling back his shoulders. "Fine. Billy, we want you to tell us everything right now. How you ended up in Mrs. Thomas' basement while she was sleeping. How her window got broken. And how you got bitten by a rat."

"I didn't mean to," Billy said, stuttering as he cried. "I was bored. I was just playing a game. Looking for buried treasure. But I never broke the window. *Honest.*"

"Bored? A game? *Really?*" His mother re-crossed her arms. "You expect us to believe that? Then who broke the window?"

"It wasn't me, I swear! The rat jumped out from the corner by the furnace, and then...then the cat broke in through the window and killed it."

"The cat?"

"My cat. It killed the rat."

"Ohhhh...so *your* cat just happened to be strolling by the window, saw you in trouble, and leapt in to rescue you? Is that what you're telling us?" She huffed, and rolled her eyes back so far that all he could see were spidery veins infesting the whites.

"Yes," Billy said, trying hard to believe it himself. "It's true!"

"You're lying!" his mother roared, flapping her arms about in a geyser of saliva. "After everything you've put us through! You are going to be punished, young man. It's time you faced the consequences of your actions, and you will learn never to lie to us again!"

"*You* lied," Billy said, spreading nuclear winter throughout the living room.

"What did you just say?" his mother seethed, her eyes sharpening into steely, bloodshot ice picks.

Billy straightened, holding his ground. "You said there was no appointment. I asked every day, and you said 'soon'. And then Doctor Patel said it's next Thursday. It was in my file. So you had to know already. You lied too."

Elizabeth Brahm shook. Then she slapped her husband's shoulder, and screamed like a banshee.

Billy had seen her mad before, but never like this – this was sad, and scary, and made no sense. He thought that he could use logic to thwart her anger. He hoped that maybe – if she could just see things from his perspective – she would forgive the mistake.

He was wrong.

"No allowance! No TV! No toys! No cat in the house! NOTHING!" Her cheeks dripped with tears, and spit, and angry sweat. "You are *grounded*."

The absurdity of her statement didn't escape the boy. He was already felled by injury, circumstance, and a streak of abnormally rotten luck. This latest blow was just his mother's way of twisting the screws right into the wood.

"What time is the appointment on Thursday?" Billy said, resigned to his fate.

"Did you *hear* me? I said you're grounded!" Her veins were now having children and grandchildren on her forehead.

"When is it?" Billy said. "Can we at least go to the fair before? I need to go there."

"You need...the *fair*?" his mother cried, waving her hands around her swollen face, knocking off her glasses. "I can't take this, Stanley. I can't *take* this!" She stomped out of the room and into the kitchen, drawers and cupboards slamming in a fountain of clatter. The room was quiet for a moment, until throaty sobs and a quavering moan flooded the house.

"Dad–?" Billy sat up, hoping for a sign of pity or understanding.

"You really hurt your mother," Stanley said, handing the boy his crutches. "You need to go upstairs."

"But Dad–"

"Go. I'll bring your dinner up later," he said, heading for the kitchen.

Billy could hear him comforting his mother as she cried. And then, as he crawled up the stairs to his bedroom, tugging on the brown shag with his rust-stained hand, Billy could hear his father begin to cry with her.

Over the next five days, Billy's mother held to her word.

He was confined to his room except for bathroom breaks. His father came in the first morning, collected the tray with the empty bowl and stale crusts of bread, and then promptly packed all of his toys and comics into cardboard boxes. His father left the walkie-talkie, but told him to only use it for emergencies.

This was ironic, considering that his appointment loomed in six days. Billy could think of no greater 'emergency' than his leg, his fear of losing it, and his need to do something about it. Yet each time he tried to speak with them and explain, he was met with shaking heads and frustrated sighs.

By the second day, the boy's fears grew. With no TV to watch and nothing to read, it was getting harder to find distractions. His sleep had grown elusive, fitful, and blank.

If only the cat were here, he thought. *He'd listen to me. He'd help me to dream.*

Billy sat by the bedroom window the next two nights, hoping for a sighting. He worried that the cat wasn't getting enough food. Or had gotten lost. Or, maybe, that he'd grown weary of all the human drama. Maybe the cat was just like the boy, preferring friendship of the four-footed kind.

By the fourth night, Billy grew desperate and buzzed on the walkie-talkie. He asked to speak with his father before bed. Heavy footsteps tromped up the stairs an hour later, followed by a knock on his bedroom door.

Billy asked him to sit down on the bed, and began to tell him the story – the real story. He told his father about the dreams, and the nightmares, and the curse. He told him how Lucy the cat helped to find the old book. He told him that he had found a way to fix himself. Billy was about to explain how, when his father held up a hand to stop him.

"Billy...*please*," Stanley sighed, rubbing his forehead.

"But Dad, I need to go to the fair," Billy pleaded, pointing to his pack hanging on the bedpost. "I have to take something there, and then he'll fix–"

"Listen, son," his father patted him on the cast, "I know this is hard. I know that you're worried. We all are. But we'll deal with it. Whatever happens, we'll work it out. But the real problem here is the stories. When you make up stuff to get out of trouble, or to get something that you want? You know how we feel about that."

"I'm not," Billy protested. "It's not a story. It's real."

Stanley brushed his son's hair from his eyes and fluffed up the pillows behind his head. "Do you really want me to tell your mother all of this? *Really*? You should know better than that. Either she'll think that you're fibbing – which means you might never be allowed out of this room – or she'll think that you actually *believe* what you're saying. And then she'll get scared."

His father's warning was a hammer, hanging in the room and threatening to swing. Billy's hands clenched beneath the covers, and he felt one of the cuts on his palm open. He clamped his eyes shut to keep from crying, and had the sudden vision of a teddy bear, waving goodbye from the window of a long grey sedan.

"No," Billy whispered. *"Don't tell her."*

Stanley nodded and patted his son's leg. "It's gonna be okay. This will all be over soon." He got up, turned out the light, and went back downstairs.

Billy rolled on his side. His leg throbbed as if it were about to burst. His skin began to itch, and he scratched himself until he bled. He stared out the window the whole night, but no stars stared back at him.

The fifth day, Tuesday, found the boy in a resigned daze.

Billy wouldn't touch any food, and his stomach ached from an awful mix of hunger and constipation. He stared at the walls, picturing the wallpaper ships floating on open seas in search of strange new worlds. Better worlds.

That evening, after an hour of pushing boxed macaroni and powdered cheese around a plastic plate, the phone rang downstairs. Billy noticed this because it was out of the ordinary – his father didn't receive any calls (except for golf on weekends), and his mother kept her gossip marathons to weekdays between ten and two.

There were footsteps on the stairs. His door opened without a knock.

"It's for you," his mother said, passing him the cordless phone with a bemused look. "I think it's a girl."

"What?" said Billy, convinced that he had fallen asleep, and into another useless dream. He took the phone and covered the mouthpiece. "I thought I was grounded?"

"Even prisoners get a phone call," his mother said, pulling the door closed with the faintest of smirks. "Keep it quick."

Billy waited to hear her descent, and then uncovered the phone. "Hello?"

"Hey buddy," said a cheerful voice on the other end. It was Lynn Jessome.

"Hey," Billy said, confused. "What do you want?"

"That's rude," she chewed gum as she spoke. "Now I don't feel bad asking if I should get checked for rabies. Didn't we share some cake?"

"Oh jeez...how did *you* hear?"

"Small towns, man. I think your Mom told Mrs. Troughton at the Save-Easy, who told Mrs. Pertwee at the bank, who told Mrs. Baker at the stables, who then told Ms. Hartnell, who has a horse with a bad bladder–"

"Okay, okay," Billy said, turning new shades of red in the confines of his room. "It's true. I got bitten by a rat, and had to go to the doctor."

"How'd you get bit?"

"You don't wanna know."

"Yes, I do," Lynn's voice softened. "That's why I called."

So, Billy told her everything. Hearing it again for the second time in two days, he could see why his father – or anyone sane, for that matter – would find it so hard to believe.

"Whoa," she gasped. "Like, *whoa*. That's messed up."

"Do you believe me?" Billy asked.

"It's crazy," she said, popping a gum bubble against her mouthpiece, "but I believe that *you* believe it. My Dad says that's all that matters. That everything comes down to 'perception', or something."

"Great. *Thanks*."

"Hey, it is what it is. But that's something, right? So, what now?"

"My appointment is on Thursday," Billy said, making a pretend cannon with his fingers and firing at the wallpaper fleet. "That's two days. What else *can* I do?"

"That's dumb," Lynn said over the sound of barking in the background. She sighed, made a spitting sound, and shouted, "*Seamus, chill out!* Sorry, Billy...yeah, like I was saying, that's just dumb."

"What do you mean?"

"Well, it's *your* leg, right?" Lynn said, a gum wrapper crackling near the receiver. "I figure you do what you have to, and don't take any crap about it."

"I'm not like you. You're a hard-ass," Billy said, deflating.

"Oooh, watch the language," she taunted. "That ain't no way for a *puss'* to talk."

"Don't," his voice thinned. "Not now."

Billy pressed the phone to his chest and wiped his nose and eyes on his pajama sleeve. When he put the receiver back to his ear, he could hear a dog whining.

"*Oh Seamus, don't be a baby. I'll be there in a minute,*" Lynn said. "Listen, Billy, I know you're sick of hearing things my Dad says, but this one might help...'cause it helped me."

"Okay," he said, closing his eyes and concentrating on her voice.

"He says that right after something bad happens – after the shock wears off – that's when the sadness comes in. And most people? They hold onto it. They hold on tight and won't let go. And soon, they forget feeling anything *other* than sad. It becomes everything they are."

"So...what do you *do*?" Billy felt a wave of helplessness wash over his body, and dip behind his ribs.

"Being sad is a *cold* feeling. It slows you down. Freezes you in place," Lynn said, lowering her voice. "When that happens, it's too late. It's like falling asleep in the snow, and not waking up again."

"Does that happen?" Billy said, picturing an icy mountainside, and a lone wolf's final breaths.

"I've seen a lot of things," Lynn said. There was an insistent bark. "*Okay, okay!* Sorry, buddy—gotta go."

"Wait," said Billy, sitting up. "You said that being sad...that it freezes you. How do you *stop* it?"

"You're the genius," Lynn said, chewing. "If something freezes, then it's like ice, right? And what happens to ice when it gets hot?"

"Well duh, it melts," Billy said.

"And washes away," Lynn said, her voice drifting.

"But that's ice," Billy rolled on his left side, and pulled his knee into his chest. "What melts a *feeling*?"

"That's easy. Just get *mad*," she said, popping a bubble in his ear. "Anger's hotter than anything I know."

"Why are you mad?" Billy asked, pulling the phone closer to his mouth.

"Sorry, puss'—gotta go. Buzz me tomorrow if you need anything. I'll be here. Promise."

"Okay. Goodnight."

Lynn hung up, and Billy did the same.

The boy rolled on his back and stared at the ceiling. He imagined the sky overhead, glittering in the depths of space. His eyes swept between stars and pushed through the crowd of constellations, until he found the fiercest one he knew.

The Hunter.

Get mad, he thought. *But good boys don't get mad. Good boys follow the rules. Good boys show respect, and do their chores, and don't complain. That makes others happy. And you want them all to be happy, right? Do you know how lucky you are? Do you know how fast it could all disappear?*

Billy sank into sleep, adrift in a sea of questions. A cold moon hung low over the graveyard on the hill, reaching through the trees to paint bars of shadow on his walls.

The television buzzed with static. It flickered and flashed. An eyeless clown waved from the set, beckoning.

Billy stood. The television disappeared, along with the living room. He was in the front hallway, and the door swung open.

The light was bright. He shielded his eyes, and stepped onto a doormat made of grass. Another step. The grass spread in all directions, and the house disappeared behind him.

The garden had moved to the front lawn. His parents were hoeing the soil, and pulling at weeds shaped like tentacles.

"*They don't stop,*" his mother said, the skin on her upper arms sagging and jiggling with blubber. "*It never stops.*" She wore a white straw hat, with a drooping brim the size of an umbrella. She held out her hand, and a drop of rain splashed in her palm.

"*Disappointing,*" she said, pushing her hand into the dry earth. She pulled at the stem of a carrot. A wad of money dangled from it. The bills fluttered and crumbled, scattering in the wind. "*This isn't what I wanted.*"

His father stood on a wooden crate at the garden's edge, surveying a tall row of corn. "*It's what we signed up for,*" he said, chewing on a strand of grass and hooking his thumbs in the straps of his overalls. "*Reap what you sow.*"

"*It's not fair,*" she said, tipping the spout of a tin watering can over the ground. Silver coins poured out, making a shiny pile on the ground. She knelt to pick up the coins, but they sank into the earth.

She dug after them, exhuming a wooden crutch from the dirt. *"See? What can I make with this?"*

"You should see mine," his father said, peeling open an ear of corn. A fat grey rat wriggled inside. He held it up by the scruff, its pink tail unfurling to the height of the corn.

"Stanley," his mother said, falling in the dirt, *"what do we do?"*

Leaves and roots wrapped around her legs and were growing fast, winding up her torso. She hacked at them with silver shears, but they kept coming.

"Ask him," said his father, pointing at Billy. *"They say he's got all the answers."*

The stalks of corn shivered, and a flurry of grey bodies burst from the swollen green sheaths. *Rats.*

They crawled up his father's legs. He dropped the one he was holding, and put another in the front pocket of his overalls, using it like the pouch of a kangaroo.

"Help!" Billy cried, and the cry rolled across the empty plains of the dream. The vines had wrapped around his mother's throat, choking her. Her eyes swelled with terror as she stabbed her shears at the plants. A serpentine root plucked them from her hand, and swung them around her bluing face.

"Useless," she croaked.

"Maybe," his father said, as the rats gnawed at his arms and throat, *"but you can cook for his friends."*

Suddenly, the garden was full of cats. They sprang from the dirt and gnawed at the roots and vines. They shimmied up the stalks of corn that had fattened into trees, and shook the rats in their teeth.

Billy's cat sat on a wooden bench beyond the garden, watching. The boy looked back to his parents. His mother now stirred a cauldron of soup, with cats on their hind legs peering over the pot's edge. His father petted the head of a burly tom as it ripped into the guts of a screeching rat. Foam peanuts spilled from its body, covering the ground like pink snow.

"*Winter's coming,*" he said, waving at Billy. "*Better not miss your bus, son.*"

Billy floated through the garden and to the bench. He sat down beside the cat, and looked down the road to the snow-capped peak in the north.

"Are you coming with me?" Billy said to the cat.

"*I am already there,*" it said, the words echoing in its golden eyes.

There was a metallic squeal, and a sharp gust of compressed air. A black bus with round windows appeared in front of the bench. Its passenger door was open.

Billy stepped inside and climbed seven black stairs. When he reached the top, the bus driver took his hand.

"*You'll need this,*" said the driver, his face obscured by a low-slung cap with an oversized brim.

Billy looked down. The symbol of the cat was stamped in red ink on the back of his hand. The ink was running.

The bus lurched forward, and the boy sat. He looked out the right-side window. The cat was gone, as was the bench, the garden, and his blue-paneled house.

He crossed the aisle and pressed his face against the glass. Mrs. Thomas stood behind a darkened window, solemn and still in a corona of flickering amber. She gave an eerie smile, waved, and then vanished.

"*Where you headed?*" asked the driver.

"The other side," said Billy.

"*That ain't kid stuff.*" The driver turned the oversized steering wheel hard to the right. The bus veered into a bank of thick fog. "*We'll have to take the high road.*"

The man pulled on a black lever poking down from the ceiling. The bus shuddered and revved, bursting through the fog and up into the sky.

Billy looked out the window at the postage stamp fields and toy houses far below. As they flew past the lone mountain, flocks of spotted geese circled the bus and honked excitedly as it steered through a rift of cloud.

"*You hear that?*" the driver said, whistling out his window at the birds. "*They're talking.*"

"Of course," Billy said, marveling at the colossal shapes carved into the clouds. He spotted the faces of cats, and dogs, and rats, and indescribable things. They all seemed to be watching him. "Everything talks."

"*So you're a Listener, huh? That's rare as reason.*" The driver pulled another lever, and the bus made a steep dip. "*You'll need that where you're going.*"

The bus burst from the clouds and skimmed the surface of a black ocean. Dark waves licked at the tires, and the bus rocked as it sped through a fleet of old sailing ships.

They pulled alongside the lead boat, its timbered hull stained with blood and its sails black as pitch. Something stood on its bow, pointing a skeletal hand to the horizon.

"*Not long now,*" the driver said, looking down. There was a copper sundial strapped to his wrist. A sliver of shadow wavered on its etched face around a wedge of orange metal.

"What do I owe you?" Billy said, reaching into his pocket. He pulled out a massive, gleaming tooth. The fang was tied to a length of silken thread.

"*Smart of you to bring them along,*" said the driver, nodding over his shoulder. "*Goin' to the same place...the long way around.*"

Billy looked across the aisle and saw Lynn. She was holding a bunch of red balloons as she blew gum bubbles. When the bubbles were about to burst, she pinched the gum near her lips and it became a balloon. She then added it to the others.

"*You can't have these,*" she said, clutching at the balloon strings, her eyes moist and sad. "*They're mine.*"

"What do I get?" asked Billy.

"*Everything,*" Lynn said. The balloons turned into floating hearts. "*But it'll cost ya.*"

Her German Shepherd hopped over the back of the seat and sat on the floor by her feet. Billy lowered his hand to its muzzle. The dog licked at the ink symbol, and barked.

"*Next stop! The other side.*" The driver pulled a lever and the door opened with a startling, arid gust.

"How do I pay?" Billy said, stepping to his side.

"*Not now,*" said the driver, cracking black-gloved knuckles, "*but soon enough.*"

He slammed a palm into Billy's chest. The boy fell down the stairs and out the door, plummeting like a stone towards the earth.

The fall was brief before he crashed into a dune, the impact rippling through his body. Billy tried to get up, but couldn't pull his right leg free of the scalding sand.

Jangling music crept over the dunes. Billy turned to see brightly coloured tents rising in a nearby valley. Huge wheels covered in blinking lights spun above the ground. Strange figures milled about in elaborate masks and costumes, many with tails. Some had gathered by cramped pens off to the side, laughing as they fed handfuls of corn to a pack of giant rats.

Stranger still were the rows upon rows of *ants*. They were the size of horses, boxes stacked high on their backs, and their black armour gleamed under the desert sun. They snapped pincers, rubbed antennae, and trudged in and out of the tents without pause or protest.

"*The Worlds collide,*" a voice thundered across the sands. "*Yours and mine.*"

"Help me," Billy said, sinking further into the dune.

"*You can forget everything. You would not lose much,*" the voice said. "*Then, for you, it is over.*"

"No!" the boy cried, as the sands crushed his leg. Billy clawed at the dune and reached for the tents in the valley below. "I've come too far. Please...*help* me."

"*We will help you,*" boomed the voice, now behind him. "*But the price will be paid.*"

Billy felt something strong grab his collar and pull him free, suspending him above the sand. He saw the thin shadow of his body cast along the face of the dune, and the imposing shape of the thing holding him aloft.

"*Pay heed to all you have seen and heard on this journey,*" said the voice. Billy knew it was the thing holding him that spoke.

"I will," Billy said, shifting his eyes for a glimpse of it. "But please hurry–there's not much time!"

Dark cloth flapped and fluttered at the edge of his vision. The boy's thoughts turned to banners marched by ancient armies, and the cloaks of legendary knights.

"*You will learn the truth of Time,*" it said, straining over the rising winds. "*But for now– be ready.*"

Grains of sand pelted Billy's face, and the grip on his collar loosened. He fell to the ground, choking on the air and wiping grit from his eyes.

"*Look to the rise of tomorrow's sun,*" it shouted through the sandstorm.

Billy covered his face and squinted through his fingers. The thing that spoke stood over him now. Its shroud spread like a dark angel's wings in the gale.

"And then?" Billy said, fumbling to his knees in its shadow. "What do I do *then*?"

The thing bent down and pulled the boy's hands from his face. "*You will know*," it growled from behind a veil of black cloth, its golden eyes revealed. "*Wait for the sign.*"

It threw its cloak around the boy, and the world went dark.

Billy's arms jerked, and he almost flopped out of bed.

He opened his eyes to see a pointy-eared shadow stretching up his bedroom wall. Rolling over, he saw the cat perched on the outside window ledge, crowned by the rising sun.

Billy pressed his palm flat against the window. The cat's eyes looked at the boy's hand, and then at the boy.

"I'll be ready," Billy said.

The cat blinked, lifted a paw, and brushed it against the pane.

There were thumps on the stairs. Billy tapped the glass, and watched the cat leap down and scamper into the blackberry bushes.

"Breakfast in ten minutes," his mother said, knocking. "And no excuses this time. You need to eat. Tomorrow's going to be a big day."

"I know," Billy said, awaiting her telltale descent. When he was sure she was back downstairs, he grabbed a pen and notepad with one hand, and the phone with the other.

You're right, he thought, scribbling furiously as he dialed. *It will be.*

XV

Of Dogs and Distractions

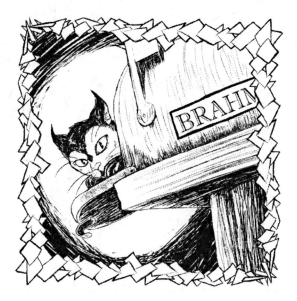

THERE WERE NO DREAMS THE NEXT NIGHT, because there was no sleep. As the cherry glow of dawn crept over the hill, Billy's mind was made.

The boy had spent his entire life being afraid. He had bent, and cowered, and surrendered to most everyone in his young life because, deep down, he felt that they deserved to be happy more than he did.

But on this day, things would be different.

Billy sat on the bed and stared out the window. The sky warmed, splashing amber waves across the meadow. Golden rays shone through the gauze of willow trees, kissing the sheen of dew that blanketed the world. Until, at last, the sun climbed over the horizon, blinding and radiant above the slabs and spires of stone that held quiet vigil in the graveyard on the hill.

Billy sat there for over an hour, waiting. He drummed his fingers against the cast, and rocked back and forth on the bed, repeating a silent prayer to anything that would listen.

He scoured his notes from the dream, desperate to find something that he might've missed. After countless reviews of underlined passages and circled words and bolded arrows of ink on the page, Billy crumpled it up and tossed it at the bin. The paper bounced off the rim, and rolled to a stop on a grooved heating vent.

I was wrong, he thought, slamming his head down on the pillows and making the whole bed shake. *It's all wrong.*

He heard his father's car honk twice. He was departing early for work to make up for taking the afternoon off. He heard his mother clomping around the kitchen. She was cooking the 'special breakfast' that was meant as some kind of consolation prize for the bad news to come.

Billy curled in a one-legged ball with the pillows around his head. He began to drift, lost in defeat and the dull thump of his own heart droning in his skull. The boy resigned himself to a brief sleep, to one last escape before his life changed forever.

But then something happened. It was an entirely unexpected something, a violent shake that freed the boy from his daze and despair.

Screaming.

Billy's mother was screaming downstairs. He heard the backdoor slam, and confusion in the kitchen. There was stomping across the living room, and a clumsy thunder up the stairs.

The bedroom door burst open, and there was Elizabeth Brahm – panting, sheet-white, with both eyes popping out of her head like an angry cartoon. She held a pair of field binoculars in her pale, trembling hands.

"What's going on?" Billy sat up, feigning sudden wakefulness.

"I need to–" she struggled for breath, "I need to *see* something." She moved to the window and held the binoculars up, smooshing her glasses askew. She squinted, bent the lens arms, and adjusted the focus knob with a shaky thumb.

"Oh no...oh no, no, NO!"

"What is it?" Billy said, pressing his face against the glass and following her line of sight. She was aimed at the back garden.

"Give me the phone," she said, holding her hand out and flapping it at him. "Quickly!" Billy handed her the cordless and she dialed from memory, her stare still fixed on the hill.

"What's wrong?" he asked, tugging on her sweat-soaked blouse. "Is there anything I can do to help?"

"Just be *quiet*," she brushed his hand away. "You've done enough already. Shhh...it's ringing. Stanley, Stanley? Damn, of all the times for voicemail–"

"He just left. He won't be at work for at least twenty minutes." Billy said.

"Shhhh!" she hushed. "Stanley? Call me the second you get in. The cat just dropped a rat at the back door!"

Billy gasped, and felt his hands start to tingle.

"Then another one came, probably one of Enid's, and it did the same thing. And then...then I see *another* cat...running down the path from the garden...and it's got a rat in *its* mouth!"

The boy pressed his forehead against the pane and cupped his hands around his eyes to stop the glare. A moment later, he spotted a familiar calico – normally so skittish and soft and shy – trotting proudly across the yard with something grey and dead hanging from her mouth.

"There's another one," Billy said, his stomach full of butterflies. "That's Minou! Oh, what a good girl—"

"I've got the binoculars, Stanley. I can see cats in the garden. They're digging it up, and chasing the things around. It's like...like they're *herding* them. I'm going back there. I'm taking the weed-whacker, the big one, and I'll scare them *all* off. Call me back as soon as you can," she said, and hung up.

"This is amazing," Billy said, as Bart – the muscled, tree-bound Tom – dropped a load of limp fur on the patio.

"This is *terrible*," said his mother, wiping the sweat from her brow and putting her glasses back on. "And it's *your* cat that started it!"

"Rodents eat vegetables, Mom," Billy said with a scholarly tone. "They're *herbivores*. If one comes, they all come. Imagine the garden tomorrow if the cats weren't here to—"

"Yes, *yes*," she sighed, massaging the bridge of her nose. "Alright. I'm going to try scaring them off. I'll take the walkie-talkie with me. When your father calls, ask if he has any better ideas. If he does, then radio me. Otherwise, your breakfast is on a plate in the stove. Make sure to use the oven mitts, and don't waste all the syrup. I'll be back as soon as I can."

"Okay," Billy said, eyeing the clock – it read 8:12AM.

His mother stepped to leave, kicking the paper ball across the carpet. "And would it kill you be tidy?" she said, bending down to pick it up. "Just because you're disabled, doesn't give you the right to be lazy."

"I'm not *disabled*," Billy shot a withering glance.

"Fine, then prove it," she said, dropping the paper into the basket and leaving the room.

Billy simmered as she moved down the stairs, through the kitchen, and out the back door. When the door slammed shut, he took her advice and sprang into as much action as a boy could with ten pounds of plaster on his leg.

He had planned his wardrobe the night before – white t-shirt, a red ball cap, denim jacket, and a pair of navy blue sweatpants. Billy had worn the pants a few times over the summer, and they stretched enough to allow his foot to slide through. The fabric was snug, but it covered the cast. He didn't want to stand out on the journey. If too many adults noticed him, they might make a fuss and try to stop him. That's why he was also leaving the crutches behind – after six weeks, his leg was either going to be fine or it wasn't – the creaky things would only attract more attention.

Billy grabbed his pack and hopped downstairs on his good leg. The living room was quiet except for the tick-tock of the grandfather clock by the wood stove. The smell of buttermilk waffles wafted in from the kitchen.

The clock chimed once. It was 8:30. There was only time to drink some milk, grab an apple, and turn off the stove.

I won't leave a note, he thought as he drank. *They'll figure it out. But the confusion should buy enough time to get me there. To finish this.*

The gas-powered trimmer whined to life in the backyard. Billy spied his mother emerge from the workshop with the machine strapped over her shoulder. She revved it twice and made her way up the garden path, the knotted rope that kept the shed door shut swinging in the stiff breeze.

Billy cinched the pack on his shoulders. Coins jingled and clanged against the sides of his piggy bank within. He hopped to the front door and checked the clock one last time. With an arc of the brass pendulum, the minute hand moved another notch.

8:33AM – seven minutes to go.

Billy opened the door and stepped outside. The groans and grunts came fast and irrepressible as he hobbled across the gravel towards the end of the driveway. Sweat pooled behind his ears and ran down his neck as he reached the mailbox.

He leaned against it to catch his breath. For the first time, the boy fully absorbed what the box was – a painted replica of his home, with a smiling family of three in the front window where the mail door opened. Billy sighed, and gazed up the highway.

 It was empty. From where he stood, you could see a long way up the road. It curved out of the valley, through the Hennigers' hobby orchard, and past the little white church to the south.

Did I miss it? the boy worried. *Was she wrong about the times?*

Billy's last bearing was from a tired old clock that his father usually forgot to give a weekly winding to. At that moment, the boy wished he still had his birthday watch that got smashed in the accident. The commercials promised that it would keep perfect time for 25 years or the rest of your life – whichever was longer.

Billy turned and scanned the shoulder of the road to the north. It was there that he had flown to a sudden, broken stop just six weeks before. It was there that the blood still stained the asphalt. And it was there that all of this had begun.

Billy heard a rustling behind him, and spotted something move through reeds. The grass parted near the mouth of the ditch. A pair of black-tipped ears poked out, followed by a salmon-pink nose and a slender, spotted face.

Billy's cat shook its head and wiped at a red smear on its snowy muzzle. It yawned, licked a paw, and wiped again.

"There you are," said Billy, crouching as best he could without crutches. "I don't know how, but you really *did* it, didn't you?"

The cat paused, sniffed at the air, and swatted at a passing fly. When the fly had fled above the reeds, the cat looked up at the boy, blinking slowly.

Billy rubbed his fingers together and leaned closer to it, "Will you come with me? Show me what to do next?"

The cat took a step from the curtain of grass, and licked the boy's fingertips with its eyes closed. Its left ear twitched and bent to one side. Billy tried to scratch its spotted chin, but the cat nipped at his finger and gave a throaty *MROWWWWWW.*

Billy pulled his hand back. This afforded him just enough time to notice the bus that was careening down the hill, and he raised his arm to signal it.

"Thanks," the boy said, but when he looked back down the cat was already a phantom in the reeds. As the squat blue bus geared down and ground to a halt, Billy remembered the cat's words from the start of his slumbering journey.

'I am already there.'

The bus door bent inwards with a decompressing hiss, and Billy hauled himself up the boxy steps with the help of a metal railing.

"Ain't you a trooper," said the driver, pinching one side of a graying moustache. "Where ya' off to, kid?"

"The county fair, please," Billy said, wobbling as he removed the backpack. "Sorry, my money's in here."

"No worries. Grab a seat. It's just you and me for a bit. You can pay when you get off."

The man had friendly eyes, surrounded by deep creases from what Billy guessed to be sunshine and good spirits. His thick salt-and-pepper hair was pulled back into a ponytail, and tied with a red rubber band. A powder-blue shirt housed wiry muscles and fading tattoos poking from rolled-up sleeves. When he smiled, it was with his whole face, and one of his front teeth – a canine – was curious in its absence. He smelled of pipe tobacco, and the kind of aftershave his father always had in the bottom of his stocking at Christmas.

As the man pulled on the lever to shut the door, Billy sat on one of the padded seats near the front.

"Now, before we go anywhere, you sure it's cool goin' off on your own?" The driver looked at Billy in the circular mirror above his window. The glass curved to give him a better view of the back of the bus, but the effect made the man's face warp and stretch to the point that he resembled a greyhound with a moustache.

"Yeah," Billy said, repeating a well-rehearsed explanation, "my Dad's at work, and my Mom's busy. I wanted to be first on the rides. They're going to pick me up in the afternoon."

"That's mighty cool of 'em," the driver said, unwrapping a stick of gum and sliding it through the gap in his teeth. "Figured they'd be awful protective after the accident. You're the Brahm boy, ain't ya?" He pointed at the mailbox, the family name painted on it plain as day.

"Mmhmm," Billy said, acutely aware that time was not in his favour. "I get my cast off today in Middleton, and then we're going away for the weekend. This is the only time I could go."

"Alrighty then," the man said, revving the engine and putting the bus into gear. "Let's stop lollygagging and put the pedal to proverbial metal." The bus lurched ahead, and the driver hit the horn and waved out his window. As the bus pulled away from the shoulder, Billy saw Mrs. Thomas waving back from the garden and scrunched down in his seat.

"You must know the old lady, right?" the driver said, grinding a gummy wad between his molars.

"Yup," Billy said, poking up his head as they got some distance from the house. Mrs. Thomas was standing at the side of the road, watching the bus leave. Not a good sign.

"Hell, you can't miss her. Not with all them cats." The driver scratched the leathery skin of his neck. "Damn things give me hives, even from here. Me? I'm more of a dog person. Comes when ya' call, fetches the paper when ya' tell it, guards your home 24/7. Talk about man's best friend. What'd a cat ever do for anyone, huh?"

"Cats were worshipped in ancient Egypt. They were kept for good fortune in Asia. They stopped the black plague from spreading by killing rats. And having one has been proven to lower blood pressure and chances of heart disease," Billy said dryly. He rested his head on the side window, and watched the countryside become a verdant blur.

"Man, you *told* me didn't ya'?" the man said, picking at his ear and chewing his gum a little slower. "Never thought of 'em that way. Huh. Everything's got its place then, don't it?"

The driver whistled, and rocked the wheel back and forth in his meaty, calloused hands. He was a nice enough fellow, but he wasn't going to win any debates with Billy Brahm anytime soon. Especially about cats.

The bus turned off the highway and onto the main street through town. They crossed the cobblestone bridge, picked up an elderly woman in front of the grocery store, and dropped her off three blocks later at the library.

They kept going, rolling past the hardware store, and the sandwich shop, and the Co-Op. Some farmers in overalls and red plaid shirts saluted as the bus passed, and the driver honked twice as he turned left. The bus crossed the river near the hockey arena, and approached the school on the other side.

"That's your school, right? Bet you ain't itching to go back in a couple o' weeks. The tragedy of summer vacation," the driver said, slowing down through the school zone. "What grade are you goin' into?"

"Six," Billy said.

They passed the paved playground with the swings, and basketball hoops, and tetherball poles that Billy knew so well. A twinge ran up his arm as he realized he was going into the same grade as the boy who broke his collarbone in kindergarten.

"A little *young*, ain't ya'?" The driver peered back over his shoulder as he shifted gears and passed the community pool on the edge of town. The smell of chlorine polluted the bus, as did the errant cries of water-winged toddlers being tossed by their parents into the deep end.

"I'm ten. Just turned. I skipped two grades," Billy said, not concealing his pride.

"Man, that's a *trip* – junior Einstein! Must be hard sometimes, though. Bein' smaller than the rest."

"Sometimes," Billy lowered his head and fiddled with the zippers on his bag. His thoughts turned to birthdays, and baseball gloves, and things that melted in fire.

"What those big kids don't get is that they're doin' you a *favour*," the driver said, holding out his arm and flexing it.

"Wow," Billy reached out to pat the man's inked and muscled bicep. It felt like granite wrapped in rawhide.

"No pain, no gain. Trust the old man on that one," he chuckled, relaxing his arm. "My ex used to say, '*Cal*, *the greatest souls are seared with scars*'. I thought that was just her way of bein' all artsy fartsy. But now, lookin' back? I can see she wasn't wrong. You smell what I'm cookin', boy-o?"

"Yes, sir," Billy said.

"Don't gimme that 'sir' crap," the driver said, picking up speed. "The name's Calvin, but you can call me Cal." He held out an open hand to the boy.

"I'm Billy," Billy said, giving the hand a nervous shake.

"Next time, gimme a *real* one. Show me you mean business. 'I'm Billy Brahm! I skipped two grades and got hit by a car! Who the hell are you?'"

The boy laughed as the man flexed and tweaked the tip of his moustache in the mirror. With a honk and a crunch of the gears, the bus blew past a doddering pickup and a pack of motorcycles bound for the highway.

Billy saw the clock on the dashboard – 9:03AM. He'd been gone for almost half-an-hour, and guessed that his mother would soon be on the verge of a nervous breakdown. She would radio the house and get suspicious when he didn't answer, or she'd soon be ready to take a break from rural pest control. Either way, she'd likely tear the insides of the house apart first, and then resort to calling his father. Then he would tell her to calm down and check across the road. After that, providing Mrs. Thomas hadn't spotted him on the bus, his mother would call the police. She might call them anyway. Billy could just picture her making a grand, humiliating opera out of the whole thing. Medics. Fire trucks. Swat teams. The six o'clock news.

But, for the moment, Billy still had some room to breathe. Calvin drove with a heavy foot – he referred to the posted speed limits as 'recommended guidelines' – and the roads were clear. At this rate, the fairgrounds were maybe twenty minutes away. Not bad.

They even had time to stop for two special passengers.

Lynn Jessome stood with her German Shepherd at the end of her driveway and flagged down the bus. Calvin skidded to a stop on the gravel shoulder, checked both directions, and waved them across.

Seamus bounded in front, pulling the leash taught and dragging Lynn behind him. His fat tongue hung like the loose strap of a seatbelt. It swung back and forth above the pavement, fanning strings of drool like a faulty lawn sprinkler. *Dogs*, Billy thought.

"That's what I'm talkin' about," said Calvin, pulling the door open. "You could put a saddle on him and ride the rest of the way!"

Seamus pawed up the steps, his claws scratching and clicking on the metal. He gave a loud bark, and Calvin held out his hand. The dog sat, lifted a paw, and rested it in the driver's palm.

"Won't see a cat doin' that anytime soon, Einstein," Calvin said, winking at Billy as he gave Seamus a rub on the snout. "*Good boy. Who's a good boy?*"

"You won't see a cat with breath that smells like poop," Billy muttered, wincing as the dog sniffed at his pack, and panted near his face.

Billy nodded to Lynn as she entered the bus. Her hair seemed blonder in the morning light, like summer wheat swaying against her shoulders. She had on the same jean jacket she always did over a white shirt, along with the same pair of frayed shorts she had worn to Tommy's party. Her skin was more tan now, with fresh clusters of freckles dotting her cheeks and nose, making her eyes even brighter than before.

"Hey, is it cool if Seamus comes on?" Lynn said, winding the leash around her wrist and smoothing a strand of hair behind her ear.

"Cooler than school, missy," Calvin said, rubbing the strip of cinnamon fur on the dog's chest. "We're not hurtin' for space. Won't even cost ya."

"Wouldn't matter. He's paying." Lynn made the shape of a gun with her thumb and index finger, and aimed a shot Billy's way.

"Oh...right," Billy said, unzipping his bag and pulling out his piggy bank. He rotated the copper-plated bottom of the tin pyramid until he heard a click, pried the panel loose, and poured a river of coins into his lap. He was slow and methodical – counting out two equal stacks according to the size and value of the coins – and then handed them carefully to Lynn.

"You're so uptight," she snorted, collapsing the piles in her hands and dumping the lot into the pay meter. She sat down across from Billy, with the dog lying down between them in the aisle.

"Ahhh, so you're both going to the fair. Am I privy to witness the first buds of young love?" Calvin popped his eyebrows up and down in the mirror.

"Pffft, no," Billy said, squelching a rising blush.

"*This* nerd? As *if*," Lynn said, rolling her sparkling blues.

"Whatever you say, kids," Calvin said, shutting the door and shifting into gear. "Whatever you say."

The bus pulled away from Lynn's house and picked up speed. A big sign on the side of a nearby barn advertised: 'COUNTY FAIR THIS WEEK!!! 15KM'. It had a cartoon tiger's face on it, with a big red arrow pointing down the road.

"No turning back now, huh," Lynn said, as Billy read the sign.

"I guess not," Billy said, biting his lip and gripping the pack a little tighter.

"People talk all the time about chasing their dreams," Lynn said, popping a fresh chunk of watermelon gum in her mouth, "and here you go, getting all *literal* about it."

"Shhhhh," Billy said, hushing her while eyeing the driver. "You *promised*."

"Relax. Cal's cool, right Seamus?" The dog lifted its head from the floor and barked. An almost *proud* look possessed its face, like he had just won the Nobel Prize, or discovered a habitable planet outside our solar system.

"Cooler than school," Calvin said, holding his thumb up in the front window. "I'll just put on the ol' headphones, crank the Floyd, and give you lovebirds a chance to get acquainted."

"Dream on, gramps," Lynn said, popping her first big bubble. She watched Calvin steer with his knees as he slid a pair of puffy headphones over his ears. When he started nodding in a smooth, steady rhythm, she shimmied to the aisle side of her chair, closer to Billy.

"Okay, I got you the bus schedule, and now I'm here, and so is Seamus," Lynn rubbed the dog behind the ears. "*What's going on?*"

"I don't know," Billy said, "but everything's come true so far. And the last dream two nights ago? I wouldn't be here, on this bus, if I hadn't listened to it."

"Come *on*," Lynn said, brushing the hair from her face and blowing another bubble. The sweet, fruity scent of the gum wrestled with the earthy bouquet of German Shepherd, winning for a few breaths. "You're no idiot, Billy. You could've gotten the bus schedule by yourself."

"Not that," Billy said, hushed and serious. "I wouldn't have gotten out of the house."

"What? Are you saying your parents are *home*?"

"My Mom is," Billy leaned close, "and she's probably calling the police any minute."

"You're kidding!" Lynn said, eyes wide and covering her mouth with her hands. "What the hell–?"

"She had to go back to the garden. There were *rats*," Billy's face grew animated and tense. "It was just like the dream. And then the cats, and...well...you wouldn't believe it. But it gave me time to call you, get ready, and sneak out."

"This is bananas," Lynn said, shaking her head. "We are on a bus headed straight for Banana Land. You're gonna be in major trouble, aren't you?"

"Epic," Billy leaned back with a long sigh. He stared at a line of rivets in the bus ceiling, tracing them with his eyes. For the first time, the boy considered just how scared and upset his parents were likely to be.

"That's pretty cool," Lynn said, flicking him on the shoulder, "even if you are wearing sweatpants."

"Yeah?" Billy said.

"Yeah—sweatpants are *lame*," Lynn teased, and popped another bubble. "But seriously, who *does* something like this? Like my Dad says—"

"Here we go..."

"Like he says, being *cool* isn't doing what everyone else is doing," Lynn wound the gum around her finger and stretched it out. "It's being crazy enough to go your own way."

"Thanks," Billy blushed. "And thanks...for coming with me."

"Whatever. It was either this, or muck the horse barn. Besides, my Dad thinks you're nice, so he's golden."

"What?" Billy bolted up, knocking his pack to the floor. "You told your *Dad*?"

"Not about the freaky-deaky stuff. Just that you wanted to go to the fair, and needed a chaperone," Lynn said.

"Are you *serious*?" Billy said, flustered. "Oh no—I didn't think of that. She'll check the phone for sure. She'll find your number was dialed, and she'll call it. Then your father will tell her—"

"—*where we're going*. Crap," Lynn said. She pulled her dog's head away from sniffing at Billy's pack on the floor. "I'm sorry, Billy, but I had to tell him."

"Why?" Billy pulled at the hair on both sides of his head. "You're twelve. You can do what you want! But now that you told him, they're gonna have people looking for *us*. Not just one lost kid. Now it's two *specific* kids, with a big, stupid dog."

"He's not stupid," she tugged on the leash as Seamus chewed at the corner of the backpack. Billy grabbed the pack by the straps and yanked it away from the dog's mouth. Seamus yelped and whined, straining at the leash in the bag's direction.

"Fine. You know what I read? That a dog is only as smart as its master. Now I *get* it." Billy wiped his eyes on his sleeve, propped the pack against the window, and collapsed into it.

Lynn studied Billy's face. She watched his breathing slow, and his jaw begin to tremble. She saw him dig two fingers into a spot below his right hip, and witnessed the wave of pain sweep through his body, making him shudder.

"I've had Seamus for seven years," Lynn said.

"Good for you," Billy sniffled.

"I've tried to love him every day since. But, some days it's hard," she said, watching the dog attempt to crawl under Billy's seat.

"I can see why," Billy scowled.

"Some days...I hate him."

There was a low rumbling, and the *pip-POP-pip* of motorcycle engines speeding past the bus. Billy turned to watch the bikes pass, trailing grey smoke from long cones of chrome. He saw Lynn grab her dog by its red leather collar, and push its face to the floor.

"*Down,*" Lynn said in the dog's ear. "*Stay.*"

Seamus whined, struggled for a second, and then flattened himself out in surrender. Lynn scratched his head, and massaged the folds of chocolate fur at the base of his neck.

"He has a thing for motorcycles. Remembers the sound, I guess," she said. "It's weird. Before I got him, my Dad did a house call in Digton one weekend. Actually, it was a 'boat call'. This fisherman had a pregnant dog on his trawler, and it was sick. The dude was scared he'd have to put her and the whole litter down."

"So?" Billy said, scratching at the skin near the top of his cast.

"My Dad saved her. He gave her some medicine, and stayed to deliver the pups – five purebred Shepherds.

"And he brought one *home* for you." Billy watched the dog roll over, wipe a crust from its own eye, and eat it.

"Nope," Lynn said, jerking the leash to bring the dog flat again. "We didn't have many pets then. Only small ones. And two dogs were more than enough for my Mom. But when he brought a picture of the pups home, I went nuts. I screamed. I cried. I even begged. I never wanted anything more in my entire life."

"Oooh, five whole years," Billy rolled his eyes, as if to give her a taste of her own medicine.

"Sure, I was only five. But I had it drummed into me early not to ask for anything, and definitely not to *beg* for it. Never. My Mom always said, '*Be grateful for what you have, and be careful what you wish for.*' But my Dad's a softie, and went to work on her. Two weeks later, they get me a babysitter, and say they'll be back the next morning. Maybe with a surprise.

"I remember the sky got dark early. Mom and Dad had their matching yellow raincoats on. They could've taken the pickup truck, but the passenger window was jammed. Mom loved the wind on her face and the smell of the countryside, so they took Dad's vintage bike with the sidecar.

"I got woken up by the babysitter just after midnight. She was crying, and stuttering so much I couldn't understand. She didn't make any sense. For some reason, she wrapped me in all these blankets. Then Mr. Varney, the old police chief? He showed up. He gave me hot chocolate and donuts, and we drove for a long time. He didn't say much, except how big the storm was, how bad the roads were, and how '*things like this just happen. They aren't anybody's fault.*'"

Billy chewed on his nails, and felt the dread climb from his guts. He saw a terrible calm in the girl's eyes then, cold and vast like glaciers.

"I fell asleep in the car. He woke me up at the hospital," she continued. "He held my hand and took me inside. Some nurses hugged me, but I still didn't know what was going on. A doctor said there had been an accident, and that my father had lost a lot of blood. They needed mine to help. I asked if my Mom was helping too. One of the nurses started crying.

"The policeman knelt down, and told me everything. He said they were caught in heavy rain, and a cargo truck cut sharp on the corner at the bottom of Beaver Hill. He said my Dad swerved to avoid it, but the truck was too big. It hit the sidecar straight on, killing my Mom instantly."

Billy had a knuckle between his teeth, and bit down so hard he almost broke skin. His eyes stung, and his cheeks were hot and damp.

"That's how my Dad lost his leg. It got smashed with my Mom when they were driving to pick up my dog. I stayed in the hospital with him the whole time. I was the one holding him when he cried. I was the one answering when he called out her name. I was the one clapping when he took his first steps on the fake leg. Then I made him a promise. I promised never to leave him for too long. To always let him know I was close in case he needed me. So that's why I told him, Billy...because I keep my word."

"*I'm sorry,*" Billy whispered, lowering his head.

"Don't be. If he had turned the other way, it would've been him instead. If my Mom hadn't buckled to my begging, they wouldn't have gone. If my Dad hadn't saved the fisherman's dog, I wouldn't have wanted *this* one. Everything has a price." Lynn looped the leash tight around her wrist, and flexed her jaw as she popped another bubble.

Without thinking, Billy reached across the aisle and touched Lynn's hand. She tensed, but he kept holding it until her gaze lifted to meet his.

It wasn't your fault, Billy thought. The feeling grew in his chest, and he pushed it to her through his eyes, and through the palm of his hand. Lynn's nostrils flared and her lower lip quivered. Her eyes glistened, turning a deeper shade of sky and sea.

"Alright, kidlets," Calvin said, dropping gears and easing off on the gas, "we are approaching journey's end."

"Thanks," Lynn pulled her hand away. She pursed her lips, and drew her hair back into a tight ponytail.

"Don't thank me—thank the one who invited ya."

"I'm here, aren't I?" Lynn said, tugging on Seamus' leash and moving to the pole by the door.

"Play nice, young lady. The real trip's just beginning," Calvin said, looking at Billy in the mirror. "And I got me a feelin' that *this* kid? He is really goin' places."

Calvin grinned, honked the horn, and banked the bus down the last off-ramp before the fairgrounds.

XVI

Of Bars and Bureaucrats

'YOU'RE EARLY.'

Billy and Lynn and Seamus stood in front of a ticket booth, sitting askew in the mud at the high-gated entrance to the County Fair. The front of it was painted white, the sides were sheets of bare plywood, and the back was open for the booth's attendant to enter, exit, and better cope with claustrophobia. Beside the bold 'TICKETS' sign that hung above the booth's barred window was a printed sheet stapled to the wood. It listed the entrance prices for Seniors, Adults, and Children.

"Hello," Billy said, cupping a mound of coins in his hands. A dime slipped through his nervous fingers and landed on its edge in the mud.

The dog sniffed at it, licked the dirt around it, then moved on to a discarded popcorn bag nearby.

"You're early," said the voice behind the glass.

Billy couldn't discern much about the ticket woman, except for her shocking girth and an abundance of *pink*. She had pink stretchy pants, a frilly pink blouse, pink fingernails, pink-rimmed sunglasses, and what appeared to be a pink wig teetering on her bulbous head, squishing against the roof whenever she stood. It was as if the booth was about to burst with a surly batch of cotton candy.

Billy counted out his money, until there was a total of $20 neatly stacked on the narrow lip at the base of the window. "Two, please."

"But you're *early*. I don't have the ticket roll. I don't have stamps for your hands. I don't even have a float yet," the woman said, sipping diet cola from a pink plastic bucket through two curly pink straws.

"I have exact change, ma'am," Billy said, sliding the coin stacks through the window. A pudgy, pink-nailed hand intercepted his.

"We're not open until ten. Come back in half an hour." The woman slid a wooden block in front of the ticket slot, turned to the pink bookmark poking out from the paperback in her studded pink purse, and began reading.

Billy vibrated with frustration. It was one thing to deal with meanness – sadly, the boy had enough experience to wrap his head around that, and then some – but a blind obsession with *rules*? People like that pushed his buttons something fierce. Billy wobbled in the mud, red-faced.

A pack of slack-jawed carnival workers watched from the gates, huddled with bottles wrapped in paper bags. Others passed through, carrying large cardboard boxes over to a row of colourful tents. A pair of burly men dragged thick coils of black cable through the muck behind the booth, grunting as they kicked a dented pop can by the boy's feet.

Billy's stomach knotted with worry. *Did Mom figure it out? Has she already called Mr. Jessome, or the police?* His eyes darted left and right, suspicious of everyone in sight. *They're playing dumb*, he thought. *They're stalling to set the trap, and waiting for just the right time to snap it shut.*

Lynn tugged on his coat. "I got this," she whispered, spitting in her hands.

She dabbed saliva around the corners of her eyes, and made two smears down her cheeks to her jaw. Then she pulled out her wad of chewing gum, slapped it in Billy's hand, and approached the booth with Seamus.

"*Please*, lady," Lynn said, knocking frantically on the booth's window, "I need your help. I'm late!"

The pink mountain shifted, and the booth leaned noticeably as the woman turned. "Calm down. What do you mean *late*?" she said, sliding the wooden block back from the ticket slot.

"Charlie here was supposed to come last week and register for the dog show, but my Mom got sick and we couldn't make it. I come all the way from Hampton to ask the judge to let me show 'im. That's why we're early."

"Well, there are rules for a reason," the woman said, pausing her sip of cola to muffle a belch in her hand. "I'm sorry, but you can try again next year."

"But don't you see, lady? There won't *be* a next year," Lynn said. "If Charlie don't win a ribbon and get a sponsor, we can't afford to keep feedin' him. Then my Daddy will take him down by the lighthouse and...and then...*please*, lady...I love him *so* much!"

Lynn threw her arms around Seamus' neck and contorted her face into a mask of tearful childhood despair. She made sure to prop the dog's chin on her shoulder, so its glassy brown eyes would be focused right at the grimacing centre of the pink nebula.

"Oh *alright*," the woman said with a sigh that threatened to buckle the booth. "Give me your hand." Lynn wiped the spit and crocodile tears on her sleeve, and put her hand by the window. The woman extracted a pink pen from the depths of her hair, and drew a star in pink ink on the back of the Lynn's hand. "There...that'll do for now. Anyone gives you a hassle, tell 'em Doris made this."

"Thank you, lady," Lynn said, holding the woman's hand. "If Charlie was a girl, I'd change his name to yours."

"Oh, goodness...why, I'm just happy to *help*," the woman beamed. "I suppose your friend needs one, too?"

"He's my little brother," Lynn said. "He's kinda *slow*, so he won't understand it if Charlie's gone. It'd kill him."

"Well, we don't want that," Doris said, tapping on the counter to get Billy's attention. Her speech slowed. "*Young man. Come here. Can you give me your hand, please? I am going to draw a pretty star on it.*"

Billy hobbled to the window, shooting Lynn a sideways glare. He held up his right hand as Lynn had, forgetting that it still contained a lump of pre-chewed watermelon gum. As the lady gripped his hand and began to draw on the back of it, she felt something decidedly unpleasant. As she pulled away upon finishing, two strands of fruity goo still clung to her fingertips.

"He likes pink, too!" Lynn grinned. She grabbed Billy by the jacket and severed the sticky connection, pulling him away from booth and into the fairgrounds.

"What was *that*?" Billy said. He couldn't help but look back at the tilted booth, and the gigantic pink posterior within.

"She has to serve hicks and boneheads all day in that box," Lynn said. She grabbed his hand, peeled the remaining gum from it, and popped it back in her mouth. "Someone like that isn't gonna help you—"

"Unless you make them feel *good* about it first," Billy said, impressed.

"You're not so slow, 'little brother," Lynn tugged on the leash, pulling Seamus away from an unmanned food cart. "And hey, I saved you twenty bucks. Those root beer floats are on you when you're outta jail."

"Wait," Billy said, clenching his teeth as a bolt of pain surged through his leg, "I need a minute."

He stopped to survey the scene. The bumper cars were parked nose-to-nose and powered down. The gaming booths were shuttered or abandoned. The midway was lifeless. The *Zipper* and the *Scrambler*, the *Tilt a' Whirl* and the *Sea Ray* – even the spinning apple carts and the old Ferris wheel – they all stood frozen, like rusted relics from a lost civilization. Except for a smattering of black-shirted workers chain-smoking by the tents? The place was dead.

"C'mon, we can't stand around," Lynn said, as a trio of grizzled carnies gave her an unwelcome whistle from behind the *Whack-a-Mole*. "Where are we going?"

"I don't know. Where do you think they'd keep a tiger?"

"Duh—with the other animals?" Lynn pointed to an arrow-shaped sign that read 'LIVESTOCK'.

"Duh—maybe if they're *stupid*, and want the others to get eaten," Billy said, loping towards the path that the sign marked.

"DUH—I'm sure it's in a *cage*, like everything else." Lynn tugged on Seamus' leash, and bid farewell to the leering men with a single finger.

The dog sniffed and snuffled at the damp ground as they followed a fence past the open-air stables and show floors. Angled girders propped up sheet-metal roofs, providing lakes of shade to tractors, horse buggies, and an array of farm equipment. Shirtless workers unhooked palettes of concrete blocks attached to chains. Later that day, the crowd in the rickety stands would cheer for (and likely gamble on) meaningless feats of animal strength and speed.

"Over there," Lynn pointed at a concrete hall with a wide, door-less entrance. "That's where they keep the bigger ones."

Billy knew that nobody in their right mind would keep an apex predator that close to prey, but he didn't have the strength to argue with her – the pain in his leg was getting worse. As he padded into the makeshift barn, Seamus looked back at the boy with the closest thing to sympathy that a dog could muster.

"It's all horses in here," Lynn said, admiring the braided mane on a mocha-skinned gelding. "Let's go out the other side."

The blue-ribbon jumpers and show ponies turned in snug stalls to watch the three of them pass through. Equine eyes widened, ears twitched, and tails swatted at swarms of biting horseflies. Halfway through the straw-matted hall, Seamus stopped to sniff at a bucket of oats by a stallion's pen. The black horse whinnied, and reared up.

"Jeez, you wanna get your head kicked in?" Lynn said, jerking on the leash. The dog barked, and the horses showed their discontent by stamping in place, biting at the air, and dropping steaming piles of dung. "Let's get out here. Horses are way too sensitive."

As Lynn and Seamus exited through the back, Billy stopped and turned in the doorway. There was a hush in the hall. Through a cloud of dust and hay, the creatures were craning their heads out of their stalls to watch the boy leave.

"Hey," Lynn called to him, "it says cats are this way." He crossed the dirt and gravel path, saw the banner hanging between the buildings, and pressed ahead.

They passed through the smaller halls, cramped with collared goats and prize hogs and jersey calves in low pens. The animals huddled in pairs on beds of straw, rising only to mob their caretakers bearing fresh water and handfuls of dried corn.

Lynn, Billy, and Seamus reached a row of striped tents, each one containing folding tables stacked with wire mesh cages. The heat within them was oppressive.

There was a cacophony of clucks and crows when Seamus poked his nose inside the first one, which held roosters and hens. In the second, rabbits of every rabbit size and rabbit colour nibbled on flavourless pellets, and culled drops of water from plastic vials suspended in their cages.

The cats were in the third tent, and it was a pathetic display. There were just twelve cages, barely big enough to hold one cat each, but some housed three or four. Billy pushed the tent flap aside and limped by each cage, sweat already beading on his upper lip.

Most of the cats were sleeping, tucked away from prying eyes and agitating fingers in the furthest possible corner of their cages. Billy spotted a skinny Angora, and a shy Birman. A grey Siamese, and a scowling Devon Rex. A wheezing Himalayan, and an aloof Norwegian Forest. A litter of listless kittens, and a pair of aging, bloated mogs.

"I don't get cat contests." Lynn watched her dog sniff the cages, risking a claw to the snout. "How do you judge who wins? It's not like they do any tricks."

Billy stopped at the middle cage on the back wall. "They don't need to *do* anything. That's what makes them special."

He slid a finger through the bars, and caressed the white tip of a sleeping long-haired's tail. The tail shivered at his touch, and the lithe form stretched and pawed at the cage's rear wall. The cat perked its silvery ears, and began to swivel a broad, misshapen skull towards him. Billy saw its mass of whiskers quiver as it turned, and caught the haunting gleam of its eye.

The colours within the orb were splashed together like swirls of oil on the surface of a puddle. Its pupil was shattered, thrusting spikes of wet blackness through the eye in all directions, like the rays of an anti-sun.

There was a metallic *CHUNK* from outside. Then came a whirring and a grinding, and the tinny loops of organ music through the fair's loudspeakers. The strange looking cat flinched, and buried its head between its paws in the corner of the cage.

"Crap, they're opening," Lynn said, standing watch at the tent-flap, scanning left and right. "We gotta hurry."

Billy bit his lip to quell the pain and loped to the exit. A sign hanging overhead was jostled as he closed the flap behind him. It read:

OPEN YOUR HEART – OPEN YOUR HOME

GIVE A LITTLE – GET A LOT

ADOPT TODAY

He followed Lynn on the path to the left, away from the fair's entrance. The tents thinned in that direction, replaced by black cargo trucks. The trucks looked just like the ones that came to Tommy Clayton's birthday party. Black cables snaked across the ground, fed from hulking generators mounted on flatbeds. Puffs of smoke and noxious vapour billowed around their heads, stinging their eyes. The air reeked of manure, sugar, and scorched engine oil.

"What now?" Lynn said, as Seamus turned in circles, whimpering.

A shot of static fuzzed through the PA system, followed by a three-tone chime. *BING-BANG-BONG.*

"*Welcome one and all to the Lawrence County Fair,*" a charming male voice crooned. "*The gates are now open. Enjoy the thrilling rides. Play the games of skill and chance. Visit the animals, and see the best our fine region has to offer!*"

"Aim high, buddy," Lynn said, squishing a fresh block of gum between her teeth.

"Today's special events include: the ox pull! Buggy racing! The demolition derby! The rock 'n' roll mayhem of 'FIRESTORM'. And don't forget, folks – starting at noon today, get your picture taken with Snowy, the Siberian tiger!"

"Where?" Lynn said to the sky. "Directions would be nice!"

"Shhh," Billy said, listening.

"And an urgent announcement–" the voice said. *"William Brahm – please report to the main gate. That's Billy Brahm. We know you're here, son. Got the good word straight from the pink lady's mouth. Your folks will be here any minute, so be a good kid – don't make us come lookin' for ya."*

"That's it," Lynn said, bursting a gum bubble. "Game over."

"No," Billy squeezed the straps of his pack so hard his knuckles whitened. "It *has* to be here!" He charged ahead through the smoke, hobbling blind and swallowing the pain that exploded through his shin.

"Come on, Billy, you're hooped," Lynn crossed her arms. But Seamus sided with the boy and tried to follow him, pulling the leash taut in his wake. The girl stood her ground for a minute, waving at the smoke around her face. "Did you know that your crazy is contagious?" she yelled, unspooling the tether so the dog could give chase.

Billy heard Lynn's words, but didn't care. He heard Seamus barking and panting somewhere behind him, but that didn't matter either. As he stepped through the wall of smoke that hovered between the trucks, something claimed his absolute attention.

A stuffed white tiger.

It hung from the crossbeam of a lone game booth. A silk noose was around its neck, and it spun a little with each gust of wind that blew through the convoy. The tiger had blue-button eyes, a pink felt nose, and whiskers made of fishing line. The thing was at least two meters long, including the tail. It was a massive, intimidating toy, and still not life-sized. For the first time, it occurred to the boy that things might not be so simple when faced with the real thing.

"Hey!" Lynn coughed as she burst through the smoke, catching up to her dog. Seamus was sitting by Billy's feet. He ignored her approach, and continued to sniff at the backpack dangling from the boy's right hand. "Wow. Well, there ya go—we gotta be close now," she said, trying to pull Seamus away from the bag. "Should we risk asking someone? They're gonna start looking for you any minute, if they haven't already."

Billy didn't respond. He had noticed something else in the booth. It was past the rows of apple baskets and the stacks of softballs between them. It was beyond the mass of smaller toy tigers, pinned to the roof by their tails like striped, upside-down bouquets. It was by itself, hanging stark against a sheet of black cloth in the corner.

A *mask*.

A chalk-white mask with a smiling mouth and thin black eyebrows. It bore the exact same face as something from Billy's dreams. Something impossible. A magical clown, that asked him for a *key*.

"*Wake up*, zombie," Lynn snapped her fingers in front of his face. "We need a plan. Fast."

Billy unzipped his pack and reached into the main pocket. He rustled around and felt for the edge of a folded sheet of paper inside. The dog watched closely, its ears standing tall and stiff. Billy pulled the sheet free, and Seamus gave a loud, anxious bark.

"*Quiet,*" Lynn yanked on the leash, looking to Billy. "What's that?"

He unfolded the paper, and Lynn saw it for the first time, just as he'd describe it – the symbol of the cat, rendered in charcoal and stamped with a bloody handprint. Billy's blood. The sight of it struck something deep within the girl. Her head went fuzzy, and her throat tightened, and her heart began to hammer in her chest.

"*What are you doing?*" she whispered.

"This is what it wants," Billy said, holding the page high for the mask to see. "The key."

Seamus growled low and guttural. He stood up on his hind legs, snapped the page from Billy's fingers, and bolted from the booth. The sudden dash jerked Lynn's arm aside, and the leash slipped free from her grasp.

"No!" Billy cried. "Come back!"

"Seamus," Lynn called after him, "Seamus, *come!*" She saw the colour drain from Billy's face, and his hands begin to shake. She saw his eyes go blank, and watched him struggle for a breath.

"*William Brahm, please come to the front gate.*" The announcer on the PA sounded annoyed. "*We've got folks looking for you. If you're lost, they'll help you find your way.*"

Billy took a step and his leg buckled. He turned to Lynn as he collapsed against the booth's counter. *Help*, he thought, digging his nails into the cheap wood. *Please...help me.*

"I'm sorry," Lynn said, strained with regret. "I'll find him...*I'll find him.*" She turned and chased after her dog, yelling its name as she ran. By the time Billy had pulled himself along the counter and around the corner, Lynn was nowhere in sight. There was just a muddy walkway flanked by sagging tents and ramshackle trailers.

Billy took an uneasy step onto the damp grass. The rubber sole of his cast slipped back, launching his body forward and crashing him into a puddle. He tried to stand but his hands kept slipping in the mud, brown water sloshing around his wrists.

Billy choked and crawled. He dragged himself over weeds and muck, over garbage and cigarette butts, and told himself the only thing he could to keep moving.

This isn't real, he thought. *This is all just a bad dream. Just keep going. Someday, you'll wake up and see.*

Billy felt something crawling on his hand. Ants. A battalion of ants trudged through the mud and converged on the wire just ahead of him. He watched them vanish on the camouflage of the black cable that slithered through the glade, and into a striped tent not ten meters away.

There, Billy thought, flashing to his dream of the desert valley – the dream with coloured tents, and giant ants, and masked things – *that's where it is*. He tried to stand, and heard voices from somewhere behind him. One of them cut clean through the carnival soundtrack, unmistakable in its shrill, maternal fury.

"*BILLY? Stop playing games, and come out here this instant!*"

Billy fell to his knee, the cast stretched out behind him. He was spent, and it hurt far too much to stand. As he knelt in the muck and struggled for breath, he prepared to meet his fate. Not just the inevitable punishment, but with what would come after. At the doctor's office.

The voices grew closer, and Billy balled his hands into fists. *Be brave*, he thought, taking a deep breath. *Just this once, show them that you're not afraid*.

He turned and was about to call to them, when blackness enveloped him on all sides. It draped over him like a chilled cloth. Billy felt a pair of arms reach under his body and lift him from the mud. He sensed motion, as if he were gliding across the ground, and heard the crowd of diffused voices pass somewhere behind. The air was stifling and smelled of salt, and mildew, and rotting fruit.

"What's going on?" Billy said, struggling in the dark. "Who is that!"

"*Hush...*" the voice said, holding him tighter. "*FRIEND.*"

The word crackled and hissed in Billy's ears. He remembered the dreams, and his blood turned to ice.

The motion stopped, and Billy was lowered to his feet. His back was against a sheet of striped canvas, and the dark fabric that surrounded him began to slide back. Cracks of light pushed through, and the boy saw it – saw the porcelain face, the empty eyes, and the chilling black-lipped grin – the magic clown's mask.

It's not REAL, Billy thought, shrinking back against the canvas wall. *None of it. I'm still dreaming.*

"*No*," the thing hissed beneath the mask. "*AWAKE.*"

"I...I tried," Billy said, the fear fat in each word. "But I couldn't get the stone. What...what happens now?"

"*The one who HEARS through Veil of Tears*," the mask hovered in blackness, grinning and eyeless, a fly buzzing in circles around it.

"What do you *mean*?" Billy whispered, terrified.

Something glinted near Billy's face. A white-gloved hand thrust from the void of cloth, a shiny key twisting between its thumb and forefinger.

"*One KEY for another*," the thing hissed, grabbing Billy's hand. It put the key in the boy's palm, and closed his fingers around it.

There was a sudden pressure on Billy's chest and he fell backwards through the flap of canvas. He landed on a cushion of loose earth, and in a mushroom of dust he saw the tent flap still swinging from his impact with it. But there was nothing on the other side. No black cloak. No masked man. There was only a swarm of flies, buzzing and circling above the puddles and mud.

"Billy," said a hushed voice behind, mingled with a low canine growl. He tried to stand and felt denim-clad arms reach under his, helping him to his feet. The pain in his leg was excruciating and his toenails looked ready to pop like corn in hot oil but, with a little effort, he was able to stand. He was rewarded with a moment's solace in a pair of friendly, sky-blue eyes.

"No time to explain. I heard my Mom out there, and then something happened," Billy said, steadying himself. "Tie Seamus up. Hurry. You can come back for him."

"But Billy," Lynn whispered, tugging on his arm.

"We're close. I *know* it. Just a little more time, and we'll find it." He squeezed the key, and felt the dull metal teeth bite into his palm.

"*Billy!*" Lynn said, pulling on his shoulder.

He spun to confront her. "What? We need to find the...*oh.*"

There was more rumbling in the shadows. At the tent's far wall, a spotlight beamed on a raised mound of earth. Seamus crouched at the light's edge, paper symbol still in his teeth. His ears were perked, his tail stiff, and his back was to the entrance. His gaze never wavered from the circle, or the mound of earth within it, or the red-barred cage upon it. The dog just growled, as if to taunt its sleeping inmate.

The girl's hush made perfect sense now. She had unwittingly followed her 80-pound pet into the bedroom of an 800-pound murder machine. This, thankfully, was as close to it as she'd ever have to get.

"So...*now* what?" Lynn whispered.

"I don't know," Billy said, which was a lie. He felt the key in his hand, and knew exactly what came next.

XVII

Of Tigers and Tea

IT WAS HOT IN THE TENT and hard to breathe. The spotlight only made it more stifling, panic and dread colluding in the air with wisps of awe.

Billy took a step.

"What are you *doing*?" Lynn said, one eye on her dog and the other on the cage. She knew that any sudden movement might spook either animal. Her father had shared some grisly tales over the years, several involving things locked 'safely in cages' – the girl had no wish to become the next dismembered anecdote.

Billy took another step and his senses narrowed. He heard Lynn speak, but her voice melted into the fair's looping calliope and the cries of adults calling his name from somewhere outside. It felt like he was underwater, sinking further and further from the world above.

"This was fun and all, but now you're freaking me out." Lynn stepped on the leash's loop and wrapped the length snug around her wrist. "We can't stay. That's a tiger! A fu—"

"It's sleeping," Billy cut her off. He took another step, and felt the firmness of the ground pulse through his leg. There was pain, but also the sense of cotton and denim brushing on his skin. Of bits of plaster grazing his hip and the base of his toes. Of the light's heat caressing his face, and coaxing the sweat from his pores.

"No shit," she said, reading the sign above the cage. "People can pay to get a picture with it. The only safe way to do that is if it's drugged. Circuses and zoos all over the world do it. That's what my Dad says. It sucks."

"Then it's safe," Billy stepped closer. He took another breath, and was clubbed by the heady scent of musk, droppings, and urine-soaked straw.

"No, it's a *tiger*. It could kill us all in a coma." Lynn pried at Seamus' jaws and pulled the sheet of paper free, drool and charcoal staining her fingers. She looked at the etching – the strange cat, caked in blood – and then at her friend, as he placed both hands on the bars of the cage. "Seriously, that's too *close*," she whispered. "This isn't cool."

The fair's PA blared again. It called Billy's name, and said something about 'police'. Tense voices clamoured outside, approaching the tent.

"Give it to me," Billy commanded, holding out his hand to her. He didn't sound like a 10yr-old boy anymore. The fear in his voice was gone.

"It's your funeral," Lynn said, stepping towards the cage. The leash tightened on her wrist as Seamus resisted, growling. She went to comfort him, but the dog flinched and whimpered like an infant. "Seamus is never like this, Billy. Can you hear that?"

"I can hear it *all*," he said, reaching back to snatch the page from her. The words twisted in his mind, and broke into shards of every dream he had had since that fateful day on the road in front of his home.

'Find the one who Hears through the Veil of Tears...'

The boy opened his hand, and the key he had been given came to rest between thumb and forefinger. It then found its way into the padlock on the barred door. The key entered, and turned, and the lock fell to the dirt.

"*No*", Lynn shrieked. "You can't!"

Billy lifted the deadbolt, slid the door open, and stepped inside the cage.

Lynn screamed into her hands and ran to the exit.

"I'm here," Billy said, hobbling towards the tiger. His plaster heel thudded and crumbled against the steel. "*I'm here.*"

"He's over here," Lynn yelled through the tent flap. "Hurry! Billy's here—*with the tiger*!"

The boy shivered as he knelt down beside the beast. He saw its massive paws, with pads worn raw from walking on metal instead of grass and earth. Its claws were cracked and discoloured, filed down to stubs. Its pale muzzle was stained pink from meals of raw, discarded meat. There were punctures on its leg, weeping holes ringed with dried poison. Feeble, laboured breaths rose and fell in the creature's distended stomach.

"Wake up," Billy said, pressing the bloodstained paper flat against that belly, a belly the size of a boy. He felt a tremor in his hand, and swooned as the vibration swept up his arm and engulfed his chest.

So that's what a tiger's purr feels like, Billy thought. The creature stirred, flexing its toes and curling the tip of its tail between the bars.

The tent-flap flew open and a mob of panicked souls burst inside. Lynn pointed and yelled. Elizabeth Brahm wailed in horror, and Stanley Brahm froze in his tracks, dumbstruck. Mr. Jessome charged in behind them, shouting instructions to a security guard. The scruffy, stocky man ran from the tent, pushing past a mountain of pink whose jaw was dropped agape in disbelief.

"I can *hear* you," Billy said, oblivious to all but the tiger. Wave after wave of the beastly hum washed through him now, cresting and crashing in his head.

The tiger opened its eyes. The boy saw his reflection in sapphire pools the size of his fists, and smiled.

"*You're free.*"

The beast roared and rolled to its feet, knocking Billy back against the far wall of the cage. Gasps and shrieks sliced through the shadows beyond the bars.

They sound so frightened, Billy thought, the hum a choir of angels in his bones. *But why?*

The great cat snorted the air and padded towards him. In its fierce and beautiful gaze, the boy's fear and pain dissolved. His sadness melted like ice, and washed away like spring rain.

Whatever happens to me, at least I did something right, Billy thought. *At least I got to help.*

The tiger peeled back sagging gums and sucked hot air between its fangs as it sniffed at the boy. There were desperate, pleading cries from beyond the ring of light. The cat cocked an ear their way, snorted, and lifted a paw.

The guard ran back into the tent with something long and grey dragging after him. Mr. Jessome shouted something, and the men fell into a line. The tiger's paw pressed down on the boy's chest, and the cries turned into screams.

Billy was smothered in blissful thrumming. Time slowed to a crawl, and the force inside of him swelled. The boy felt himself *expand*, a newfound awareness stretching with him in all directions.

He felt the tiger upon him, and knew its urge for freedom. He heard the dog whimper in the darkness, and understood its fear.

Billy grew.

He reached Mr. Jessome, and felt the love the man had for his daughter, and the crippling guilt he carried over the loss of her mother. Close by, Billy could feel Lynn's thoughts mirror her father's in every way.

Billy grew.

He felt the anguish gripping at the hearts of his parents. In that sliver of time, Stanley Brahm knew he had failed to protect his son, and wished more than anything that his own father had taught him how. This, as Elizabeth Brahm relived the early loss of her parents, and tasted the unbearable grief that would come with burying her only child. In that moment, she was staggered by the cruelty of life, and her utter insignificance in the face of death.

And still, Billy grew.

Past the tent-poles and garbage bins. Past the power cables and fire hoses. Past the security guard who drenches his loneliness in whiskey and baseball cards. Past the woman in pink who dreams that someone will notice her, and tell her that she's special.

Billy felt himself and the hum reach the tent's edge. The boy was aware of everything, every cell and atom and particle of space, and felt it all singing inside of him. The balloon of his mind swelled to the verge of bursting.

And then it did.

Billy became an impossible wave, rising and rushing out in all directions at once. In less time than a thought, he touched every blade of grass in his town. In less than a blink, the entire planet spun within him. In less than a heartbeat, galaxies were born in his belly. In less than a breath, he burned at the heart of a billion, billion suns.

The light shone so bright there was only Light. The hum grew so loud there was only Hum. All things disappeared, collapsing into endless nothingness. And then, at the edge of eternity, the Emptiness awoke. And it had a thought.

I was a boy once. And I was searching for something.

The black sea shimmered. The void began to boil.

'Find the one who Hears through the Veil of tears, with the fang o' the Great Cat's Maw.'

A bolt of light cried as it pierced the membrane. It pushed through the tear it had made, crossed the threshold, and fell into a new place. The light sang as it fell, a soft song like falling water, and then it *became* falling water. And then, as the water fell, it sang and *became* the shape of a boy. Until, at last, the boy himself pushed through – through the light, through the waterfall, and through *himself* – and stepped into another world.

The shining grotto.

He was stunned by it. The water murmured, the grass swayed and hummed, and the white cliffs sang as they scraped at the heavens. The air was alive, crackling with magic. It was all exactly as the boy had dreamt it, more real than the world of dirt and blood and broken bones could ever dream of being.

"Welcome," a voice said.

Through the waterfall's gleaming mist, Billy saw it. The thing sat on the edge of the stone pool as a person would sit. It wore its long robes as a person would wear them. But this wasn't a person. This was a *tiger,* holding a silver teapot in its striped paws. It hovered over a pair of rounded cups. One was black, the other white.

"Come," the beast said, and Billy found himself stepping into the flow of water. Stones pillars rose to meet his feet. It looked as if the

boy was a wayward leaf, afloat on a river that would carry him to rest by the pool's edge.

"*You have traveled far. Pierced the Veil,*" it said, filling the cups with a mossy green liquid that sighed as it splashed within. "*This is no small thing.*"

"THE VEIL–?" Billy boomed. His voice was like thunder in this place. Like cannons, and engines, and flocks of screeching gulls. He grimaced at the sound.

"*The Veil of Tears. Drink,*" the tiger said, lifting the white cup to Billy's lips. "*It will hurt less.*"

Billy sipped. The tea dissolved on his tongue, filling him with soothing warmth. It smelled of flowers, and mint, and something old and unknowable.

"*Better?*" asked the tiger. Its tone was soft and concerned, almost motherly.

"Yes," Billy said, his mind quieting.

"*Good,*" it raised the black cup to its furred white mouth. "*When things are good, it is because we remember a time when they were not. When there was pain. But now the pain is gone, so things are 'good'. When we hurt, it is because we recall a time when we did not. When there was no pain. But now we suffer, so things are 'bad'.* The tiger sipped from the cup, peering at the boy over the rim. Stars swirled in its eyes. "*Good. Bad. The cup holds both.*"

"Where am I?" Billy said, swirling bits of leaf and broken stems in the bottom of his cup.

"*Here,*" said the tiger.

"Who are you?" Billy asked.

"*Myself,*" it said, placing the cup down on the stones with a dainty *chink*. It draped a massive paw in the water, and gently made a ripple on its surface.

The water went dark, and a scene rose within it as it had in Billy's dream. The scene was vivid with colour and dimension, but frozen in time like a picture. It showed a metal cage with a white tiger inside. The tiger held a small, brown-haired boy beneath its paw.

"That's...me. That's *me!*" Billy said, awash in sensation as the memories came flooding back to him. "I remember. I remember it all! And the tiger? Is that—?"

"*One and the same,*" the creature said, regarding the pool. "*But also not. We fall asleep, and walk in a world of dreams for too long. It is so easy to become confused. To grow pale, and forget the truth of one's self. To know only the shadow of it.*"

Billy drained his cup and set it down on the stones. He skimmed his fingers in the water, sending tiny waves rolling across the scene.

"Is that what all this is...?" Billy asked as he watched the ripples warp him in the water. "Did you *kill* me?"

"*Goodness no, child,*" the tiger said, its chest heaving in what resembled laughter beneath its scarlet robes. "*You are very much alive.*"

"Then what happened *after*? What am I doing here *now*?" Billy asked.

"*Nothing has happened...yet. Or maybe it has. It is hard to say. The flow of things is different here.*" The tiger smacked its paw on the pool's surface. The image vanished, and the pool filled with waves. "*You were drawn to us because you listened. You can hear the Hum of all worlds, breathing beneath the waves. And to hear it is to speak it – to commune with Shadows. This is the gift that comes to those who listen. It is the thing that will heal you. But it comes with...a price.*"

"You told me that before. In the dream," Billy said, entranced by the splashing, shimmering waves. "What do you want?

"*Sometimes, bad things must happen to make something better,*" it said, the waves glinting in its azure eyes. "*It is the way of change. At first there was Nothing. Then the Hum came. It filled the black ocean, stirring it* to life. *Waves were born, giving form to all things that were, are, and will be. But, soon enough, the waves must collide.*"

The ripples in the pool peaked and crashed together, swallowing each other. The water went flat and dead.

"I don't understand," Billy said. He suddenly felt dizzy, and found it hard to breathe.

"*You straddle the worlds now, child,*" the tiger leaned forward and wrapped its paws around Billy's shoulders. "*Something dark stirs beneath the waves. We must prepare. Wake the Shadows. Find the Key. Deliver the MESSAGE.*"

"The *key?*" Billy said, his vision twisting in a kaleidoscope of light. "Didn't I find it already? And what message? What am I supposed to–?"

"*There is little time, and much to learn. But you shall have a guide. A Watcher.*" The beast caressed the boy's face with a silken pad on its paw.

Billy watched the shining threads on the tiger's robe slither and coil like golden serpents. The boy tried to smile, but trembled instead. He tried to stand, but felt as if his insides were going to erupt from his skin.

"Who...are...YOU?" Billy slurred, reeling.

"*Tao. Call me Tao,*" the tiger smiled as only a tiger could smile. Its eyes hung like winter moons, with icicle whiskers and snowcapped peaks for teeth.

Billy reached into the cat's maw as he had done in the dream, and touched a shining fang. It vanished in his fingertips. "WHERE–?"

"*I already gave it to you, child,*" Tao said, squeezing the boy's shoulders. "*Remember...deliver the MESSAGE.*"

Tao shoved him from the pool's edge and into the water. Billy dropped like a stone, lost in sheets of bubbles and cold, wet darkness. He flailed as he fell, trying to pull himself back up to the gleam of the grotto. But the light above him disappeared, and another sparked in the blackness far beneath him.

The boy fell, faster and faster, but was running out of breath. Billy thought he might drown before he hit bottom, or perish from the impact when he did. The light beneath him brightened, the water got colder, and he heard voices as he fell. The voices grew as the light devoured the darkness, and Billy heard them for what they really were...

Shouts, and cries, and screams.

In a burst of incandescence, Billy slammed back into his body. He was flat in the cage as a jet of icy water sprayed through the bars. The adults approached with a fire hose in hand, targeting the tiger's face.

"Billy! Now's your chance," Mr. Jessome called from the front of ranks. "Crawl out of there!"

Billy scrambled across the cage floor and out the door, sliding it shut behind him. The hose kept spraying, and the boy looked back at the poor beast huddled in the corner, soaked to the white-and-black bone. There were few things more pathetic than a wet cat, but a big wet cat was one of them.

Amidst the loud, embarrassed, blame-filled, and lawsuit-threatening madness that followed, a few incredible things happened before Billy Brahm left the fairgrounds.

As he was pulled from the tiger's tent, he saw Lynn Jessome. There was no anger or fear in her eyes. Instead, there was a hint of amazement. She nodded at Billy, and mimed a small 'X' in front of her chest.

When he limped past the ticket lady, Billy paused in the shadow of her pinkness. He smiled and said, 'You're special'. In that moment, Doris' face went pinker than her outfit for the first time in recorded history.

Outside the tent, when a fair official offered Billy a wheelchair, he waved it off. He shunned the crutches too. Instead, the boy held his head high as he was escorted through the crowd.

And there was one more thing.

It happened on the way out, near the small-animal tents – by the cat tent, to be precise. That's when Billy felt something jab into his thigh, and he stopped to reach into his pocket.

The thing was smooth, and curved, and sharp at the tip. Billy clenched it tight, and remembered. His mother told him to keep moving, but he ignored her.

Instead, he closed his eyes, and *listened*.

It was then, as he held the great cat's fang in his hand, that he heard them. Through the din of whirling machines and children's laughter and the carnival's hollow refrain, Billy heard voices. They were sweet, jubilant voices, rejoicing as one.

"We remember! We remember! We are AWAKE!"

XVIII

Of Freedom and Fire

THE TRIP TO THE DOCTOR'S OFFICE went pretty much as the boy expected it would.

Billy's mother wept and cursed and blustered from the front seat, making mounds of crumpled tissue balls in the car's cup holders. Amidst a litany of admonishments and declarations of 'eternal shame', she took the opportunity to showcase newfound veins on the back of her neck.

Meanwhile, Billy's father drove in silence. His skin was wan and eyes vacant as he attempted to fathom the morning's unfathomable events. Every few streets, he'd look in the rearview mirror to steal a glance at the boy in the back seat, searching for answers to the brown-eyed riddle staring back at him.

At the clinic across the river, his parents grew somber. They said little as they met with Dr. Lim – a pleasant enough woman in a crisp white lab-coat – and held each other's hands behind a pane of smoked glass as Billy's leg was x-rayed.

After, in the waiting room, they both folded their hands in their laps, and stared at the clock on the wall. With each tick, their shoulders slumped a little further, and the skin around their mouths seemed to sag that much closer to the perfectly polished tiles.

There was confusion when Dr Lim called the Brahms back into the examination room. His parents had fully expected the next meeting to take place in the doctor's office. There, they would officially receive the bad news. Stanley and Elizabeth would then console their son, schedule the surgery, and explore the various prosthetic options and 'lifestyle adjustments' to come.

But that didn't happen. Instead, the doctor asked Billy to hop back up on the exam table, and shook his hand.

"Congratulations, young man," Dr Lim said, smiling. "You've made an astonishing recovery."

"What?" Elizabeth said, lifting a shaky hand to trembling lips. "But we were *told*–"

"The prognosis *wasn't* good, Mrs. Brahm. But these things aren't set in stone." The doctor flicked a switch beneath a panel on the wall, lighting up three black x-ray sheets. "As you can see, both the tibia and fibula have healed well, and there's no sign of the vascular damage that had concerned the operating physician. No blood pooling in the limb. No permanent tendon or ligament damage. No need to re-break and insert an intermediary rod. And we certainly won't be taking anything *away* from Billy anytime soon."

"But...how?" Stanley said, looking as confused as he did elated.

"Everyone heals differently. And, contrary to popular opinion, I believe that much of the responsibility falls to the patient. They need to *see* a positive outcome. Visualize it like it's *real*. With that, there's evidence that we can work miracles on ourselves." The doctor patted Billy's leg.

Billy thanked the doctor and turned to his parents. They responded with strained smiles. They were still upset with him, but the boy sensed another struggle. Guilt. They had hidden the truth from him, which his mother had always said was no better than lying. And now, they knew without question that *he* knew it too. The grievances were deep and mutual. It was a stalemate that Billy could live with.

The doctor hoisted his leg up on the table, and grabbed a handheld circular saw from a tray of implements beside it. She pressed a button, and it whirred and whined down the length of the plaster. Chalky dust sprayed in its wake as it cut. With a thin wedge of metal, the woman pried the cast apart at the seam and removed it from his leg.

Peeled it from him would be more accurate. The cotton mesh lining of the cast stuck to the limb, mud-brown from six weeks of no showers in the height of summer. The doctor cleaned the leg with cotton pads soaked in alcohol, and carefully removed the scabs along the boy's new scar. When she was finished, Billy put his legs side-by-side to compare. The injured one seemed strange and alien, a slash of red running down the side of its pale, emaciated shin.

"Will it always look like that?" Billy rubbed the leg and bent the knee up and down.

"It atrophied a bit, but the muscle will come back," the doctor said, wiggling his foot back and forth. "This one will always be a little shorter, though. You won't be running any marathons, I'm afraid."

"That sucks," Billy said, picking at plaques of psoriasis that had bloomed behind his knee.

"*William*," his mother stood. "Count your blessings, and don't look gift horses in the mouth."

"Horses can *run*," Billy scowled. He hopped down from the table, and took a step towards the door.

On the way home, they stopped at a drive-thru for dinner. Billy ordered a double-burger with cheese and bacon, large fries, and some chicken nuggets. As he wolfed the food down, he imagined it moving into his leg to fatten it up. This was also his justification for having a double-scoop strawberry cone for dessert.

"That's called a hollow leg. Better get another x-ray," his father teased, slurping a ring of onion from its fried shell.

His mother was quiet as she finished her fish burger and sipped the dregs of a diet iced tea. Before they left the parking lot, she lowered the vanity mirror and tilted it to look at her son. She remembered the giggling boy with strawberry ice cream that had tumbled down the stairs seven years ago.

That boy was so small, and needy, and helpless. She thought of how much had changed since and wondered what, if anything, had remained the same.

The sun was low in the sky as the Brahms pulled into their driveway in the heart of Appleton. Billy had passed out in the back seat, but stirred as soon as their tires touched gravel. He got out of the car, and the first thing he did was go to the mailbox.

"What are you doing?" his mother said.

"It's my job. I haven't checked it in forever," Billy said, opening the mailbox door with the happy family painted on it. There was only a flyer inside, printed on pink paper. It bore a smiling tiger on the front, above an ad for the county fair.

"Well, what is it?" she said.

"Junk mail," Billy said, folding the sheet and shoving it in his pocket. He grazed the tiger's tooth, and turned towards the old Thomas house. Some cats scampered through Enid's garden, and chased each other around the stone arch.

I can't wait, Billy thought, squeezing the tooth in his hand. *I can't wait to hear all of you.* He waved at the house, hoping the old woman would see him through her dusty, darkened windows. He hoped she would let him visit soon, so he could explain everything. He hoped that she would forgive his selfishness.

"That's enough. Get away from the road." Elizabeth said, clearly annoyed. "You don't want to tempt fate."

Billy headed back to the house as the sun set beyond the mountain. As he opened the front door and crossed the threshold of his home, the sky blossomed in amber and rose behind him.

"We'll talk in the morning, young man. You can be sure of that," his mother said, reaching for a glass in the kitchen cabinet. "By hook or by crook, things are going to *change* around here."

"Yes, mother," Billy said. He walked to the stairs, savouring the tickle of shag carpet on both feet for the first time in six weeks.

"And be ready for chores out your eyeballs," she said, uncorking some wine and filling her glass to the brim. "Looks like someone left the shed door open. Probably in a panic, as she tracked down her delinquent runaway. You can spend tomorrow taking everything out, and putting it all back in neat and tidy. *With* the gas topped up!"

"Yes, *mother*," Billy said, rolling his eyes at the top of the stairs, and thinking of Lynn as he did it.

"And then? Ohhh...then it's time for litter duty," she bellowed, "because you love *cats* so damn much!"

Billy smirked as he walked down the hall towards his room. His mother thought she was punishing him, but she was right – he *did* love cats. And there was one particular cat that he loved more than anything else in the world.

Billy eased the bedroom door open. The cat was curled tight beside his pillow, fast asleep. The boy sat on the bed, and laid his head down next to it. He placed his hand upon it as gently as he could, and stroked its fur from the snowy crown of its head to the inky tip of its tail. The cat's lids flicked open, it pupils retreating in the room's electric light.

The cat looked at the boy, and the boy looked at the cat. They both lay there for a time, silent and staring, until the boy removed the tooth from his pocket. He held it near the cat's face, and twisted it between his fingers.

The cat's eyes narrowed. Its nose twitched, and its ears stiffened.

"Hello," Billy said, soft and anxious. "Can you hear me?"

"*Yes*," the cat said, its mouth unmoving. The voice seemed to skip across the air like flat stones on a lake, ending with an echoing splash in the boy's head.

"Thank you," Billy said. "Thank you...for everything."

The cat blinked once, but said nothing.

"I don't know where to start. There's so much. Everything that's happened. And all the dreams. And then what Tao told me–" Billy's heart raced, and his words slurred together.

"*Be calm*," the cat said, pupils pulsing. "*A path is made one stone at a time*."

"I'm sorry," Billy said, taking a breath. He gazed deep into his friend's golden eyes, and tried again from where most friendships begin. "What's your name?"

"*Close your eyes*," the cat blinked, "*and listen*."

Billy did as the cat asked. The first thing he heard were voices – his parents bickering downstairs. He let them fade, focusing instead on the chirps of crickets, and the frogs croaking in the marsh. Soon, they faded too, dwarfed by the sounds of breath flowing through his nose, and the drum of his own heartbeat. Billy stayed with both for some time, drifting in the dark behind his eyes. He listened and he waited...

And then he heard a *hum*.

Purring. The sound swept across the bed, deep and slow, until the boy felt his skin tingle. There was a soft *meow*, and Billy opened his eyes.

It was dark. The cat was perched on the windowsill. The drapes swayed in the evening breeze.

"*Come*," said the cat, turning to the boy with flames in its eyes. It leapt from the sill, and into the night.

"Wait," the boy said with a hush, leaning out the window. A spotted shape skimmed over the yard, and sailed across the meadow to the top of the hill. He looked back to his door, waiting for an angry hand to flick the light on.

A warm gust blew through the room. The wallpaper's glowing boats dipped on hand-drawn waves, and their sails rippled in the wind.

"Wait for me!" Billy shouted. He hopped up on the ledge and dove out the window, safe in the knowledge that he was dreaming. The boy pushed his arms out as he fell, and willed himself to fly.

Billy soared across the grass in a gentle swoop. He arced high above the fields, and through the trees, and along the path that led up the hill. He hovered to a stop at its end, descending until he felt twilight dew caress his heels. He lifted the rusty latch, and let the iron gate swing open with a squeal. The sound rolled down the hill, and across the slumbering valley.

Billy floated into the cemetery. He had never been there at night. The headstones and crosses and monuments looked no scarier now than they did during the day. They seemed at home in the dark, safe in a cradle of fences and trees.

But there was something else in the graveyard now. Something *alive*. It was as big as a man, maybe bigger. It crouched on the slab in the far corner, and Billy knew that it was watching him. Yet, strangely, he wasn't afraid.

"Hey," Billy said, hovering between the graves and towards the shadowy mass of cloth and fur.

"*Sit*," the figure said, holding out an arm to the adjacent slab. His voice was commanding, rumbling with bass in every vowel. Billy approached, gliding across the clover and dandelions, and sat on the stone next to him.

"Can I see you?" Billy said, peering at the dark space beneath its hood.

"*You know my face*," the cat said, eyes gleaming within the cloak.

The boy caught a glimpse of whiteness around his eyes, and a dark strip running between them. As he turned away, the dim light struck his broad pink nose, flat and wet.

"What is your name?" Billy asked.

"*Where I am from, no word can name you. Your whole being is your name. Your scent. Your marks. Your clan*," he growled. "*Your spirit.*"

"I don't know those things," Billy said. He saw a huge black paw emerge from the shroud, and drag across the slab. Even in the darkness of the dream, the boy could see its shining claws and knew that they were being sharpened. "Everything has a name. It's how you make sense of things."

"*Sense? Your world has none, child.*" He flexed the paw in front of his face, and blew on the claws. Dust scattered in the wind, sparkling as it drifted away. "*It is heavy there. So many trapped for so long. Sleeping. Until we are so small, so thin, we become naught but dust and shadows.*"

"In the grotto...the tiger, Tao, said that. '*Wake the Shadows*,'" Billy said, watching the willows bend and sway, branches reaching across the graves. "Do you know him?"

"Her," the cat said, a smile in his voice. *"Yes, She is known."*

"Well, if that's what you *are*...then that's what I'll call you, if it's alright with you," Billy said, shifting on the stone. "Shadow."

"Hrrrrm," the cat purred, lowering its head. *"That would be better suited for the Grey clan."*

"Someone once said that all cats are grey in the dark," the boy smiled, leaning closer.

There was a flash of gold from amused eyes. *"Fine. I will take the name."*

"Tao told me other things," Billy said, as fireflies rose from the grass and weaved between the headstones. "She said I had to deliver...*a message."*

The blacks of Shadow's eyes grew, engulfing the gold to drink in more light. He watched the flickering bugs flit about and rise into the night. He leaned back upon the slab. His long cloak shrouded him in blackness, except for his whiskers and the bright fur around his nose.

"Look at the sky with me."

Billy watched the steam of Shadow's breath rise from flaring nostrils, and climb past the trees. The boy reclined on his own stone, and looked up at the night sky.

"What do you see?" Shadow said, his voice softening.

"Stars," Billy said, as the fireflies danced overhead. They rose and multiplied in the velvet veil, forming threads and webs and constellations of light.

"This is my sky." Shadow lifted a paw to trace invisible lines between the shimmers. *"The first Watchers. Lion and leopard. Tiger and puma. And others. The Wolf. The Rat. What lies between them. And what lies Beneath..."*

"It's beautiful," Billy said, awed by the strange yet somehow familiar sight. "So different."

"*But also the same,*" Shadow pointed to a patch of sky and circled his paw. "*Look.*"

"Oh wow...*Orion,*" Billy gasped, tilting his head to be sure of the shape that he knew so well. He quickly found the feet, and the belt, and the curve of a jeweled bow.

"*What does it mean to you?*"

"Well...he's the hunter. The legendary Hunter in the sky," Billy said, and the stars shone brighter with his words.

"*Yes. But something else,*" Shadow lowered his arm to the slab. "*Something more.*"

The cat opened his mouth and drew in breath, his chest rising off the stone. When he exhaled, a deafening hum rattled his jaws and shook the air, bending the trees themselves away from the graves.

"What's happening?" Billy said. He clutched at the sides of the slab, afraid that the rising wind would pick him up, and carry him away from the dream.

"*A great horror comes. A war for Creation,*" Shadow growled, silver whiskers shuddering in the starlight. "*We tried to stop it. But They move beyond the Veil. And too soon, the Key is turned.*"

"The key—?" the boy said.

The stars began to vanish. Billy had seen this before in a nightmare. The dread clawed at his belly, and climbed into his chest. The stars were snuffed out, until just two crimson flames burned in the black above them.

"*A gate has been opened,*" Shadow said. He rose from the slab, pupils collapsed into slivers.

Billy sat up. The graveyard had changed. It was covered in sand, and the stones had all become other things – pillars and obelisks, statues with the heads of animals, and three gleaming pyramids capped with crowns of gold.

There was a flash of light and heat, and the cemetery burst into fire. The flames spread quickly, turning the trees to ash as they climbed.

Billy looked up and saw the red stars flare and spin. Suddenly, it was as if a million specks of darkness twisted and writhed in the void above, forming a face to hold the burning eyes that stared down upon them.

"*It begins,*" Shadow said, with a frightened mew.

"*DO YOU SEE IT, WATCHER? DO YOU HEAR IT, LISTENER?*" shrieked the devil in the sky.

"I...*I know that voice,*" Billy stammered in terror.

"*WE SLEEP NO MORE!*"

And then the sky screamed.

Shadow's form flickered as the scream split the air, and his cloak flapped violently in a sudden gale. A bolt of lightning crashed from the sky and struck the fence, hot sparks showering the ground.

In a whirlwind of light and darkness, Shadow *changed* – the shrouded beast became a simple cat again, perched on the stone's edge. He screeched at the sky with ears flat, tail puffed, and a spine arched in rage.

Billy ran to the graveyard's gate and fumbled with the latch. The iron was aglow, searing the boy's hands. Strips of charred skin hung from his fingers.

He looked down the hill, and saw something flutter towards him. A white bird. It soared up the path, unfurled its wings, and landed upon his shoulder.

"*It's alright,*" the bird whispered in Billy's ear, slicing through the screams and yowls and madness of the dream. "*You can wake up now.*"

Billy knew that voice. He looked at the bird, and he knew its eyes as well. He knew the kindness in them, and the warmth and understanding in their creamy jade. The boy was struck by thoughts of sunflowers and lemonade and warm apple pie...

And then he woke up.

The piercing howl had crossed between worlds, wailing through the walls of the house. Billy leapt out of bed, and saw Shadow scratching wide-eyed at the base of his door.

"What's happening?" Billy said, opening it.

The cat raced out of the room and down the stairs. Billy's parents stumbled from their bedroom in matching gown and pajamas. Confused and bleary-eyed, they made their way to the staircase.

"What a horrible sound," Elizabeth said, glasses askew on her pillow-creased face.

"You should stay in your room, son," Stanley said, matting down a flap of hair. "It's late."

"No," Billy said, still shaken from the dream. "I need to see."

The Brahms clambered down the stairs. They didn't need to turn on the lights to make their way, as the windows were bright from something outside. The cat was waiting for them at the front door, and gave a yowl that sent chills through all of them.

"He said they could sense disaster," Billy's mother said, remembering the vet's words as she unlocked the door and pulled it open.

The wall of heat struck them dumb, and the sirens deafened them. Two pump trucks were parked on the road with an ambulance, and a squadron of men in yellow coats and pants were putting on helmets, unrolling hoses, and converging on the old Thomas house.

"What about Enid? Jesus...did they get her *out*?" Elizabeth's lips quivered, and tears streamed down her cheeks.

"There. Look," Stanley said, pointing to the ambulance. Two men were loading a stretcher through the back doors, carrying a grey-haired figure with a mask strapped to its face. The doors closed, and the vehicle's siren and emergency lights flared to life as it sped north.

"*Thank god*," Elizabeth said. She put her arms around her husband and her son, and pulled them closer to her.

The house was engulfed in a hellish tunnel of flame. The fire licked and clawed at the sky, its embers riding a wave of charred smoke that eclipsed the stars. The oak and cedar and old cherry wood popped and hissed as they burned, and there was an awful *cracking* of stones as the blaze reached its peak.

But the boy heard other things as the sirens blared, and the firemen yelled, and his parents held him close. There were cries through the smoke. Curses in the flames. Prayers, and pleas, and frightened final breaths.

"I can hear them. *All of them*," Billy whispered, the tiger's tooth pressed tight in his trembling young hand.

"*I know*," said Shadow, crouching by his feet. The blacks of his eyes had disappeared, drowned in burning pools of gold. "*And that is the price.*"

Billy Brahm was wide-awake, but trapped in another nightmare. It wasn't made of blood, or bullies, or a broken leg like the first. This time, the pain wasn't his. Instead, it was all around him, and he felt it like it was his own.

That night, Shadow took the pillow next to Billy as the fire burned across the road.

The cat purred, and did not sleep.

The boy wept, and did not dream.

EPILOGUE

NOW

THE HEAD OF A MATCH dragged across granite, flaring to life. The flame swelled in that place, feeding on the stench and drinking the fumes like wine. It kissed a charred wick on a greasy stub of wax, and one became two.

"*Come close, childrennn,*" he said above the squeals, and writhing grubs, and drops of filth that fell from the walls to strike the pool below.

Cracked lips parted. A stygian tendril licked at coils of smoke. Gaunt fingers pushed the burning match against the tongue, extinguishing it with a wet *FSSShhhhh* that filled the room.

"*Closerrr*," he said, flies treading the corners of his mouth and flitting inside. The bloom of candlelight swept across dark walls to reveal marks and scratches. As the light settled in place, a picture formed in the gouges and cracks – a scene, carved on the walls of a nightmare.

"*Let USsss tell you a story...*"

When the cold Winds blow and the Waters flow

Upon the distant shore

And the Fires burn, and the Earth doth churn

And the Swords are raised for war.

Then plant them deep as the Watchers sleep

and abandon all Ye know

of the Blood and Stones for the Lover's bones

Ere Ye reap from what Ye sow

Find the one who Hears through the Veil of Tears

with a fang o' the Great Cat's maw

When the Stars are right, let the Clans unite

and bequeath the Black Dog's claw

Then ye have but Two of the Devil's due

and the magic's sure to fail

with the Blood and Stones for the Lover's bones

'less you cleave the Servant's tail.

So now with Three, far beyond the sea

and within Orion's breast

O'er golden sands in the Shadowland

Will ye face the final test

For the Key is bound 'neath hallowed ground

To release It, ye need Four

When the Scarab flies
Then the Gates swing wide
And We shall sleep no more
And We shall sleep no more
And the Dead shall sleep...

"*NO MORE,*" he growled, and the room went cold.

The candlelight flickered, and the marks on the wall of stone began to *move* – the carved scene had come to life. A great sailing ship rocked and dipped on jagged waves. A tempest raged all around it, and a devil's face loomed overhead in the storm.

From above the chamber, sifting through a mantle of iron and stone came a grinding, hollow thrum. Beyond that, the bitter swell of a late summer tide. And further still, atop a lonely peak, the skies spit thunder and an old wolf howled.

Beneath the world, cold fingers snuffed a dying flame, and the Grey Man howled back.

BOOK II
PROLOGUE

SMOKE

DAWN CAME, AND THE WORLD WAS DEAD.

Chunks of ash fluttered in the air like fattened moths struggling in a stiff breeze. An acrid haze hung low and thick, blanketing the scorched earth. Charred timbers thrust out from walls of cracked, blackened stone. Vast puddles choked the singed lawn, their waters fouled by soot and oil and shards of glass.

And bones.

The tall grass behind the trampled sunflower garden shivered, and then parted. A narrow face poked through, sniffed at the air, and coughed. A notched, misshapen ear bent left and drooped. Silver strands on its cheeks twitched, their broken ends probing the haze for a sign in the awful stillness.

The old grey cat stepped onto the lawn, coughed again, and gave a pained mew. "*Come out,*" Smoke said, wheezing between his words. "*Come out and be counted.*"

He closed his eyes and listened. His hearing was only now returning after the deafening clamour – after the nightmare of fire, and the Yellow Men, and the terrible howl of their mammoth machines.

The cat heard branches creak and bushes rustle. He heard pebbles shift and faint footfalls in the mud. He heard coughing, and trilling, and even a frightened yowl.

Smoke took a sharp breath and loped along the garden's edge, doing his best to hide the pain in his legs and lungs. His head was low to the ground as he moved, whiskers twitching to guide him along until he reached the spot he knew so well at the yard's edge. It was the place where they would listen to him.

The cat sniffed at the vine-wrapped base of the birdbath, tensed his haunches, and leapt up to the stone basin. He almost slipped from its rim, but his rear claws dug in and held fast to the perch.

Tired old fool, he thought, steadying himself before lapping at the basin's shallow pool. *They need to see strength now. Give it to them.* He shook the drops of water from his muzzle and turned to sit on edge of the perch.

"Our eyes are dim in this place," Smoke said, slapping his tattered tail on the stone. *"Our scents are tainted by fire, and oil, and death. Make your voices heard, with the names given by Kind Mother."*

The assembled cats heeded the battle-scarred tom, and spoke their given names. Smoke acknowledged each of them, and took note. When the mewing and trilling and hissing had ceased, the count had reached twelve.

"Let us honour the lost," Smoke said, closing his eyes and lowering his head. *"Let us Hum for those who Dream no more."*

The cat's chest swelled, and a raspy purr came from him. The other cats followed suit, though some were slower than others and less wholehearted. Still, their purring grew and spread, and the air itself shook. A cool wind rose, the willows swayed, and the haze began to clear.

A golden light crested the eastern horizon, making a halo for the old cemetery on the hill. A ray spilled down and lit the ground a few meters from the stone arch by the front of the burnt house. Flowers still clung to its bleached stone surface, somehow undamaged by the heat of the blaze the night before. As the sky brightened, their petals trembled and unfurled.

"*There is little time,*" Smoke said, ceasing his purr and opening his eyes. "*We must go. Quickly.*"

The grey cat, weary and pained, hopped clumsily down from the birdbath and made his way back towards the tall grass. The other cats moved to follow, some of them reluctantly, but stopped at the sound of a thin cry.

"*Wait!*" cried the small voice, and all turned to spy the speaker in the haze. A marmalade kitten stumbled through the beam of morning light, and scampered towards the group. "*Don't leave me...*"

Some of those gathered hissed at the little one as he neared, but Smoke gave a throaty growl to quiet them. The cats moved aside, and allowed the kitten to approach.

"*I do not know you,*" Smoke said to it, swishing his tail with authority. "*You have not walked beyond Kind Mother's walls before?*"

"*No,*" said the kitten, crouching in the grass near Smoke's front paws, allowing his head to be sniffed. "*This is my first time.*"

"*What did She name you?*" Smoke said, brushing his dry nose across the raw, fire-kissed tips of the kitten's ears.

"*Lucky,*" it mewed, scratching at the dirt.

"*You must be,*" Smoke's voice softened, warming to the poor thing as it tried to show the sharpness of its claws. "*Come...you will journey by my side.*"

"*A journey?*" Lucky said, hopping to the edge of the curtain of grass. "*Is it far?*"

"*Yes,*" said Smoke, holding the kitten in his murky, emerald gaze. "*And many of us will not finish it.*"

The kitten's eyes widened. "*Then why? Why do we have to go?*"

The scarred tom pushed a paw into the base of the tall grass, bending a swath of it to make a path. "*We are Watchers, child,*" Smoke said, the black slits of his eyes growing as he stepped into the grass. "*That is why we are here. To bear witness.*"

Another step, and Smoke was gone in the green. Lucky watched apprehensively as the twelve survivors followed the grey cat's trail, and they too disappeared into the field behind the old Thomas house.

The marmalade kitten gave a final look back at what had been his home – at the place where he had been raised, and fed, and shown love for the first time – and knew that he would never see the likes of it again. He hopped into the tall grass, and it shivered once more before closing behind him.

The winds rose, and the crumbling husk that had been their refuge sighed its last breaths of smoke. The dark wisps climbed towards the clouds, and were soon caught in their steady drift. The rifts of grey moved west, inching their way towards a lonely mountaintop.

A wolf howled, the sky rumbled, and the rain began to fall.

ABOUT THE AUTHOR

BROOKE BURGESS was born in a tiny town on the eastern coast of Canada. Cats had a presence in his home from the very beginning. They became his siblings, friends, and (benevolent) masters. An old graveyard on a nearby hill was a real (and beautiful) thing. This probably influenced his love of (somewhat) scary stories. Brooke has written for videogames, animation, comic books, and film. He loves mythology, travel, really good TV, and frozen yogurt. Many of the things in this book (dreams included) actually happened.

The Cat's Maw is Brooke's first novel.

www.brookeburgess.com

ACKNOWLEDGEMENTS

TO ALL *THE CAT'S MAW* BETA READERS – Susan Vaziri, Aleisha Friesen, Nazima Ali, Trish Maisonville, Michelle Deighton, Tanya Mundy, Richard & Andrea Hetley, Nathan Frost, Julie Zakar, Trasie Sands, Soracha Cashman, Shannon Brooker, Tobias Tinker, Zoe Curnoe, and Tyler Blancard-Mackinnon – your efforts were treasured, and your insights were invaluable.

To Seamus Cashman – your expertise was timely, welcomed, and infinitely appreciated.

And, of course, to Sarah Plochl – I can't thank you enough for your belief, and your gift of finding diamonds in the dross.

To those who opened their hearts (and wallets) to make this project possible – my fine friends, family, and fellow worshippers of all things feline – this is just the beginning. I hope I've afforded you some teensy measure of pride, and a wee smile of patronly satisfaction.

And, finally, to the countless cats that have crossed my path (yes, even the black ones) and graced my lap (yes, even the fat ones). My life is better for having witnessed your beauty, your grace, and your divine mystery. I shall listen for each of you in the Great Hum, until we purr together once more...

In the Shadowland.